BAD MEDICINE

THE MEDICAL STUDENTS
BOOK TWO

JAMES B. COHOON

Relax. Read. Repeat.

BAD MEDICINE (The Medical Students, Book Two)
By James Cohoon
Published by TouchPoint Press
Brookland, AR 72417
www.touchpointpress.com

ISBN-13: 978-1-952816-67-3

Editor: Kelly Esparza
Cover Design: ColbieMyles.com
Cover Images: Woman in surgical mask by Jacob Wackerhausen (iStock, Getty Images);
Saline solution by thekopmylife (Shutterstock)

First Edition

Printed in the United States of America.

To Rozanne, who has made me the luckiest guy in the world, and to Everett and Beckett, my two grandsons, who have brought so much joy to me while I've been writing this book.

Chapter 1

Dr. Matthew Preston and Dr. Torrey Jamison were living the dream. As newlywed medical residents at a great Kaiser hospital in San Diego, they lived in an ocean-view condo in La Jolla, an upscale seaside community wedged between Del Mar to the north and Pacific Beach to the south. La Jolla is one of those "walkable" towns—walk to beautiful beaches teeming with seals and surfers, walk through gorgeous neighborhoods dotted with miniature "Little Free Libraries" adjacent to wide tree-lined streets, walk to favorite restaurants and coffee shops.

They had gotten married in the few weeks between their June 2019 Stanford Medical School graduations and the start of their residencies. Five months later, it still felt like they were on their honeymoon in spite of living and working on minimal sleep due to the seventy to eighty-hour work weeks and the 36-hour on-call rotations.

The two of them were having their early morning breakfast of green smoothies, croissants, and coffee when Matthew's phone buzzed. Matthew stared at the text message as he put down his coffee cup. Torrey noticed the furrowed brow. "What is it, honey?" she asked, assuming that the call was from someone at the hospital.

Matthew slid the phone over to Torrey so that she could read the short message. Torrey wiped flaky croissant crumbs off her fingers and then turned the phone so that the message was right side up. Neither spoke for several seconds.

"Are you positive you didn't tell anyone?" asked Matthew finally.

"Of course I am." Torrey stiffened, raised her eyebrows, and stared at Matthew. "Did *you* say something? Maybe to your Uncle TJ?"

Matthew didn't deign to answer that question directly. "Don't look at *me*," he scoffed. "Maybe you let something slip when someone asked you about what happened?"

Torrey was incredulous. "Puhleez! You seriously think that I would *accidentally* tell someone that I committed murder?"

"Then no one could possibly know anything," replied Matthew with more hope in his voice than conviction.

"Well, someone knows something," Torrey countered with pursed lips.

Matthew gave Torrey a hug and tried to sound confident. "Let's not worry just yet. This could be a prank, or a text sent to the wrong number." Even to him, Matthew's words rang hollow.

They both looked down with hunched shoulders and huddled over Matthew's phone. Torrey read the text out loud: *I know what really happened at San Quentin.* "Should we just ignore it?" asked Torrey.

"I don't see how we can." With that, Matthew looked at Torrey and with unspoken agreement, typed a short reply. *What do you want?*

The reply arrived within seconds and was equally abrupt. *I want in.*

Torrey deliberated for a second. "Hmm, I guess it's not a joke," she mused, "or a text intended for someone else."

Chapter 2

Torrey grabbed the phone and without asking Matthew, typed, *Who is this?*
A friend. I need your help.

Torrey and Matthew's eyes met for an instant. "Maybe this is some
sort of trap," whispered Torrey.

"I don't see how it could be," Matthew whispered back. "And why are
we whispering?"

They both gawked at the phone screen as if willing it to provide
more information. It didn't. Matthew slowly typed a reply, raised his
eyebrows at Torrey, got a nod of assent, and pushed SEND. Matthew
realized that he had only bought a short reprieve by indicating they
would have to consider the request, but they truly needed some time to
talk it over. He knew that his bride had far more brain power than he
would ever have.

"So, what do you think?" Matthew asked as he rubbed his signature
one day's worth of stubble.

"What I think is that we need to meet with this guy, determine what
he knows, and find out what he means by '*I want in.*' Maybe we're being
paranoid. There really is no way for anyone to know what happened in that
prison room besides me. And you, of course, after I told you. But only
Nash and I were in there. We were out of range of the video camera system

when I stabbed him. And dead men tell no tales, as they say. So, no one else could *know* anything."

"All of that's true. But then where's this coming from?" Matthew paused and snapped his fingers. "I have an idea. Why don't I call my private investigator who's surveilling George Rincon for us? Maybe he could help."

"I don't know about bringing another person into the loop on this. And the investigator told you that he'd be finished with Rincon in about a week. I don't want to disturb that work. I vote that we set up a meeting in a public place and hear what this guy has to say. I'm apprehensive, but I'm more curious than anything. I want to know who this is and what he *thinks* he knows."

Matthew shrugged with upturned palms. "I guess I don't have a better idea."

● ● ●

The rendezvous was scheduled for the next day at 10:00 a.m. at Mabel's Coffee Shop around the corner from the Kaiser hospital where both of the residents worked. Mabel's, which had been serving breakfast and lunch since before the hospital was on the drawing board, was where Matthew and Torrey met whenever they could steal a few minutes away together in the midst of their grueling schedules. Dressed in matching blue scrubs, they usually sat at a window table to watch the passersby and to soak in some natural sunlight, but today they sat side by side at the table farthest from the street entrance with their backs against the wall and their hands clasped together in Matthew's lap. To quell their nerves and to decrease their anxiety levels, they ordered coffee and—Torrey's favorite— croissants. They had a clear view of the front door. The shop was nearly empty at this time of day, except for the waitress who kept glancing their way, pencil ready to add their order. As they were waiting, Matthew drummed his fingers on the table. Torrey reached for a croissant but stopped mid-grab when Matthew exclaimed, "How can you eat at a time like this?"

"I can multitask," remarked Torrey with a wry grimace, but she reluctantly acquiesced and pulled back her hand. She was not happy about it. Saliva pooled in her mouth.

At the appointed time, a familiar face walked in and headed directly towards them. Matthew stood and pointed. "You?" he gasped. Torrey was too surprised to speak. She simply rose and gave Edwina Steed a big hug.

Matthew and Torrey knew Edwina from their medical school rotation at San Quentin prison. Edwina was the guard who ran the video surveillance for the medical clinic. She was male when they first knew her, but she had since transitioned to female. At that time, her name was Ed, but almost everyone had called her Mr. Ed, a reference to a popular, but ridiculous, 1960s TV sitcom about a talking horse. Hormone therapy and facial feminization surgery had softened most of her masculine features and reshaped her nose. All traces of facial hair had been removed. With shoulder-length hair and makeup, she was now quite striking. After the transition, her closest friends were invited to call her Mrs. Ed. Today she was dressed in tailored high-waisted pants and a fashionable silk top. Her long brown hair was pulled back in a ponytail. Her head was covered with a scarf tied under her chin, and she wore oversized designer sunglasses, like a movie star who was trying to go shopping incognito.

"How are you, Mrs. Ed? What's going on?" asked Torrey quizzically.

"I'm super-duper," said Edwina with a forced smile as she set down her sunglasses on the table. "Actually, I'm not super. Or duper." Edwina, eyes downcast, sat down directly across from Matthew and Torrey. "I'm so sorry to contact you in the way that I did—with the dramatic language. I just had to be sure you'd take me seriously. That you wouldn't just brush me off." She looked up and spoke with sincerity. "You know I'd never hurt either of you in any way. I know what really happened with Ted Nash, and I wanted to let you know that I'm down with the way you two exterminated that rat."

Matthew and Torrey remained silent for a few seconds. Matthew, feigning shock, blustered, "What do you mean?"

Edwina locked eyes with Mathew. "C'mon, Matthew," she said with exasperation.

Matthew's face reddened as he set his square jaw. "C'mon what? Tell us what you're talking about. It sounds like you've created some sort of false narrative in your mind."

Edwina took a deep breath and chose her words carefully. "Look, you know I love you guys. The three of us shared a life-changing experience at San Quentin. But before I really got to know you, I was suspicious of you, Matthew, because you were not the type of medical student who typically volunteered to rotate through the prison system. I did some checking with the help of my brother, who did some sort of secret government work, and I learned that your father was murdered in a home invasion robbery when you were a young boy. And that the killer, Ted Nash, was incarcerated in San Quentin."

While Edwina spoke, Torrey swallowed hard and squeezed Matthew's hand so tightly that Matthew had to loosen her grip with his free hand. He was afraid to look at Torrey for fear that his eyes would give something away. Matthew's mouth tightened, and his heart skipped a beat as Edwina continued. "It seemed too coincidental that you showed up to do a rotation, not just at any prison, but at the very facility where your father's killer was jailed. Then I noticed that you and Torrey were a couple. And then, miraculously, Torrey happens to get attacked by Nash during a prison riot, and she kills him with a scalpel that she conveniently had hidden in her lab coat."

Torrey, ever the wordsmith, decided to challenge Edwina's assumptions to see if she had anything more than supposition. "So what? He attacked me," Torrey prompted in a light, even tone. An uneasy silence fell over the table. Torrey blew on her cup of hot coffee and sipped.

"All right. If you insist that I say more, I will. I get where you're coming from." Edwina stared at Torrey as she continued. "I went back later and looked at the videotapes of the interaction between you and Nash. You took great care to position yourself along the wall where you weren't visible to the surveillance camera. And by the way, I remember you asking me about that blind spot during your initial tour of the clinic. I remember because no one else had ever asked me about that in all the years I worked there. The lazy, apathetic detectives did a slipshod investigation of the killing. They conducted a half-assed review of the video and concluded there was nothing there to contradict your story. They spent no more than five minutes in the video room. To them, a convict was killed during an assault—big deal. But I studied the tape frame by frame. I saw your hand reach out and gesture for Nash to come towards you. And when he got close, I saw the tips of your fingers grab his shirt and pull him toward you."

Matthew shifted in his seat and shot a look at Torrey. Getting more uneasy by the minute, Matthew pursed his lips and made no attempt to hide his irritation. He paused, looked back at Edwina, and finally said brusquely, "What's your point, Mrs. Ed?"

The question hung in the air while Edwina stared at them and searched for the right words. "I would never tell a soul what I know about you and Nash." Edwina mimed zipping her lips closed. She continued in a hushed voice, "What you guys did was fantastic. I'd observed Nash during his frequent visits to the medical clinic and saw firsthand how he treated people, always pawing the nurses and the female doctors. He was an unredeemable murderer. I also know that he was scheduled to be released on parole. And I know that his release would've been a travesty of justice. Some people are so evil that even life in prison is too good for them."

Torrey was starting to calm down. She took a turn to get clarification. "Mrs. Ed, we need to know the endgame here. We adore you, but I'm confused about why we're having this conversation."

Edwina knew this was the moment of truth, but she only paused for a moment. "As I said in my first text, I want into your circle. You two understand that the system doesn't always punish the bad guys. Sometimes we have to take matters into our own hands. You did it with Nash, who was your bad guy. For all I know," said Edwina with a shrug, "you guys chose Kaiser in order to administer real justice to someone else. I noticed how surprised your Uncle TJ was about your residency choice on Match Day. He was genuinely perplexed.

"You two being here is fortuitous for me. I suspect I may need your help to deal with a different bad guy. But here's the wrinkle—my bad guy is a doctor. I need your medical expertise to confirm whether my suspicions are correct. If they are, I intend to make him pay the ultimate price."

"Mrs. Ed," replied Matthew as his face clouded and his arms crossed, "I think you've gotten the wrong idea about us."

"Matthew," pleaded Edwina, "I can't turn to anyone else for help. I have no proof of his heinous crime. And even if I did, what would happen to him? A slap on the wrist? A few years in a Club Fed? A country club prison? Criminals get away with murder these days, as you well know."

Before Matthew could say another word, Torrey patted Matthew's knee and said with thoughtful eyes, "Tell us about this doctor." She edged her chair closer to the table, gently putting down her coffee cup onto the table. She unconsciously stuck her right hand into her pants pocket and fingered the surgeon's scalpel that she always carried since her stint at San Quentin Prison as a medical student.

Chapter 3

Matthew sighed impatiently and looked at the ceiling. Torrey smiled and without looking at him, said lightly, "I can see your eyes rolling from here, Matthew. Let's hear Mrs. Ed out. I think we owe her that much."

Matthew nodded reluctantly and craned his neck around, checking for patrons who might overhear their conversation. The other tables were still empty, and the sole waitress was busy wiping down the counter by the cash register. A man in a suit carrying a newspaper came in while Matthew was looking around, but he sat far away at a window table. "No one can hear us," said Matthew. "So, what's going on?"

"There's a doctor who claims to be conducting clinical trials for children diagnosed with certain kinds of cancer. His name is Albert Toohey. His office is located in San Diego, not far from here. He—"

Matthew's pager buzzed. As he glanced down at the screen, Torrey's pager also buzzed. They were being summoned back to the hospital. "Mrs. Ed, I'm sorry, but we have to get back. We're on a 24-hour call, and one of our patients is having a seizure."

"But this doctor killed my niece who had a brain tumor!" Edwina wailed softly. "You can't go now!"

Torrey froze in her seat when Edwina said the words "brain tumor" and "niece" in the same sentence. She imagined Edwina's niece being about the same age as Torrey's sister when she died of a brain tumor. "Look," said Torrey gravely, "I promise we'll meet you again for as long as it takes right after our shifts end today. Right now, we have to get back, or we'll be fired. As soon as I have a minute, I'll text you our address, and we'll meet you there later. Okay?"

"Okay," Edwina muttered reluctantly.

Matthew threw some bills on the table. The three of them got up quickly and headed towards the door. As they passed the man with the newspaper, Matthew noticed that the man was staring at Edwina over the top of the open sports page, while pretending that he wasn't. He was wearing a dark grey sharkskin suit, a white shirt opened at the collar, and a gold chain around his neck. His eyes were dark and humorless. The man was extremely tall and muscular. Matthew had taken years of martial arts. He could tell by the size of the man's neck and his posture that he could handle himself in a street fight.

Once they were outside, Edwina stiffened and tugged on Torrey's elbow to usher her down the sidewalk. Matthew quickened his pace to keep up. Edwina started talking so fast that neither Torrey nor Matthew could understand her. Torrey told her to slow down and to take a deep breath. Edwina no longer sounded sad and upset. She now sounded scared. "That man! That man by the door! He's been following me!"

• • •

Matthew immediately dropped behind and kept an eye on the door while Torrey and Edwina almost ran to the hospital entrance. When he joined them a minute later, he announced that the man had not left the café. "He's just sitting there reading his paper," said Matthew.

"I'm telling you!" exclaimed Edwina with a raised voice and her arms spread widely. "He's been following me! The first time that I noticed him was when I was leaving Toohey's office after going there to confront him. The man followed me home to my apartment in Pacific Beach!"

Matthew gave her a pat on the shoulder as he hurried towards the lobby elevator. "We'll see you tonight after work. Try not to worry."

• • •

Torrey desperately wanted to speak with Matthew about the Edwina situation, but the seizure patient and their other duties required their undivided attention. Medical residents are the life blood of the hospital system. They provide the manpower that allows hospitals to function, at a profit, or at all. They are overworked, underpaid, and stressed to the max.

The boss of the residents, Dr. Anne Peterson, was none too happy that neither of them was around when the seizure began. After the patient was sedated, and there was a break in the action, Dr. Peterson sat the two of them down in the physicians' lounge. "You two may have been big deals in medical school, but here you are first-year residents with no special privileges. You are expected to be on the floor of this hospital during your shifts. And if you have to step out for a moment, you are expected to reply immediately when you get paged. Neither of you replied, and neither of you gave your pager to your senior resident. You just showed up long after the emergency began. That's not acceptable. Any questions?"

"No excuses," said Torrey contritely.

"It won't happen again," added Matthew.

After Dr. Peterson left the room, Torrey said, "Well, that's not going to help our reviews. Anne has a reputation for being laid back, but she was pretty upset."

"We can't blame her. We weren't there when our patient needed us. We can't lose our focus just because Mrs. Ed wants our help. By the way, what did you make of her suspicion about Toohey, the clinical trial doctor? And what about her idea that someone has been following her?"

Torrey replied, "I guess I'll reserve judgment on everything until we meet with her again. But if there is anything to a doctor endangering a child with a brain tumor, we have to help."

11

Matthew looked into Torrey's sky blue eyes and saw the icy fire that flared whenever she was reminded of her sister's treatment during her last days of life. He changed the subject to cool her down. "I have to tell you. That man by the door who was reading the newspaper did look out of place in there."

"He looked like a thug to me."

"Well, he sure was a well-dressed thug. And he was staring at us as we walked by. If he's following Mrs. Ed, I wonder what he wants."

Chapter 4

After their 7:00 a.m. to 9:30 p.m. shifts, both Matthew and Torrey were, as usual, physically and mentally exhausted. But they had arranged for Edwina to arrive at their condo at 10:00 p.m. sharp. They had barely made it home and started a late dinner when the doorbell rang. Edwina was right on time.

Matthew answered the door. "Come on in, Mrs. Ed. We were just going to sit down for a bite to eat. We have plenty for you. Please join us. How about a beer to get started?" Before following Edwina into the condo, Matthew stepped out onto the porch and looked around. No one was in sight.

They let the stew continue to simmer while the three of them sat in uncomfortable silence in the living room. Matthew tried to look nonchalant in the recliner while Edwina and Torrey sat with rigid backs next to each other on the sofa. Mrs. Ed stared out the window at the ocean. "Love your place. It's got a nice beachy vibe. And look," she exclaimed, "you can see bioluminescence light in the crashing waves!"

Matthew looked blank, so Torrey explained, "The waves glow from the light emitted from certain marine organisms like phytoplankton." To Edwina, she said, "Yes, it's a wonderful place to live. I just wish we were home more to enjoy it. It feels like we're here only to sleep and shower."

Most medical residents could not afford the steep rent of an oceanfront condo, but Matthew was the sole heir to his father's fortune. His father had come from nothing, but he had created and sold a next generation browser. After Matthew's father was murdered, Mrs. Preston created the Grant Preston Foundation, dedicated to assisting deserving non-profit charities. Upon Mary Preston passing, Matthew was gifted a generous lifetime allowance sufficient to rent or outright buy any home in La Jolla.

After another awkward silence, Matthew said with a forced smile, "So, where do you want to start?"

Torrey interjected. "Wait a minute. Let's just catch up a little first, shall we? Mrs. Ed, you said you're now living in Pacific Beach. I love the fun atmosphere there. I gather you're no longer working in the prison system?"

"No. Too stressful. After that whole thing with the escape attempt, I was through." Then she added with a smirk, "Although, I did get awarded 'Guard of the Month' with my picture in the lobby."

Torrey laughed. "So, what are you doing now?"

Edwina exhaled and dropped her shoulders, finally starting to relax "Well, I took a few months off, but," she added with a flip of her hair, "I've just started doing some modeling and commercial work. Believe it or not, I just shot a shampoo commercial which I'm told might air during the Super Bowl!"

"Look, you two," grumbled Matthew with a grimace, "can we catch up later? And let's put the man who has been following you on the back burner for a minute. Tell us about this Dr. Toohey fellow. Don't leave anything out."

"Okay," said Edwina as she sat up tall. "Don't forget that I'm not a medical professional. I'm just going to tell you what happened."

"Fair enough," said Torrey.

"My brother, Jefferson Hawke—everyone just calls him Hawk—and his wife had a beautiful little girl named Emily. She was the center of their lives, and mine, too because I have no kids of my own."

"Wait a minute." interrupted Matthew. "When we met you at the prison, your last name was Steed, not Hawke. I remember because it was funny that your name was Ed Steed, and everyone called you Mr. Ed."

"My given last name was Hawke. But when I told my father about my plans to transition to female, he disowned me. He said he was ashamed of me. Questioned why I couldn't be more like my he-man brother. Said I was dead to him. I was naively optimistic for a while that he would have a change of heart and accept me. He never did. So, I decided I didn't want to carry his name anymore. I had it legally changed to Steed."

"What a shame," murmured Torrey.

"No worries. His loss. I'm over it. And I think Steed has a nice ring to it. Anyway, as I was saying, about a year ago, Hawk's daughter—my niece Emily—started having headaches and dizzy spells. And she began to slur her speech. Her pediatrician sent her to Lady of the Angels Hospital for a brain scan. The MRI showed a golf ball-sized, high-grade tumor that, according to her oncologist, required surgical removal, followed by radiation and chemotherapy. The neurosurgeon who was going to perform the surgery told my brother that she was going to have to open Emily's skull, and there was a good chance that Emily would lose language skills and motor functions. Plus, there was no guarantee of survival beyond one year."

Torrey became visibly upset as Edwina told her story. Through tears, she grabbed Matthew's forearm and squeezed tightly.

Edwina's voice broke several times as she continued, "Hawk's wife, Angela, was scared out of her mind about the surgery. A few days before, a hospital nurse—well, I guess I'm not sure she was a real nurse—they said that she was a young employee with pink hair; she wore scrubs and had a little desk at the end of the second floor hallway. The woman took Angela aside and told her that she knew a doctor who could cure Emily, without surgery or radiation. Naturally, in retrospect, that sounded too good to be true. No one asked for my input, and Angela was willing to do anything to spare Emily the recommended treatment. She convinced Hawk to go with her to meet Dr. Toohey at his office."

"So, what happened then?" asked Matthew. "I gather that the parents decided to go with this Dr. Toohey rather than doing surgery at the hospital?"

"In a word, yes. Dr. Toohey told them that he had been conducting a private clinical trial for five years, in which he administered a combination of what he called 'anti-cancer' drugs to kids with various kinds of brain tumors. He claimed he could reduce the size of any tumor by ninety percent without any surgery or side effects. But here's the rub. Toohey said his clinical trial was at capacity, and there was no more room. And even if space were available, the treatment was very costly at a $125,000. Angela said they would pay anything, and glory be, an opening became available the next day."

Matthew adjusted the recliner so that he was now sitting straight up with his feet flat on the floor. But he forced himself to hold his questions so that Edwina could finish her narrative. Even though Torrey sat statue-like, she was shaking with anger.

"Hawk and Angela mortgaged their house, emptied out their retirement accounts, and hand delivered a cashier's check to Dr. Toohey's office. Emily started treatment the next day. Within three months, Emily was dead. I suggested an autopsy to Hawk and Angela, and they agreed, over the objections of Dr. Toohey. The medical examiner discovered that Emily's tumor had nearly doubled in size in the months before her death. I went to Dr. Toohey's office and confronted him with the autopsy results. Without a hint of remorse, he just told me the same thing he'd said to my brother—that no treatment is foolproof, and that Emily must have been too far gone for the medicines to work. Of course, he brusquely refused to refund their money."

Torrey came out of her trance with a vengeance. "Mrs. Ed, you can't possibly know how sorry I am about Emily. What can we do to help you, Hawk, and Angela?"

"Having worked at San Quentin for all those years, my BS radar is well tuned. Look, I know I'm not a doctor, but what my brother and

Toohey told me doesn't make sense. I'm positive that Toohey is running some sort of scam. I just don't know what it is. I need your help, as doctors and friends, to figure out what he did and how he did it. And like I said—if I'm right, I want to burn the bastard."

Matthew took the last swallow of his beer while he weighed whether to reply to Edwina's last statement. He exchanged a glance with Torrey and saw her resolve. He knew in that moment that Torrey was all in, and that frightened him. He decided to return to the topic of the man in the coffee shop. "You say that you're being followed?"

"Yes, I suspected it before, but I'm sure of it now."

"Any idea who he is or why he's following you? Has he spoken to you?" asked Matthew.

"No and no. I can only imagine that he's somehow involved with Dr. Toohey. I started noticing this guy shortly after my run-in with Toohey. And he looks like some kind of an enforcer. Maybe he's trying to intimidate me into keeping my gut feeling to myself. But if that's true, then he now probably suspects that I've told my story to you two doctors. After all, at the coffee shop, you were dressed in scrubs, and we were right next to the hospital."

Torrey sniffed. "We're not afraid of some hood. No promises, but we'll help you figure out what happened. Right, Matthew?" she said pointedly.

Matthew knew there was no point in arguing at that moment. "Of course," he said without conviction.

The three of them devoured every bite of a delicious dinner. They talked into the night until they had some semblance of a plan.

Chapter 5

Joe Cook, a former UCLA fraternity rush chairman and football star, had been a LAPD homicide detective before deciding to open his own private investigation agency. He had grown tired of the politically correct government bureaucrats and the red tape that had prevented him and his fellow officers from doing their jobs. Not to mention all of the violent criminals who were being set free. And no one seemed to care, except for the victims. As his own boss, Joe enjoyed answering only to himself.

Joe had done some prior work for Matthew Preston, and he was always happy to do more. Matthew was not just a high-paying client. Joe had a soft spot in his heart for Matthew, knowing that Matthew had lost his father in a home-invasion burglary when he was just a boy.

Joe couldn't put his finger on why Matthew was so interested in George Rincon. When he was in medical school, Matthew had asked him to do a detailed background check on Rincon. Now Matthew's current directive was to follow Rincon all over creation. It was puzzling, but he had learned long ago to ask only about the *what*, not the *why,* of his assignments. Therefore, although the exercise seemed pointless, he dutifully recorded Rincon's daily movements. He had been tailing Rincon for three weeks of a month-long job. So far Joe had established that Rincon lived alone (divorced), had no friends (the guy was a weirdo), and he had no noticeable direction in his life (again, the guy was a weirdo). Rincon had no current job, as far as Joe could tell, and no obvious schedule.

Joe had started this new mission already knowing that Rincon was a retired school counselor and that he was receiving treatment for Crohn's disease at the Kaiser hospital where Matthew now worked as a medical resident. Part of Joe's assignment was to find out exactly when Rincon went in for his treatments and whether anyone accompanied him to the hospital. Joe had witnessed Rincon going for two treatments so far on the fifth floor of the hospital, but they had been on different days of the week and at different times of the day. Matthew had asked Joe to figure out if Rincon visited the hospital on some sort of regular pattern. So far, no.

In the last few weeks, Joe had been constantly amused by Rincon. Although Rincon was fifty-six years old, his hair was dyed jet black, except for the gray roots. He wore the millennial uniform of skinny jeans, brown dress shoes, and a backwards baseball cap. He wore a different vintage T-shirt every day. Joe's favorite so far was *THAT'S TOO MUCH BACON, said no one ever.* Joe had seen that shirt before, on the high school kid that lived down the street. It just seemed funnier on a guy near the age of penalty-free 401k withdrawals. Rincon spent his days going to shops, bars, and eateries where people under thirty congregated. Joe watched from a distance as the young people awkwardly feigned interest and then laughed behind Rincon's back. Joe almost felt sorry for the moron.

Joe would report to Matthew in another week. Matthew had no end of family money, so maybe Joe could finagle this assignment into a long-term gig. It was a little boring, but it beat taking videos of cheating husbands with long-range lenses.

Little did Joe know the assignment was about to end abruptly.

Chapter 6

First-year medical residents are referred to as interns, and they are not allowed to practice unsupervised medicine. At Kaiser, there was a congenial collection of fourteen residents who came from medical schools all over the country. Matthew and Torrey had attended Stanford Medical School, but they had interns in their residency class from medical schools all over the West Coast and from as far away as Harvard, Yale, and NYU. Matthew knew well why he and Torrey chose Kaiser San Diego, and he sometimes wondered—although not curious enough to inquire—about the reasons the other residents had for that choice. He wasn't keen on making "bffs," so he had coffee or lunch with Torrey, or by himself.

Torrey, on the other hand, had become quite gregarious since the San Quentin episode. Her celebrity preceded her as news of her exploits spread quickly among her peers, as well as the hospital staff. She made quick friends with a fellow intern who grew up in India, then attended a university in London, and against her parents' wishes, had gone to medical school in Boston, where the summers are humid, and the winters are icy. Torrey had asked her directly how she came to the decision to do her residency in San Diego. She laughed and gave an intellectually shallow, but honest answer: "The weather."

After the intern year, residency can range for an additional two to six years, depending on the area of specialty. Because Matthew was interested in practicing internal medicine with his uncle, he was planning to spend as little time as possible on his post-medical school training. Torrey, on the other hand, knew that her goal of becoming a pediatric neurosurgeon would require a six-year long residency—the longest of all medical specialties—plus one or more fellowships for additional training. She had chosen this path at age fifteen when her little sister passed away.

As interns, Matthew and Torrey were at the bottom of the physician hierarchy, so they were constantly taking orders from more senior residents, fellows, and of course, the attending physicians. To make matters even more complicated, often there were private doctors whose patients were admitted to the hospital. These doctors were typically non-specialists, but they were frequently loath to take treatment advice from hospital personnel, especially from lowly interns.

Of all the private physicians with whom the interns came into contact, the unanimous least favorite was Dr. Andrej Volkov, a heavy-set, ancient-looking Russian with few medical skills and even fewer people skills. However, he seemed to have a lock on the local Eastern European ex-pat community, which provided him with an unlimited supply of compliant patients. He invoked his long-standing hospital privileges to unnecessarily admit patients who could easily be treated in his office. The hospital residents suspected that this practice was a ruse to inflate his bills with unneeded medical tests and treatment, all at the expense of his low-income clients.

Torrey was not the first intern to be infuriated by Dr. Volkov, but she was the first to call him out—in the nicest possible way, of course. Torrey was in the midst of a 24-hour on-call shift when her presence was requested in the ER at 11:00 a.m. for a consult. In conjunction with the chief resident, Travis McKnight, Torrey's job was to make a diagnosis and to determine whether the patient should be admitted to the hospital. Two problems surfaced immediately. First, Dr. McKnight was busy with a gang member suffering from a gunshot wound. Second, the patient, a young woman named Eva Berzinski, was under the primary care of Dr. Volkov.

Volkov was nowhere to be seen, but Ms. Berzinski was holding a letter on Volkov's office stationery stating that she had Irritable Bowel Syndrome and that she should be admitted for a full volley of tests over several days. The letter also demanded that the hospital start her on a regimen of antidepressant drugs and antibiotics to relieve her symptoms.

Like she had been trained to do, Torrey took a detailed history from the patient. Eva complained of severe abdominal pain and diarrhea. After learning the details and the temporal relationship between Eva's diet and the onset of her symptoms, Torrey was not convinced of the IBS diagnosis, the need for invasive testing, or the reasonableness of the prescribed drugs. She strongly suspected celiac disease, which could be controlled with a gluten-free diet. Instead of following Dr. Volkov's orders, Torrey wrote out a detailed nutritional plan for Eva, and to get things started off right, Torrey personally delivered some wild salmon and fruit from the cafeteria. She sat with Eva until the plate was empty, all the while talking about Eva's hopes and dreams as a recent immigrant.

When Volkov came to the hospital the following day and discovered that his patient was not receiving any *treatment,* he went on a tirade. He demanded to know what *idiot* screwed up his patient's treatment. Torrey was still on call. She was summoned to Ms. Berzinski's bedside.

"Who the hell are you to ignore my orders for my patient!" demanded Volkov. "I gave specific instructions for this patient's care. And the instructions," said Volkov with a dismissive sneer, "were *in writing*! I don't need or want some fresh-faced girlie doctor interfering with my medical practice."

By this time, the entire floor could hear the dressing-down. A nurse practitioner paged the chief resident and whispered that he needed to get down here immediately. "Volkov is on the warpath against a new resident."

Torrey showed no visible reaction to Volkov. She just calmly stared at him, which seemed to infuriate him even more. "What's wrong with you! Are you mute?"

"Are you finished, sir?" asked Torrey, chin set, in her sweetest voice. "Because if you are, I have a few words of my own." Volkov turned red with rage, but before he could hurl any new insults, Torrey continued, "It is apparent, sir, that you have fallen down on your duty to keep up on medical literature. Ms. Berzinski is suffering from your lack of knowledge."

It was a dead heat as to whom was more stunned—Volkov or the hospital staff who were watching and listening. Torrey utilized her photographic memory to call up all of the medical literature she had read on celiac disease. She calmly recited a recent study, which concluded that some doctors are unaware that celiac disease is often misdiagnosed for IBS because the symptoms are similar. However, the causes and treatments are vastly different. "Did you know, sir, that Ms. Berzinski has had two miscarriages, which is a red flag for celiac disease? Did you know, sir, that I did a quick blood draw, and I found that Ms. Berzinski's calcium and vitamin D levels are so abnormally low that they are off the chart? And the same blood draw showed that she tested positive for the celiac gene?" asked Torrey.

Volkov tried to interrupt, but Torrey never left an opening. "Did you know, sir, that Ms. Berzinski's diet consists almost exclusively of pasta, bread, and cereal—all high in gluten? And that it's obvious that her immune system is reacting to the gluten protein, which is very likely the cause of her pain and bowel issues?"

By now, Dr. McKnight was present, but he was enjoying Torrey's rebuke far too much to intervene. A shock of Volkov's wild white hair fell out of place, and beads of sweat started to run down his forehead into the creases of his jowls. His eyes were crazed as he looked at the chief resident and the other staff who had gathered around. He screamed at Torrey, "You're fired, you little bitch!"

Before Dr. McKnight could point out that Volkov had no authority to fire anyone at the hospital, 5'3" Torrey squared her hips, used her hands-on-hips power pose, and finished the conversation. "I may be small, and it is true I'm a female, but I will make it my gift to the medical profession to see to it that your hospital privileges are revoked. This isn't entirely based on your failures as a doctor, of which there are many, but mostly on your failures as a decent human. You are clearly unaware of your own patient's history. IBS is diagnosed by excluding other causes, and you have failed to eliminate celiac disease, or anything else. And you clearly put your own financial interests above the well-being of your patients. The tests and treatment you prescribed are unnecessary. Ms. Berzinski's symptoms are going to improve and then disappear within weeks of starting the new diet that I've discussed with her. All with no invasive tests, no drugs, and no risks of additional medical complications. Oh, and I almost forgot. You are clearly a misogynist who should not be allowed within a hundred yards of any female."

"How dare you!" Volkov cried. He looked at the chief resident and the nurses as he yelled out another clever rejoinder. "Don't just stand there! Do something about her!"

The corners of Torrey's mouth turned up just a bit. Not quite a smile but very close. "I have an idea," she said. "You wanted us to prescribe Lotronex to control Ms. Berzinski's diarrhea. Yes, that's a drug that can activate receptors in the nervous system, which can reduce bowel contractions. But that medicine is also known to cause ischemic colitis, a life-threatening condition." After a slight pause, Torrey added, "Why don't you do us all a favor and prescribe that for yourself?"

Volkov stormed out. Eva squeezed Torrey's hand gratefully. And the onlookers applauded.

● ● ●

"You know, most new residents are plagued by self-doubt," said Matthew that evening over dinner. The table was filled with Matthew's favorite foods, including thick rib eyes and a lovely store-bought salad. But he was

24

too flabbergasted to eat. "You really said all that?" asked Matthew with raised eyebrows.

Torrey sipped her glass of Pinot and smiled demurely. "That and more. I just gave you the highlights."

Matthew gazed at his lovely wife in wonder. She never failed to delight him.

After some thought, Matthew asked, "Don't you feel a little bit sorry for doctors like Volkov who grew up in an atmosphere of misogyny? Back in the day, female doctors were a rarity and likely threatened the men. They could insult women without the fear of backlash."

"No!" said Torrey. "I'm not applying yesterday's standards to today's conduct, which is problematic at best. I don't care what he did thirty or forty years ago. I agree—those times were different. I'm applying today's standards to today's conduct. These guys need to change with the times, like all businesses do. If they don't, then shame on them. Deal with the consequences."

"What did Dr. McKnight say about your interaction with Volkov?"

"He said he would have to report the entire incident to Dr. Peterson and maybe to the chief of staff."

"Uh-oh," said Matthew.

"I'm not worried," replied Torrey with a soft giggle. "McKnight was smiling when he said it. Besides, if I'm not mistaken, he was clapping the loudest after Volkov left."

Matthew, bewitched as always, loved her giggle. He leaned over and gave her a hug. "That's my girl."

Chapter 7

Matthew was between patients when his phone buzzed. It was Edwina with a text message in all caps: *MAN FROM COFFEE SHOP IS KNOCKING AT MY DOOR!*

Matthew quickly replied: *Don't answer.*

Matthew's instructions echoed Edwina's gut instinct. She readily complied. She did not answer, or make a sound, but her miniature wiener dog, Koa, didn't get the memo. She barked nonstop until the knocking ceased. The man at the door yelled out, "Miss Steed, I need to talk to you. I just want to ask you some questions!" Edwina remained motionless beside her new IKEA dining table for fifteen more minutes, trying to avoid the hiccups that her nerves sometimes caused. Then she knelt, poked her head up, and peeked out a front window. The man was now sitting in his car across the street. She couldn't get to her Prius without being seen. So, she did the only logical thing. She grabbed Koa, snuck out the back door, cut through the alley, ran three blocks, and called an Uber. She rode to Kaiser and texted Matthew to come to the lobby as soon as possible.

• • •

Rocco Washington, aka Big Rocky, sat in his just washed but unremarkable late model black Crown Vic for another two hours. He had chosen his vehicle knowing that the San Diego police department issued its detectives the same model. Originally from Newark, with a heavy New Jersey accent, Rocco had grown up a tough-guy fixer in a rough neighborhood. At 6'5" and a solid 285 pounds, he had used his size and fists to get by. Rocco was a pretty common name for guys in his neighborhood, and every one of them went by the nickname, Rocky. But none of them were as big as he was. He was the only Big Rocky.

When he moved out to California at age twenty-five, he had made a concerted effort to change everything about himself. He realized that breaking knuckles for a living was not sustainable, although he continued to carry a gun by force of habit.

When he arrived in Southern California, he learned how to speak softly. He practiced his manners, and he began to rely upon his brains, rather than his brawn. The one thing he couldn't change was his size. To his chagrin, his old nickname was revived when his new boss, thinking he was being witty and creative, introduced him as Big Rocky to his fellow subordinates.

The cheap coffee and the Hostess cupcakes that he had purchased at 7-Eleven were gone in the first twenty minutes of his surveillance of Steed's apartment. He threw the empty Hostess wrapper out the window, so there would be no trace of his secret weakness in the car. The guys at the bar would never let him live it down if they knew.

He was positive that Steed was in her apartment. Her car was in her assigned parking spot outside the complex, and he had seen her peeking out a window. He adjusted his shoulder holster and used his cell phone without taking his eyes off of Edwina's unit. No polite greetings were necessary. "She knows I want to talk to her. She refused to answer the door. She is either hiding inside her apartment now, or she somehow snuck out the back way. What do you want me to do?"

"Keep on her for now. As you know, we need to know what she knows. And make sure you catch her alone. Impress on her what is at stake.

27

What about the two doctors you saw her with? Do you think they know anything?"

"I suspect that she confided in them. After the three of them left the coffee shop, Steed left with the female doctor, and the male doctor lagged behind, obviously to see if I followed. I didn't."

"Try to find out who the doctors are, Big Rocky. Then report back." The call ended without a goodbye. Rocco ran his fingers through his shoulder length black hair as he looked at himself in the rearview mirror.

By force of habit from his days in New Jersey, he checked the safety on his non-registered firearm. He had only used it once since moving to California—having nothing to do with his job—to break up a fistfight between a pimp and one of his girls. After that encounter, the pimp was out of business.

• • •

Matthew's first question in the hospital lobby seemed a little dramatic, even to him. "Were you followed here?"

"I don't think so," said Edwina. "The guy was driving one of those old, big black sedans—like the gangsters use in the movies. I took an Uber to get here. I turned around and looked behind us the whole way. I didn't see him following."

Matthew was thinking, *Us?* But then he noticed the large rolling backpack that was parked beside Edwina. A dog's snout was peeking out. Matthew exclaimed, "How on earth did you smuggle that dog in here?" Edwina shrugged. "Never mind," said Matthew. "I know where there's an empty exam room on the third floor. Let's go there just in case he figures you came to the hospital. I don't want you to get roughed up on hospital property." Edwina wasn't sure whether Matthew was being facetious. But neither of them smiled.

It took Matthew about fifteen minutes to calm Edwina down. Then he scribbled an address on his prescription pad. "There's a dog park in our neighborhood. Why don't you grab some coffee and hang out there for a few hours? I'll be in touch. And cover up that dog before you head out!" whispered Matthew.

• • •

Matthew texted Torrey, but there was no reply. Torrey had decided not to wait for her supervisor to call her in about the Volkov situation. Instead, she showed up unannounced at Dr. Peterson's office. Torrey could see through the open door that Anne was meeting with the chief of surgery. After a fifteen-minute wait, Torrey was waved in.

"Well, Dr. Jamison, what a coincidence. You were on my list to talk to today," said Dr. Peterson wryly.

"I imagine you talked to Dr. McKnight," said Torrey as she sat down.

"And to the president of the hospital, who got a call from Dr. Volkov's attorney."

"I would like to add to what Dr. McKnight might have told you."

"I'm listening," Dr. Peterson replied evenly as she leaned back in her chair, waiting for an apology.

Torrey pulled no punches, and she led with a right hook. "Dr. Volkov is a bad doctor. He should have his privileges pulled." Dr. Peterson looked at Torrey, stunned into silence. So, Torrey continued, "I spent a lot of time with his patient, Ms. Berzinski. She was sent to the hospital without Dr. Volkov having even met her, much less having taken her medical history. She arrived with an undated and unsigned form note, which was obviously generated by Volkov's secretary. The other doctors in the ER confirmed that such notes are Volkov's standard practice, which is below the standard of care and a disservice to his patients. Plus, he ordered tests and treatment based on an improper diagnosis, which could have caused irreparable harm to Ms. Berzinski."

"Torrey, that's no excuse to—"

Torrey interrupted. "I know what you're going to say. But it's more than Volkov's negligence. He treats the hospital doctors, especially women, like second-class citizens. His attitude alone should disqualify him from our facility."

"You did not let me finish my thought, Torrey. As I was saying, I cannot excuse your outburst in front of patients and staff."

Torrey interjected, "No one has ever accused me of being a people person."

Dr. Peterson tried to hide her amusement. "But," Dr. Peterson said in a lighter tone, "I can understand why you did what you did. I cannot condone your methods, but I can justify them to the legal beagles."

Torrey slowly digested those words. She then coyly exclaimed, "Really?"

Dr. Peterson finally smiled. "And the president agrees. We are cancelling Volkov's privileges for all Kaiser hospitals. We are also submitting a comprehensive report to the State Medical Board, which will hold a hearing to determine whether he is censured, suspended from the practice of medicine, or has his medical license revoked. If we get sued, so be it. By all accounts, this should have been done years ago. I had heard murmurs before, but no one had ever put the case together like you did."

Torrey jumped up out of her seat. "That's wonderful! I'm so happy!"

"But Torrey, you know what I'm going to say now, right?"

Torrey paused and looked up at the ceiling like she was deep in thought. With a twinkle in her eye, she joked, "Hmm, can I get back to you on that?" When Dr. Peterson failed to laugh, Torrey said in a mock serious tone, "If I have a problem in the future with a doctor, I should come talk to you, correct?"

Dr. Peterson nodded solemnly and added for good measure, "So are we clear?"

"Crystal," replied Torrey in a military tone as she walked towards the door to leave. Just before she disappeared from Dr. Peterson's sight, Torrey heard a few final words trail after her. "Good work, doctor."

Chapter 8

Joe Cook followed his normal routine in the morning of what was to become a day to remember. Before leaving his house to start another 5:00 a.m. to midnight shift of following Rincon, he ran through his mental checklist of inspecting his equipment and selecting what he might need for that day or night. In his basement office, he unlocked a steel cabinet where he kept the tools of his trade, including surveillance equipment, cameras, night goggles, and enough first aid paraphernalia to rival a walk-in medical clinic. He grabbed what he needed and made a pile. He then opened his antique Wells Fargo bank vault, where he kept his guns. Some were legal in California, others not. He packed everything he might need in his work vehicle, a nondescript sedan, and set out at 4:30 a.m.

By 5:00 a.m., Joe was sitting in his usual spot, across the street from George Rincon's house. Over the last few weeks, Rincon's customary practice was to leave his home at about 8:30 a.m. and head out to get coffee. Today, instead of his usual millennial garb, Rincon was dressed in costume like he was going out trick-or-treating on Halloween night. Joe did a double take. It took him a few seconds to process what he was seeing. But it quickly dawned on him that Rincon was wearing an outfit from a *Star Wars* movie. It had been a while since Joe had seen any movie from that franchise, but he could swear that Rincon was dressed as Luke

Skywalker, complete with a baggy shirt, a size-too-small pair of stretch leggings, and a lightsaber hanging on his belt. Joe laughed out loud and said to nobody, "What the hell?"

Rincon gingerly slid into his car, taking care not to wrinkle his outfit. He slowly backed out of his driveway and then sped up, heading towards downtown. Joe settled in about four car lengths behind, wondering where Rincon was going. He couldn't help repeating under his breath every few blocks, "What the hell?"

Joe followed Rincon into downtown, through the Gas Lamp Quarter, to the Embarcadero. Rincon was darting in and out of traffic, and Joe had to step on it to keep up. Joe wondered what the damn hurry was. Joe almost lost him when an elderly man pulled out from the curb in front of him and then proceeded to drive his late model Cadillac at a frantic fifteen miles per hour. The man was dressed in a blue suit, white shirt, and blue tie. Joe figured that this guy had given birth to the saying that "Conservative people drive conservative cars conservatively."

Joe passed the Cadillac at a yellow light, looked both ways, and spotted Rincon pulling into the Convention Center parking lot. Joe made a left turn and followed Rincon into the lot. Joe was going a little too fast as he turned down a row of cars, searching for a parking space. He had to slam on the brakes in order to avoid a trio of superheroes—Green Lantern, Supergirl, and Captain America. The sixty-something, plump, gray-haired lady parading around as Supergirl, turned around and gave Joe the finger. The teenage Captain America, probably the grandson of Supergirl, yelled at Joe, "Watch it, you freak!" Joe looked up and saw a big-screen billboard: WELCOME TO COMIC-CON 2019.

Because it took him fifteen frustrating minutes to find a parking spot, Joe had lost track of Rincon. Joe figured he could find him again once he got inside, but he didn't count on the fact that in his ticket line alone, he counted six Luke Skywalkers, not to mention three Darth Vaders, and a Chewbacca. In the time it took Joe to get to the front of the ticket line, the Obi-Wan Kenobi, who was standing behind Joe with a youngster dressed as a Droid, had quipped at least a dozen times to passersby, "This is not the Droid you are looking for." Each time Obi-Wan said the words, he and his sidekick would laugh so hard that Joe thought they might keel over from lack of oxygen.

Joe didn't know whether to laugh or cry at the assortment of sights and sounds outside the venue, but he definitely cringed at having to pay sixty-three dollars for a one-day pass to the four-day event. The ticket seller told Joe he was fortunate that there were any single-day tickets available; they usually were sold out weeks in advance. Joe didn't feel lucky as he handed over his credit card. The entire event seemed childish, but the prices were definitely adult-sized. He hoped Matthew wouldn't question this item on his expense report.

Once inside, it wasn't easy, but he eventually found Rincon, who was busy glad-handing and trying to hit on every young-looking Batgirl and Catwoman in the place. Rincon even stopped to say hello to a young Judy Garland look-alike who was dressed as Dorothy. Joe got close enough to overhear Judy ask Rincon, "Toto, too?"

Naturally, Rincon, while leering at Judy, replied, "Yes, Toto, too."

Joe watched Rincon shell out eighty dollars in cash for the autograph of a bored-looking Mr. Sulu from the original *Star Trek* show. For some reason, Joe was glad that Captain Kirk and Spock were not also there hawking their autographs.

Dressed in chinos and a blue sport coat, Joe felt and looked like a fish out of water. He bought a fifty-five-dollar cheap-looking Iron Man mask from a vendor in order to better blend in with the crowd, but he still followed Rincon at a respectable distance. After an hour or so, Joe noticed that another person, dressed head to toe in an Imperial Stormtrooper costume, was also following Rincon. At first, Joe thought he must be imagining it, but for the next 30 minutes, Joe saw that wherever Rincon went, the Stormtrooper followed. When Rincon stopped, the Stormtrooper stopped. When Rincon paused to greet a green-painted bodybuilder who was growling and posing in tattered pants and a ripped T-shirt as The

Incredible Hulk, the Stormtrooper stood to the side with folded arms and watched.

When Rincon wandered to the farthest reaches of the convention center, with no one around except a group of Zombies taking selfies while passing around a joint, Joe saw the Stormtrooper walk up to Rincon, grab his arm, and begin talking in his ear. Rincon tried to pull away, but the Stormtrooper kept talking and would not let go. After a few seconds, the Stormtrooper jerked Rincon behind a display wall promoting the latest *Avengers* movie. Joe continued to watch from his distant vantage point. After a few seconds, the Stormtrooper came out from behind the temporary wall and began marching briskly away. Rincon did not reappear. Joe hurriedly walked over to the display wall and pulled off his mask. Glancing over his shoulder, he saw the Stormtrooper disappearing into a sea of people. When Joe raced around the end of the wall, he saw Rincon lying in a pool of blood. What looked to be a knife handle was sticking out of Rincon's chest. Joe knelt over the body and felt for a pulse. There was none. Rincon's lightsaber was still in its sheath. The Stormtrooper's blaster was on the ground next to the body.

As Joe surveyed the huge room while heading back towards the entrance of the convention center, he realized he faced several insurmountable problems. First, the few security personnel he saw looked like they were high school age, and they were too caught up in the general hubbub to be of any real help. Second, there were any number of marked exit doors as well as unmarked doors leading to who knows where, that the killer already could have used to escape. Third, even if the killer had not yet left the building, there were countless Stormtroopers in his field of vision. And they all looked the same.

Chapter 9

The news that Dr. Volkov would no longer have privileges at Kaiser spread like wildfire. Torrey became a hero to the hospital staff, especially the female nurses and residents. The next day when both Matthew and Torrey had shifts in the emergency room, Travis McKnight brought in a platter of cupcakes with the letter *T* in fancy script written on each one. Dr. McKnight gathered all the employees who happened to be in the ER and yelled, "Everyone grab a cupcake! I want to propose a toast." As they all lifted their cupcakes into the air, he proclaimed, "To Dr. Jamison! May we never set eyes on Volkov again!"

As complimentary shouts and cheers filled the room, Matthew grabbed Torrey and swung her around. "I'm so proud of you. See, every once in a while, the good guys prevail! And the bad guys get what's coming to them!"

Being the modest young woman that she was, Torrey worked hard not to respond with a shout and fist pump.

• • •

The light mood changed in an instant as an announcement over the loudspeaker boomed, "Code Silver. I repeat, Code Silver." The staff started to scurry around, wheeling patients out of the ER common area and into separate exam rooms. Matthew asked Torrey, "What in the world is a Code Silver?"

"Active shooter! Active shooter in the hospital! Employee manual page thirty-seven!"

Matthew looked at his wife in amazement. He was reminded once again that she had a photographic memory and a staggeringly high IQ to analyze what she had memorized. "I guess I missed that page," quipped Matthew as his adrenaline began pumping.

His eyes were drawn to the glass entrance doors to the ER as they slid closed and locked with a loud clunk. He saw a security guard, gun drawn, appear out of nowhere outside on the sidewalk. The voice over the loudspeaker confirmed what was happening, "The hospital is now on total lockdown. Move to the nearest safe, enclosed room and await further instructions. No one is allowed to enter or exit the hospital until further notice."

From the ER, faint gunshots and screams could be heard. The sounds grew louder as the shooter got closer. The ER patients who could move on their own stormed the exit doors. The doors would not open. A young man with a bandaged foot banged on the door and shouted, "Why are we locked in? We're trapped like animals! Let us out!"

Dr. McKnight, Matthew, and Torrey herded him, the other patients, and nurses away from the common area and into exam rooms. The three of them then huddled together to figure out what to do next. But before they could agree on anything, they heard another gunshot in the hallway leading to the common area. The gunman would be there any second. Matthew shouted for Dr. McKnight to take Torrey and hide behind the nursing station. Dr. McKnight began pulling Torrey's arm when they heard a loud voice barking, "WHERE IS SHE? WHERE IS THE LITTLE BITCH?" Torrey's thoughts started to race. There was no mistaking that voice. Her eyes widened in alarm. Dr. Volkov was on the rampage, and she was the target.

Torrey swatted at Dr. McKnight and broke free from his hold.

"Matthew, that's Volkov! He's gone berserk! We have to stop him!" Looking around at her co-workers and the patients who were going to be in the line of fire, her fearful adrenaline rush quickly turned into resolve.

Matthew took charge. He calmly issued orders, "You two, go over by the exit doors. When he comes in, I'll take him out while his attention is diverted. Travis, if he gets by me somehow, don't let anything happen to her."

"Count on it," Dr. McKnight vowed, as he again grabbed Torrey's arm.

A few seconds later, Volkov burst into the room, a gun in his right hand and a handful of bullets in his left. His eyes were wild, his stark white hair was a mess, and his face was beet red. The employees still in the ER hit the floor. Torrey jerked free from Dr. McKnight's grip and stepped out from behind a partition. She yelled to Volkov, "Hey! You looking for me?"

Just as Matthew was muttering "Really?" to himself, Volkov started screaming and charged at Torrey, gun raised. Before he had taken two steps, Matthew's 6'2" frame and 210 pounds of muscle charged into Volkov and knocked him to the floor. Matthew landed five or six vicious blows to Volkov's head for good measure. Matthew's Wheaties box face was untouched. The gun slid across the floor and was recovered by Dr. McKnight.

• • •

As the police assessed the crime scene, Dr. McKnight, automatically reverting into his role as chief resident, decided that Volkov needed some medical care to his bloody face before he was taken into custody. Torrey volunteered to do the honors, while Matthew and Travis restrained the barely conscious patient. The doctors jointly decided that Volkov needed no local anesthetic. Volkov did not get a vote. Torrey actually whistled while she worked. After she finished with her trusty scalpel, sutures, and bandages, she bent down and whispered in his ear, "I want you to never forget me."

She was usually very good with her scalpel and suturing work, but somehow, as Volkov would discover when his bandages were removed, her handiwork in this instance left Volkov with permanent scars. On each cheek, in perfect 12-pt Times New Roman font, was the letter *T*.

Chapter 10

Police were still everywhere. Orderlies were busy mopping up blood splatters, remnants of the beating that Matthew had given to Volkov. Dr. McKnight was running interference for Matthew and Torrey with hospital administrators so that they could sneak away to wash up and change into new scrubs. Just before they were ready to head back out to the floor, both Matthew's and Torrey's phones buzzed with a text from Edwina. *Are you two okay? I saw on the news that something is going on at your hospital.*

After sharing a conspiratorial look, Matthew pointed to his chest, indicating that he would reply to Mrs. Ed. *Nothing to see here. Move along.*

Edwina, familiar with Matthew's dry wit, guessed that there was plenty to see but decided to get the details later. *When can we meet again? We need a plan. I'm worried about Toohey's enforcer.*

Where are you now? asked Matthew.

Laying low at the dog park you told me about.

Don't go back to your apartment. Come stay with us. We have an extra bedroom. We should be home early tonight, probably by 7.

Edwina spent the next few hours checking her neighborhood for the enforcer's car. Satisfied that it was all clear, she ignored Matthew's warning, ducked into her apartment, loaded up her car with some essentials, and then went to the local Safeway for several bags of groceries, including the breakfast of champions—Lucky Charms cereal, Wonder bread, and freshly squeezed orange juice. She also picked up a bouquet of flowers. She hated to go anywhere without a hostess gift. She arrived early and waited patiently on Matthew and Torrey's porch, Koa by her side, until they got home.

Torrey was the first to arrive. "Hi, Edwina! Who's your little friend?" Torrey bent down and gave Koa an appreciative pet.

"I hope you don't mind. Koa is my fur baby. I didn't have anyone to leave her with. Matthew said to come right over, so—"

"Hey," said Torrey. "It's all good. I love animals, and I've been trying to convince Matthew to get a dog or cat. Maybe having Koa around will do the trick."

They went inside the condo, and Koa started running around the living room. Edwina looked embarrassed and said, "I should give you a heads up."

"About what?"

"About Koa. She likes to race around wildly until she drops from exhaustion. She tries to jump up on the furniture, and she'll bark loudly when it's time to feed her."

Torrey smiled as she watched Koa circle the coffee table. "Hmm. So, what you are saying is that Koa is a dog. I think we will somehow survive Koa's peculiarities." After a pause, Torrey knelt down and rubbed Koa's protruding belly. And then lightly, and ever so politely, said, "She seems a little chubby."

"She's not fat. She's just big-boned!" Edwina mildly protested.

Torrey whispered in singsong directly in Koa's ear as she continued to stroke her stomach, "Are you just big-boned? Huh? Are you? That's a good girl!" Torrey turned to Edwina with a smile, saying, "You know, if Koa doesn't get more exercise, her bones are going to get even bigger." Edwina laughed, but inside she was scowling.

· · ·

When Matthew arrived home, he was still amped up after the adventure with Volkov. Edwina, after hearing all the details of the episode, had only one question. "Torrey, that's all super interesting, especially the part about the gun, but tell me, how do you keep your hair on fleek after all that activity?"

Torrey grinned. Matthew looked puzzled, but they all had a laugh as Torrey pretended to shape her pixie cut with her hands and said to Matthew, "I'll explain it later." Then, they buckled down to work.

"Okay," said Matthew, "let's figure out what needs to happen and which of us is best suited for each task. Off the top of my head, it seems to me that we have to do the following. I think—"

"Wait a minute," interrupted Edwina. "What about that guy who's following me? Should we call the police? I don't like hiding out or imposing on you. I can't stay with you guys forever."

Torrey exchanged a look with Matthew and said, "Mrs. Ed, if that guy wanted to hurt you, he would have by now. He was knocking on your door, not shooting holes in it. He probably just wants to threaten you, so you don't go to the authorities about Toohey. But I agree he sounds like bad news, so staying here with us for the time being makes sense."

Matthew said, "As I was saying, I think the first step is to have my investigator find out everything there is to know about Toohey. One of us needs to interview the nurse who referred Hawk and Angela to Toohey, and one of us needs to meet with Toohey himself."

"I'll do both. I'll meet with the nurse and Toohey," interjected Torrey.

"Hold on, we haven't gotten to the division of labor yet," replied Matthew.

"I'm just saying, I'm the logical choice to meet with those two. I can put on my actress hat and present myself as a mother who will do anything for her cancer-stricken child. And I really don't have to act because that's how I would be," she said gravely. "So that's settled, right?" Torrey looked back and forth between Matthew and Edwina.

Matthew glared. Edwina held up both hands. "Don't get me into the middle of your marital bliss. But what Torrey says does make sense, Matthew."

Matthew grimaced at his petite wife. "You think it's a good idea for you to be the front man, so to speak, when there is some hood tracking us?"

"I came up with it, so of course it's a good idea," said Torrey with a sugary-sweet smile. "Plus, you said yourself, the guy is a well-dressed hood. How dangerous could he be?"

"Fine," said Matthew. "Just stick to the script, and I'll be just a stone's throw away if you get into trouble."

"I'm not worried," said Torrey nonchalantly, as Matthew groaned. "And don't give me that hang-dog look," added Torrey while blowing a kiss.

Edwina had to laugh, remarking, "You guys are so cute together."

Matthew threw up his hands in defeat. "So, if that's settled, I want you," he said, gesturing to Mrs. Ed, "to set up a meeting for you and me with Hawk and with Angela if she's up to it about exactly how Toohey presented the treatment that he was suggesting. And we need to identify other parents who paid Toohey money. In the meantime, I'll talk to my investigator about the steps we want him to undertake." After a moment of thought, Matthew snapped his fingers and added, "And I'll talk to a few people to see if they've heard of Toohey's clinical trials."

Chapter 11

The following day was routine, but after the previous day in the ER, routine was refreshing. Both Matthew and Torrey were busy, but what else was new? The only interruption was when they each were separately cornered and interrogated by Dr. Peterson, who wanted to see if their stories jibed with what she had heard from Dr. McKnight. She seemed satisfied. Fortunately, she hadn't asked, and none of the three had volunteered anything about Torrey's first aid on Volkov's face.

When they got home, Edwina was out. A note left on the counter said that she was visiting her brother. Matthew was glad that he was alone with Torrey. "I got a call earlier today from Joe Cook," Matthew told Torrey after they had finished with the dishes and were relaxing on the living room couch.

"Oh really?" said Torrey. "What did he say?"

"Well," said Matthew as he placed his hand over hers, "as you know, I had asked Joe to keep tabs on George Rincon for a month or so in order to track his movements, his friends, and his medical appointments."

"I know. So, what did Joe say? What's Rincon up to? I'm anxious to figure out what to do about him."

Matthew paused, looked Torrey in the eyes, and burst out triumphantly, "Rincon is dead! Murdered yesterday!"

Torrey's initial puzzled expression turned into dark anger within seconds. "Wait, what?" Torrey started to tear up. Instead of looking happy, she exuded defeat.

"Why are you crying?" asked Matthew in surprise. "You hated that jerk! We took this residency at Kaiser so that we could somehow get revenge for what he did to you. Someone else took care of him for us. He's dead!"

Tears flowed unchecked, and Torrey's face became distorted with rage. "Don't hate me, but I wanted to be the one to get revenge," she burst out. "I wanted to see his face! I wanted to stare into his eyes and say, 'Remember *me*, you creepy bastard?'"

Matthew got up, pulled Torrey to her feet, and into his arms. He could feel her shivering, even though the breeze through the open windows was at least seventy-five degrees. He stroked her hair as he said softly into her ear, "I know you despised Rincon. We both did. But now he's been executed without us having to take any risks."

They didn't speak for several minutes as they embraced. Torrey's mind was working overtime. She finally broke the silence. "Who did it? Who killed him? How do they know it was murder? What did Joe say?"

"Rincon was stabbed while he was at the Comic-Con Convention downtown by someone dressed in a *Star Wars* costume. Joe learned all about it from a fraternity brother who works in the San Diego police department. I guess it didn't take them long to figure out who did it. They knew it wasn't a robbery because Rincon had about $200 in his wallet when he was found. As is usually the case, the police started looking at family, friends, and motive. They learned that Rincon's daughter and son-in-law had taken out a restraining order against Rincon last year because they suspected that Rincon had molested their five-year-old daughter. They couldn't prove it, so Rincon was not prosecuted. But apparently the son-in-law screamed at the judge during a hearing that Rincon should be on death row. The police went to the daughter's house with a search warrant. They found a blood-stained Stormtrooper costume in the closet just as the son-in-law came home from work. He confessed within minutes. Everyone in the family knew that Rincon went to Comic-Con every year, so I guess the son-in-law came up with a plan to obtain his own brand of justice."

As Matthew lovingly swayed her in place, like they were slow dancing, Torrey numbly drifted back to that day in high school when the trusted high school counselor, George Rincon, raped her in his office. Ostensibly, Rincon had been counseling her after her little sister's death, but what he had really been doing was grooming her for compliance. Then she imagined Rincon lying in a pool of his own blood at the convention center. She was happy he was dead, but why did she feel that justice had not been served? Was it simply that she wasn't the one who did the killing? Was it that her repressed shadow self was robbed of her moment?

Being a super-fast reader in conjunction with her memory had allowed Torrey to satisfy her voracious appetite for scientific knowledge and philosophical principles. She had always been curious about and intrigued by the works of psychiatrist Carl Jung who proposed the concept that our minds are divided into the persona and the shadow self. We may view ourselves as good persons, and we may well be. We might follow the Golden Rule. We might project steadiness, maturity, and love for mankind. From a young age, we all learn what are acceptable behaviors, and most of us adhere to laws, social mores, and Christian values. And the world is the better for it.

But, Jung wrote, just because most of us don't act on an impulse to steal, cheat, say hurtful things, or kill, doesn't mean that such thoughts never occur. This dark aspect, which most of us push down into our unconscious, or ignore altogether in order to not feel shame, is the shadow beneath the surface of who we think we are.

Torrey thought about that day at San Quentin when she had sliced open the neck of the inmate who had murdered Matthew's father. Blood was everywhere. Then she had stabbed him in the heart, twice. With her religious upbringing, she had always believed that she was opposed to vigilantism, much less murder. But that was before she met Matthew. Before hearing about Ted Nash who shot Matthew's father in cold blood and destroyed Matthew's happy childhood. Before Matthew's mother had died of a broken heart. Before she was suddenly and unexpectedly face-to-face with Nash in the prison clinic and white-hot rage filled her heart. Before she orchestrated the fictional narrative that Nash had attacked her. Before she experienced the profound satisfaction of watching his face go lifeless as she struck him multiple times with her scalpel. Before there had been a paradigm shift in her belief system.

Society dictated that she should have been sorry for killing Nash. But she wasn't. She should have felt a tsunami of guilt. But she didn't. When she told Matthew how the killing actually happened, she didn't even feel embarrassed, much less shame or regret. She only felt that justice, though delayed, had been served. And that justice had freed Matthew's psyche from a lifetime of pain.

But now she wondered. Did she have some dark proprietary need for vengeance? Had she just been pretending her entire life that her moral compass was unwavering? Had she just been avoiding a confrontation with the picture she had of herself? What else could account for this crushing feeling of loss?

Chapter 12

Now that Joe Cook's surveillance of George Rincon was over, Matthew had a new assignment for him—find out everything there was to know about Dr. Albert Toohey. Joe was up to the task. He knew that with the investigation skills that he had honed as a burglary detective and then a homicide detective, he could discover more in a week about an individual's habits, secrets, and desires than the individual's mother or wife would learn in a lifetime.

Joe retreated to his basement home office and fired up his two powerful computers, each tied to a giant monitor. On computer number one, he listed each item of information he wanted to uncover. As was his wont, he verbalized his thoughts as he typed. He actually talked to himself a lot. Not consciously. In fact, he usually wasn't listening to himself, even when he heard the words come out. But it helped him to focus. "Okay, this guy is a medical doctor, so I need his education documentation, his employment history, and his personal information. Married? Kids? Regarding his current job, I need bank records and credit reports to know money earned compared to money spent." He gently rocked in the wooden rocking chair he used at his desk while he poured himself a cup of black coffee from his French Press. While he continued to think, he stared at the vintage Wells Fargo bank vault that he used to store his guns, knives, and night vision surveillance equipment. He wasn't above using force, but he doubted he would have to open his vault for this assignment.

As he slurped his coffee, he logged into computer number two where he could access the professional-grade databases to which he subscribed as a licensed investigator. He started with the TLOxp and the Tracers Info software and found Toohey's social security number, home address, and phone number within seconds. Toohey, age fifty-six, had married Hillary Flint, age thirty-two, five years earlier, no kids, no pets. DMV records showed that Toohey and Hillary owned two vehicles, an older Toyota Camry and an almost new Boxster. Joe had to chuckle about the choice of cars. Just like the Porsche SUV is simply a VW Touareg in disguise, anyone who knows cars realizes that a Boxster is a fake Porsche. No power, no styling, and no point in owning one other than to impress other non-car people.

Joe knew from Matthew that Toohey worked at his own private clinic, but oddly enough, Toohey did not maintain a website or a social media presence. He had no LinkedIn page or reviews on Yelp. *How does this guy get any patients without an online presence?* Joe wondered. *Does he even treat patients?* The American Medical Association listed Toohey as an inactive member. The California Medical Association showed he had graduated from a third-tier medical school twenty-two years ago, which apparently had limited him to finding initial employment in the federal government, at the U.S. Food & Drug Administration. He started as a glorified librarian, where he catalogued published medical research papers for three years. In a typical example of the Peter Principle in government work, he gradually was promoted over the next seventeen years, eventually attaining the title of Principal Researcher. For reasons unclear from the public records, Toohey left the FDA five years ago, after which he opened his own office. Fortunately, Joe had a friend, Everett Beck, in Homeland Security who could easily gain access to the FDA's sealed files to learn the backstory. Everett, known to all by Big E, was a Sigma Alpha Epsilon fraternity brother from college. Joe knew from past experience that the information would only cost him two cheeseburgers and a pitcher of Heineken. And maybe two Dodgers tickets if the information was particularly sensitive. An SAE brother can unlock—for another brother—the most secure doors. And the fact that it's the largest fraternity in the country means one brother can find another in any city, whenever needed.

Joe knew that Everett couldn't talk freely on his office phone, so Joe called Big E's personal cell and left a coded voicemail that only an SAE brother would understand: *Am looking for a True Gentleman, J.* Less than five minutes later, Big E had left his office, gone around the corner for coffee, and called Joe back. After explaining that he was not looking for any national secrets, Joe convinced Big E to help. In addition to dinner and beer, Big E wanted a piece of pecan pie and a promise to join him at the next Homecoming game at UCLA. Ten minutes later, Joe's email dinged, and courtesy of Big E, he was looking at Toohey's entire FDA employment file. The subject line dictated that Joe would also have to spring for a plate of sweet potato fries.

Joe muttered to himself as he read, "Ha! Wait until Matthew hears about this! The guy was fired for sexual misconduct. He was carrying on with one of his lab technicians—a young woman by the name of Hillary Flint, now known as Mrs. Albert Toohey."

Joe instinctively knew that he had to learn more about the Toohey couple. A little surveillance can tell a lot. Joe was the proud owner of two vehicles. For his personal use, he had treated himself to a tricked-out, late model Range Rover, which allowed him, as a confirmed never-to-marry-again bachelor, to simultaneously impress the ladies and indulge his passion for off-roading in the desert. For business, he utilized an uninteresting looking, four-door, 1990 Nissan Sentra sedan that had a large trunk and a bench seat for catnaps. The area behind the driver's seat was perfect for a large cooler and several coffee thermoses. In a plastic container on the passenger floor, he kept a hand-held urinal for those times when he couldn't leave his car during a lengthy surveillance. Joe had modified the vehicle with several secret compartments to hold two handguns, ammunition, black-market surveillance equipment from China, and his extensive first aid kit. He had started accumulating medical supplies after a fellow private eye got shot by an angry husband who was caught cheating on his wife. The private eye had called 911 but had bled out before an ambulance arrived. Joe swore that was not going to happen to him.

As it was late afternoon, Joe decided to wait outside Toohey's clinic and then follow the good doctor home. It didn't take long for Toohey to emerge from the uncovered parking lot next to his beige-stucco, three-story, nondescript building. Joe was surprised that Toohey was driving the Camry rather than the Boxster.

Toohey headed northwest, as expected, towards the beach community of Solana Beach where the Tooheys owned an average-priced home, according to Zillow. However, Toohey took an unexpected turn about a mile from his neighborhood and drove several long blocks to a small self-storage facility. The place was old and rundown, probably a mom-and-pop operation, nothing like the fancy Public Storage facilities that had cropped up all over the country in the last twenty years. Toohey looped through the maze of buildings and stopped in front of Unit 206. Joe parked on the shoulder of the adjacent main street and watched through binoculars as Toohey opened his car door, threw a spent cigarette on the ground, and removed a cardboard box from his trunk. The garage door on 206 was protected by an oversized combination lock. Toohey balanced the box between his hip and the wall while he used both hands to spin the dial. When Toohey pulled up on the door handle, Joe could see that the visible portion of the locker contained several tables that were covered with boxes and stacks of paper. Toohey placed his box on one of the tables, walked back to the doorway, and looked left and right. He reentered and pulled down the roller door. Five minutes later, Toohey emerged, the box, now empty, dangling from his hand. He put the lock back on the storage unit door, threw the box into his trunk, got back in his car, and drove away. Joe recognized suspicious behavior when he saw it, and he knew two things for sure. First, whatever Toohey was up to, he wanted no witnesses. A dilapidated storage facility meant no guards, no rules, and no paperwork. Second, whatever Toohey had taken into the unit was still in there. Joe had to figure out what it was.

Joe followed Toohey home. As Joe suspected from the value of Toohey's house, Dr. and Mrs. Toohey lived on the wrong side of the street. Although their modest looking home was worth over one million dollars, it had no view and almost no usable land. The palatial homes that were on the other side of the wide road were on expansive treed lots boasting manicured lawns which rivaled the most exclusive country club fairways. The owners made certain that the attractive landscaping was mostly hidden from prying eyes behind tall brick walls with ornate iron gates. Closed circuit security cameras were in style. The only things missing were drawbridges over moats. Of course, because these houses were sitting on the edge of a cliff overlooking the Pacific Ocean, they were selling for five times as much as the houses on Toohey's side of the street. *The perks of the one-percenters*, Joe reflected.

As Toohey made a slow left into his driveway, Joe pulled over to the curb, three houses away, on the other side of the road. The only movement on the street were gardeners mowing and blowing. From this vantage point, he saw Mrs. Toohey come out of the house to greet her husband. Joe was rarely surprised about marital relationships, but today he was dumbfounded. Whereas Dr. Toohey had the look of a balding, paunchy Neanderthal, Mrs. Toohey was a knockout. Dressed in short shorts and a low-cut sleeveless blouse to show off her long legs and show-girl figure, she pranced over to Toohey, stood on her tippy toes, and kissed his cheek. With her freshly curled and bleached blonde hair, high cheekbones, and moon-like eyes, she reminded Joe of a Stepford Wife, except for the lit cigarette dangling from her left hand. "Hot damn," breathed Joe with a soft whistle. He involuntarily rubbed his hands together as he whispered, "Now that's what I'm talking about." He hoped Toohey and Hillary would linger outside, but they walked together towards the house. Joe noticed Toohey's hand start to wander as they crossed the threshold and closed the door behind them.

Just as Joe was about to leave, his attention was drawn to another car, a black Crown Vic, parked on Toohey's side of the street, under a stand of trees. Although the Vic was a good hundred meters away, Joe could see a huge man sitting in the driver's seat. The windows were rolled down. Joe couldn't see a face, but he clearly saw a sandwich in one hand and a Coke in the other. Joe had been on enough stakeouts to know one when he saw one. Whoever he was, the man was watching Toohey's house.

Chapter 13

Matthew knocked, even though Anne Peterson's door was wide open. Anne looked up, smiled warmly, and gestured to the guest chair closest to her desk. Anne tried not to have favorites among the residents, but Matthew's leadership abilities, earnest efforts, and good nature had won her over. She was also curious about his marriage. Torrey seemed to be his complete opposite. Anne wondered what had brought them together.

"Hello, Matthew, have you disarmed any maniacs today?"

Matthew grinned. "No, there seems to be a shortage of gun-toting crazies this morning. But I'll keep an eye out."

"Thank you. What can I do for you?"

"I'm interested in participating in a clinical trial, and—"

"As a patient or a researcher?" Anne deadpanned.

It took Matthew a second to appreciate Dr. Peterson's attempt at humor. "Touché," Matthew replied as he laughed. Leaning forward in his chair, Matthew explained, "I'm thinking about medical research as a career focus. I know you're the principal researcher on an ongoing study looking at the carcinogenic effects of weed killer. I wonder if you could tell me more about that."

"Well, as you know, a clinical trial is where human participants are treated with different interventions pursuant to research protocols. Often the researchers are comparing one drug to another to see whether one is more effective in treating a specific disease. Or they might want to learn whether a prescribed drug works at all by administering it to one group while another group gets a placebo. As you probably know, my lab is doing animal studies rather than clinical trials. Our study has been in progress for almost ten years now. I'm proud to say that our work has been the foundation of a number of successful lawsuits against the maker of Roundup, a systemic herbicide. Even though the EPA has found that the active ingredient, glyphosate, is not carcinogenic to humans, our research shows that it causes non-Hodgkin's lymphoma, a common cancer among users of Roundup. Are you interested in working in my lab on this study?" Anne said hopefully.

"Not exactly. I'm wondering if you know of any clinical trials that are ongoing in the San Diego area having to do with pediatric brain cancers? As everyone with ears knows, my wife, Torrey, is passionate about becoming a brain surgeon, and I thought I could support her by doing some research in that field. I know that the FDA has to approve all clinical trials, and I've gone through the registry database maintained by the NIH. I couldn't find anything local. I thought you might know of some trials that are not yet listed. Or perhaps you know of some doctors who are conducting clinical trials that have not been approved."

"I'm not aware of any such trials. The Office of Good Clinical Practice sets the policies for clinical trials, and no one, medical doctor or not, can conduct a clinical trial without the blessing and oversight of the FDA. So, if the database doesn't show any clinical trials in San Diego, then there aren't any."

Anne was impressed that Matthew wanted to learn more about Torrey's area on interest. A supportive spouse is hard to find. "So, Matthew, yes, I know that Torrey wants to become a pediatric brain surgeon, which is quite a lofty goal. That's a long and grueling specialty, not lightly undertaken. I know she can do it. I read her application papers, which touched on her family circumstances. Can you tell me more about what lead Torrey to her monumental decision?"

Matthew took a long breath. "Her little sister, Leia, died of glioblastoma when Torrey was just a teenager. There were issues with her sister's care. And her family didn't have the resources, on top of treatment costs, to move from California to Oregon which had a 'Right to Die' statute allowing people to die with dignity. It affected her deeply, and she is dedicated to doing everything she can to help other families in that situation. She wants to have a clinic where everyone, especially children, can get the treatment they need without regard to finances."

"I love her commitment to children with cancer," said Anne.

Matthew reflected that Anne could never guess just how committed Torrey was.

• • •

Matthew had been meaning to drive up to LA to visit his Uncle TJ. He missed his mother's brother, and he knew that he owed a lot to his uncle for helping him get through his father's murder and his mother's passing. As a bonus, he figured he could pick TJ's brain about clinical trials.

Torrey was excited to make the trip with him. They intended to stay overnight in Matthew's Pacific Palisades childhood home. No one had lived there since Matthew's mother had passed away, but between the frequent visits by a caretaker and a gardener, the house and grounds looked immaculate. They arrived in the early afternoon. TJ was scheduled to arrive around 7:00 p.m. for a late dinner. "So, what shall we do while we're waiting for TJ?" asked Torrey while they lounged in an oversized hammock in the large, park-like backyard.

Matthew looked around. "I know, we could play croquet!"

"You're joking, right?" There was no reply, so Torrey repeated, "Please tell me you're joking!"

"Haven't you ever played?" asked an astonished Matthew.

Torrey, having grown up on the wrong side of the tracks in poverty-stricken East Palo Alto, couldn't resist having some fun. "Well," mocked

Torrey, "only after a rousing game of polo, when my string of ponies needed some rest."

"It's fun! Don't knock it until you try it!" Matthew said with a sheepish grin.

"I notice that you didn't tell me about your secret croquet obsession until after I married you," said Torrey playfully. Before she was able to make even more fun of her husband, her phone buzzed. "Uh-oh," said Torrey. "I wonder if this is Dr. Peterson. I asked her to call if—" She held up her pointer finger to signal that the call would just take a minute. "Hello, Dr. Peterson?" Matthew listened to Torrey's side of the conversation. "Yes, I still want to participate . . . yes, I can be there in a couple of hours . . . thank you very much for calling!"

"Matthew," Torrey exclaimed, "someone fell off a roof and was just brought into the ER. He has a closed head injury. They're going to operate this evening after the swelling goes down. Dr. Peterson thought that I, being the overly enthusiastic surgical resident that I am, might want to observe the surgery from *inside* the operating room!" She gave Matthew a giant hug.

"Well, better you than me. No, really, I'm happy for you." He returned the squeeze. "Take my car. I'll take the train tomorrow. I'll have TJ take me to the train station."

"Thank you, Matthew. I sure am lucky to have you." Then she added with a wink, "Even if you like to play croquet."

"Hilarious," he dryly replied. "Now get going. I'll walk you to the car."

• • •

TJ was disappointed to miss Torrey, whom he hadn't seen since her intimate wedding to Matthew in the Muir Woods near San Francisco. A week after graduating from medical school, Matthew and Torrey had exchanged vows while standing in the hollow of a giant redwood tree. The day was magical with Torrey wearing a vintage lace gown and carrying pink roses, the favorite flower of Matthew's mother. The only other attendees were Torrey's parents. TJ had stood in for both of Matthew's deceased parents and proudly acted as the officiant.

Matthew's Uncle TJ had been a physician for more than twenty-five years, with a small general practice in Santa Monica, not too far from where his nephew grew up. TJ had gladly assumed the role of surrogate dad after Matthew's father was shot during a home robbery when Matthew was eight years old. TJ had been thrilled when Matthew decided to go to medical school at Stanford, TJ's alma mater. Of course, he had no idea that Matthew's motivation to go to *any* medical school was to become a physician at San Quentin, so he could "treat" his father's murderer with a fatal dose of medicine. As it turned out, unforeseen circumstances had caused Torrey to take matters into her own hands.

Matthew cooked up the steaks and opened the wine that TJ had brought. They sat at the large, intricately carved cement slab table in the backyard where Matthew had enjoyed many family dinners growing up. Matthew's dad had commissioned the design and construction of the table for his wife's thirtieth birthday. The table stood under a wooden trellis around which thick Wisteria vines climbed. The backyard was still filled with flowering trees and pink roses. During the pleasant dinner, TJ inundated Matthew with questions about his residency and married life. TJ was thankful to hear that Matthew and Torrey and their marriage were thriving in San Diego.

After the interrogation ended, Matthew asked about TJ's familiarity with clinical trials. TJ admitted that his experience was limited to referring patients over the years to doctors and researchers who were engaged in trials that might help one of his patients.

"Have you ever heard of a doc by the name of Albert Toohey?" asked Matthew.

"No, what kind of practice does he have?"

"I'm not really sure. He's based in San Diego, and he apparently claims that he's running a clinical trial for terminally ill children out of his private clinic. But I can't find him listed on any FDA database. What do you make of that?"

"There may be a good explanation, but I can't think of what it could be. Why are you interested?"

Matthew chose his words carefully. "Do you remember Edwina who came to our Match Day? She was the one who worked as a guard at San Quentin and helped me to subdue that prisoner who was trying to escape."

"Sure. She transitioned from male to female after that, right?"

"Yes. Anyway, she came to Torrey and me about Dr. Toohey's treatment of a family member—specifically, Edwina's niece. The niece was diagnosed with brain cancer, and she died during some sort of special treatment that Toohey was providing. Edwina's brother told her all about it, and Edwina is suspicious of the circumstances. She wants Torrey and me to investigate."

"Why doesn't she just go to the police or to the Medical Board?"

"Doesn't trust either of them."

"So, what is Edwina's brother going to do with the information that you uncover?"

"Well, he's a former Army Ranger, and if it turns out that Toohey was running some sort of scam which killed his daughter, then he certainly will want Toohey punished."

"Punished how?" TJ asked with alarm.

Matthew realized that he had gotten too comfortable after a couple of glasses of wine and had said too much. But he couldn't stop himself from responding honestly. After a long pause, Matthew said, "Put it this way. The brother, Hawk, served overseas. He saw his buddies get killed, and he became a big proponent of the 'eye for an eye' philosophy. Can't say that I blame him."

TJ put down his fork and stared at Matthew. Matthew glared back. "You're quoting the Old Testament? An eye for an eye? I didn't think you were religious anymore," TJ said.

"This has nothing to do with religion. Just a basic law of justice. Of human nature. If someone kills my loved one, the only adequate remedy is his death."

"Matthew!" TJ exclaimed. "If your mother were here, she would be horrified!"

"Sorry, but that's how I feel. And you know better than anyone, my mother *would* be here if not for the murder of my father and the decision of the Parole Board to release his killer. After that corrupt decision, my mother—your sister by the way—withered away until she died. By any measure, had the killer been adequately punished? Can the State be trusted to uphold the rights of victims? We both know the answer to those questions." Matthew's normally compassionate eyes blazed.

TJ squinted at Matthew and shifted uncomfortably in his seat. He hardly recognized the young man sitting across from him. TJ had helped to raise Matthew. He knew Matthew like a son, or so he thought. "Matthew, this is all hypothetical, right?"

"Oh, sure," said Matthew. But TJ sensed otherwise.

"You know that my love for you is unconditional. But regardless of what you find out about Dr. Toohey, please tell me that you aren't going to be a part of any revenge by Hawk."

"Of course not," said Matthew offhandedly and without conviction.

They finished their meals in silence. When Matthew got up to make some coffee, TJ followed him into the kitchen. He leaned against the refrigerator while he watched Matthew pour coffee beans into the grinder. "Matthew, I've avoided talking to you about Ted Nash's death in prison, which occurred right before he was scheduled to be released. But now that I hear you talking so freely about vengeance, I have to ask about the fact that it was Torrey who killed your father's murderer."

"What about it? You know what happened. Nash attacked her during a prison lockdown. She used a scalpel to defend herself."

"I know that's the story. But it is quite a coincidence that your then-girlfriend, now wife, happened to be the one and only medical student who was attacked by the one and only prisoner in San Quentin who you think should've been executed." TJ added slowly, "Unless it *wasn't* a coincidence."

Matthew kept his back to TJ as he worked on the coffee. "What do you mean?"

"Matthew, I've lived a long time. I know some things about life."

Turning on the bean grinder gave Matthew an extra ten seconds to think. He could either utter another lie, or another platitude. Matthew chose option three—no response at all. "I only know what Torrey told me," he said over his shoulder. He then turned around, looked at TJ, and politely asked, "Do you still take a little cream in your coffee?"

"Nice deflection. Are you forgetting I taught you that trick when you were in high school? And while we are still on the topic, did Edwina coerce you and Torrey into choosing a residency in San Diego because of Toohey? That always struck me as odd. You could have both matched at a hospital in Los Angeles or San Francisco."

"TJ, I promise you that Toohey had nothing to do with our choice of residency."

Chapter 14

Matthew was scheduled to work the following day, but he felt guilty about lying to TJ about the circumstances regarding the death of Ted Nash. He decided to stick around for an extra day, so he could help TJ with his typically heavy Monday morning parade of patients. He called a fellow Kaiser resident to negotiate a trade. Matthew would cover his friend's upcoming Friday night shift in exchange for working Matthew's Monday shift.

Torrey was understanding, and truth be told, she wasn't altogether unhappy that Matthew was staying an extra day. Now she could do her own investigation without Matthew trying to micromanage the details. First up, an early morning visit to the Lady of the Angels Hospital employee who was apparently siphoning distraught parents to Dr. Toohey. Torrey figured she could find out what she wanted to know within fifteen minutes, which would give her enough time to get to Kaiser for the start of her shift.

Even though Torrey did not know the name or job title of the young woman described by Edwina, she had no trouble finding the object of her search at the end of a dead-end hallway next to a supply room. The pink-haired girl, who Torrey immediately identified as an orderly, a nurse's helper, was staring into space. None of the nurses on the floor seemed inclined to ask for her help. Torrey appreciated the reluctance because the girl looked like a female Gilligan, chewing her gum while waiting for instructions from the Skipper. There was a giant-size Burger King soda cup on her little desk.

As Torrey approached, she observed that, in addition to her iridescent bright pink hair, the orderly had a gold nose ring and a bicep tattoo of a smiley face on a yellow sun poking out from her short-sleeved scrubs. Torrey stifled a scoff as she read the name tag pinned to the girl's scrubs top: "Hi there! I'm Ms. Sunshine."

The girl noticed Torrey's interest in her name tag and said, "Oh, that's not for real. It's just what everyone calls me, so I had them put it on here," she beamed as she pointed a finger to the plastic badge. "You know what I'm sayin'?" Sunshine said as she looked up at Torrey. A wad of gum was plainly visible inside Sunshine's mouth.

Torrey had a clever retort on the tip of her tongue, but she settled for, "That's really cute. By the way, I love your hair."

"Oh thanks, I just had a blowout."

"I can tell." Torrey thought back to the last time she had the patience for a salon visit—her wedding day. "Say, I wonder if you could help me," Torrey whispered as she looked around, then bent down close to Sunshine. "Have you worked here long?"

"Almost two years!"

"That's great!" Torrey said, unable to comprehend how Sunshine could have kept any job for that long. "My daughter has a brain tumor, and I don't like the treatment plan that the doctor here is suggesting. I don't trust the doctors or nurses to tell me about better options that might be available at other places. You look like you know what is going on around here," Torrey lied. "Have you heard about any other doctors who might be able to help my daughter?"

Sunshine sat up a little straighter. Then she looked over at the nurses' station to be sure they weren't paying any attention to her. They weren't. She stopped chewing her gum and lowered her voice. "As a matter of fact, I know a doctor who's much better than anyone around here."

"Oh really? Who?"

"Dr. Albert Toohey. His office isn't far from here."

"How do you know him?"

"I'm not supposed to say, but he's my stepfather's brother."

"Why is Dr. Toohey so good?"

"He cures people. I think he's a genius or something."

"Oh really?"

"True dat," Sunshine replied as she snapped her gum.

Torrey played along with the fanciful claim. "Wow, who told you that?"

"My stepfather. He introduced me to Dr. Toohey. Then Dr. Toohey got this job for me. Me and him have a deal."

"What do you mean?"

Sunshine looked around again, then cupped her hand over her mouth, so no one could read her lips. "Well, Dr. Toohey gives me a thousand dollars for every patient I refer to him, but," she said, quickly adding, "I would do it for free because, OMG, he's so great. Like, I think he's famous or something."

"How many people have you referred to Dr. Toohey?"

"I've mentioned him to quite a few parents, but not many actually changed over to him. I guess they don't know what's good for them," Sunshine said with a shrug.

"No, I guess not. So how many parents would you say have taken their kids to Dr. Toohey for treatment?"

"Like I said, not many. Probably only twenty or twenty-five. Enough for me to buy a new Prius. So, I'm not only helping the patients, but I'm helping save the world from global warming. Or maybe global cooling, I forget." When she grinned at Torrey, her gum fell out. Sunshine picked it up and threw it into the waste basket beside her desk. Torrey saw the wad of gum land on top of a bunch of candy wrappers, of the same type that might be left on a bedside by parents for their sick kids. "So, do you want Dr. Toohey's phone number?" Sunshine asked eagerly.

• • •

Matthew arrived back home just as Torrey was opening the door to their condo. Torrey was anxious to tell Matthew about Sunshine referring patients to Dr. Toohey. But Matthew wasn't as excited to hear about it. "You did what?" Matthew groaned. "I thought we had an agreement that we were going to talk strategy before you approached Dr. Toohey's runner!"

"I just wanted to keep the ball rolling while you were gone. And let's face it, the sooner we get to the bottom of this thing, the sooner Mrs. Ed can go back to her own apartment and out of ours," Torrey said as she did an almost imperceptible sashay with one hand on her hip.

"Well, when you put it that way, what's next?"

"You're so easy!" Torrey said with dancing eyes.

"I know," agreed Matthew with a huge grin.

Chapter 15

That evening, Matthew and Edwina met with Hawk and Angela to get the details of their interactions with Toohey. After introductions and the pouring of some adult beverages that went untouched, Edwina told her oft-repeated story about how she and Matthew had forged a lasting bond by saving the day at San Quentin. Unsurprisingly, Edwina played a more exaggerated role with each telling. Hawk wanted details about how Matthew and Edwina had subdued the gigantic prisoner who was holding a doctor hostage during an escape attempt. The way Edwina told the story, Matthew was more or less a bystander. Angela was polite but sat ramrod straight, expressionless, still in mourning, waiting for the conversation to turn to her daughter.

Matthew looked around the living room as Edwina bragged about their exploits. On the door jamb leading from the living room to the kitchen, he noticed a series of pencil marks tracking Emily's height over time. The fact that there wouldn't be any more marks was heartbreaking.

The home was filled with photographs of Emily. Matthew could see that she was a beautiful freckle-faced girl, having inherited curly red hair from her mother and strong features from Hawk. In one of the photos, Hawk, Angela, and Emily were dressed in matching white linen shirts. Matthew realized with a jolt that it resembled a similar family photograph from his own childhood, taken just months before his father was murdered. Matthew had been trying to remain emotionally distant from the circumstances of the Hawke family tragedy. He wanted to look at the facts with his brain, not his heart. But after meeting the family and seeing the photographs, he realized he was becoming as invested as Torrey was in helping Hawk, Angela, and Edwina.

Matthew tore his gaze away from the happy family photo and focused on another picture where Hawk, in military fatigues, was holding a newborn Emily. It prompted Matthew to ask a question he had been wondering about. "Hawk, what did you do in the military?"

Hawk was the opposite of Edwina. No bragging. "Oh, a little of this, a little of that."

"Don't you believe it," protested Edwina proudly. "Hawk was a special forces Army Ranger. And a hero. Most of his work was classified, but I know that he parachuted into dark territory in Afghanistan. He took out an entire rat's nest of bad guys, including at least one who had helped plan 9/11. He's like a good-looking Jack Reacher." Edwina, younger than Hawk by five years, loved and admired her older brother despite their strained relationship growing up. Hawk, as the athlete, the renegade, and the decorated eagle scout, was the favored child of their strict military father. Edwina, more subdued and closer to their mother, grew up in her brother's shadow. It didn't affect their outward relationship, but both children recognized the division of love, and both felt guilty about it.

Hawk looked at Matthew. "Edwina conveniently left out the fact that I was one member of a squad. I played a marginal role." Angela squeezed Hawk's forearm with pride.

"You don't have to downplay your service heroics on my account," Edwina protested. "I didn't volunteer for the army, but it wasn't because I thought that, as the black sheep of the family, I could never measure up to your accomplishments. I just decided to live my life differently. And I'm happy with my decisions." She added in a challenging voice, "All of them."

Hawk tried to move on. "Look, Edwina, let's not bring up past history. I—"

Matthew broke into the family argument and deftly changed the subject by thanking Hawk for his service and Edwina for her courage and strength of will. Then he turned to Angela and again expressed his sorrow for their loss. Finally, Matthew jumped to the purpose of his visit.

"I honestly don't know if I can learn anything about Dr. Toohey that you don't already

know, but I'll do what I can to investigate him and his supposed clinical trial. Why don't you tell me about your meetings with him and about the treatment he said he would provide to Emily? You could start by telling me what kind of tumor Emily had. Edwina only said that it was some sort of brain cancer."

Hawk and Angela looked at each other. Matthew could tell that Angela was in no shape to discuss the details. "Well," said Hawk, "you probably know that we first took her to Lady of the Angels Hospital because she was having headaches and trouble holding and lifting things. We thought she was just sick, but then she had a terrifying seizure. They did a bunch of tests." Hawk gestured to the stack of medical records piled on the coffee table. "They diagnosed Emily with what they called a golf ball-sized high-grade glioma, whatever the hell that is. All we heard was *brain tumor*."

"You said they did tests. Who are *they*?"

"There was a neurologist and a pediatric oncologist. They sat us down in a little office, offered us coffee, and told us that our little girl needed brain surgery. That they were going to cut open her skull."

Matthew glanced over at Angela who had a faraway look on her face. Tears were running down her cheeks. She dabbed her eyes with a wad of Kleenex. She whispered, "I'm so sorry," as she ran out of the room. Matthew, Edwina, and Hawk looked at each other.

Hawk did not need to explain, but in a low conspiratorial whisper, he offered that Angela was so vulnerable now that any talk of Toohey caused her to crumble. "She says she blames herself for 'talking me into' Toohey. Of course, she didn't. I was fully on board."

Matthew was all too familiar with depression caused by the death of a family member. He had watched his mother waste away after his father was murdered. But he knew that he had to keep the ball rolling with Hawk and stay focused on the present. "I'll read through those medical records, but what were you told about Emily's prognosis if you had agreed to the surgery?"

"They used a lot of technical medical jargon, most of which we didn't understand, but I remember them saying that the tumor was in the cerebral part of the brain. Oh, and that Emily was likely to lose some of her ability to speak and move, even if the operation was successful. They repeated several times that the tumor was aggressive and had to be removed, or Emily would be dead within months. In the next breath, they said that although the surgery was absolutely necessary, there were no guarantees that she would make it out of the operating room. I'm sure they were competent doctors, but their little CYA speech reminded me of some of my superiors in the military who would give an order and then spend most of their energy figuring out how to avoid responsibility when shit hit the fan." Hawk's face darkened.

"How did you find your way to Toohey?" Matthew had been briefed by Torrey about Sunshine, but he wanted to hear it directly from Hawk.

"It was actually sort of strange. Angela and I were in Emily's hospital room, both of us in despair and in tears. Emily was asleep. This nurse walked in and started talking to us in hushed tones, like she didn't want anyone else to hear. We were taken aback by her appearance. She had weird hair, tattoos, and a nose ring. And very young. Anyway, she said that she knew a doctor who was running a clinical trial involving some experimental drugs for brain cancer. She said he had good success without any surgery. As you can imagine, Angela was on board immediately. So, we went to visit Dr. Toohey the next day."

"Before you tell us about Toohey, what happened when you told the hospital doctors that you were taking Emily elsewhere for treatment?"

"They said we were making a huge mistake. That Emily couldn't get better treatment anywhere. Of course, they wanted to know where we were taking Emily, but Toohey had warned us not to mention his name or his clinic."

"Did Toohey say why the need for secrecy?"

"Yes, he said that the drug combination that he'd invented was so new and untested that he couldn't get government approval or funding. And that kids would die if the authorities shut down his clinic on what were mere technicalities. That was also the reason he had to charge patients a lot of money to do his life-saving work, although he hated to do it."

Matthew's eyes darted to Edwina. Hawk said in a tone full of remorse, "I know how this sounds. Like we were complete fools to leave the hospital. Like how could we entrust our child to someone who admitted freely that he was operating outside of normal channels?"

"Hawk," reassured Edwina, "nobody is blaming you."

"And," Matthew added supportively, "who can say what would have happened if you'd chosen to remain at the hospital? Medicine is unpredictable. Then when you add in the emotion of hearing that your daughter might lose cognitive functions, or worse, you and Angela chose what felt like the best of two bad options." Hawk exhaled a bit, calmed by Matthew's knack for saying exactly the right thing. "So," Matthew gently continued, "getting back to Toohey, tell us about the meeting you had with him."

"Maybe it was all an act, but I will say that Toohey seemed to really care about us and Emily. As people. And coming from the hospital where those doctors were so cold and clinical, like robots, Toohey seemed like a breath of fresh air. He explained that he used to work at the FDA, so he knew how ridiculous the approval process was for new drugs. He said he had been conducting his own non-sanctioned clinical trials for years to test a new mix of medicines he had invented for childhood brain tumors. They work, he told us, and he didn't want any more kids to die waiting for government approval, which would take years."

Edwina leaned over and gave her brother a hug. "We'll get to the bottom of this." She looked at Matthew and said with conviction, "Won't we, Matthew?"

Chapter 16

Torrey and Matthew sat outside Toohey's office building in Matthew's vintage Mustang. "Now remember," Matthew said. "I'll be loitering in the lobby while you go up to Toohey's office."

"You've mentioned that. Several times," deadpanned Torrey.

Matthew ignored the pointed comment. "Do you remember what you're going to say?"

"No, I think we better go over it three *more* times," said Torrey in her exaggerated mocking voice.

Matthew pretended that he didn't notice the sarcasm. "So just to summarize, keep your phone line open, don't let Toohey know we are suspicious of him, and above all, abort if you see Toohey's enforcer up there."

"Yes, sir!" quipped Torrey while giving a West Point salute.

"Very funny. Can you be serious for a moment?"

"Matthew, I'm deadly serious. You know that. I'm just doing some reconnaissance. I'll be back before you know it." She gave him a kiss on the cheek before she opened the car door, bounded up the steps to the front entrance of the building, and disappeared inside.

Torrey stared at the directory board in the lobby. The Medical Offices of Albert Toohey, M.D. was listed as occupying Suite 202, in between

New Age Holistic in Suite 201 and Helping Hand Massages in Suite 203. She had no idea what New Age was, but she had a pretty good idea about the massage parlor. So far, not impressive.

The waiting room of Toohey's office was similarly uninspiring. Spartan furnishings, no plants, no prints on the walls, and only four uncomfortable-looking chairs. The only sign identifying the tenant was a laminated plaque, which was posted behind the reception desk, "*Dr. Albert Toohey, FDA.*"

The receptionist was not your typical cute, twenty-something wannabe actress with a pencil skirt and high heels. Almost six feet tall and solid. Not just frumpy, she was like a forty-year-old, middle-European bodybuilder. Unattractive and hard. Severe features. Blunt bowl haircut. Pinched frown. No makeup or jewelry. Her manner was consistent with her appearance. She just looked up at Torrey through the square of the open glass. No greeting. No offer to fetch a hot cup of coffee or a cool glass of water. No "Can I help you?" The receptionist simply stared at Torrey with disinterested eyes. Torrey immediately diagnosed the receptionist with "stridor," indicated by loud wheezy breathing caused by partially blocked airways. Against the silence of the office, it sounded like a high-pitched dentist's drill with every exhale. Torrey resisted the urge to stare at the source of the noise, especially in light of the feathery mustache above the upper lip.

Torrey had learned during medical school, with Matthew's patient tutelage, how to get people to open up and talk. She was not one to suffer fools lightly, but Matthew had taught her that sometimes you had to pour the honey on thick. *Be friendly, smile, and use the person's name.* Unfortunately, Ms. Olympia 1988 wore no name tag, and there was no nameplate on the counter. Just a pack of Camels and a half-full ashtray. "Hello," said Torrey with her warmest smile, "my name is Bella Swan. I'm here to see Dr. Toohey."

"Appointment?" the receptionist asked with a heavy eastern European accent.

"No, but—"

"Dr. Toohey sees no one without an appointment."

"I'm sorry for just showing up, but it is an emergency. Dr. Toohey's niece told me that he could help my daughter who has a brain tumor. Please, I must see him!"

Torrey could feel cautious eyes studying her. "You talked to Sunshine?"

"Yes, over at Lady of the Angels hospital. She said Dr. Toohey is a miracle worker."

"Wait here," said the receptionist as she left her post and vanished down a hallway. Torrey noticed that Ms. Olympia was dressed all in black except for white orthopedic shoes. Torrey tried to steal a look at the open appointment book bearing an FDA logo, but not only was it upside down to Torrey, but the handwriting was small and indecipherable, like it was some sort of code.

When Ms. Olympia returned, she opened the door leading to the inner office and grunted something that Torrey could not understand. When Torrey failed to move, Ms. Olympia raised her voice, "Follow me!" Torrey scooted into the hallway before the door locked her out.

They passed two closed doors on each side of the hallway before Ms. Olympia stopped in front of the last door and knocked as she pushed it open. Without a word, she turned and walked away. Torrey assumed that was her signal to enter and meet Dr. Toohey.

Toohey rose from behind his desk and walked over to greet her. His physique was almost slight, except for a pronounced pot belly, which reminded Torrey of the malnourished kids seen in *National Geographic*. His head was enormous, with thin lips and freakishly bushy eyebrows that were almost connected. He had a weak chin and small reading glasses hanging from a chain around his neck. Older, gray-haired doctors can look distinguished, but his cemented down comb-over was counter-productive. And it did nothing to disguise his bald patch anyway. As they shook hands and exchanged introductions, Torrey quipped, "Friendly staff you have here."

"Oh, don't mind Mrs. Borsky," he said with a genial smile. "She doesn't do perky. But she is very protective of me. And she happens to be my brother's cousin. Came over from the old country to work for me when I opened this office." He gestured toward an empty chair. "Please sit down."

Torrey glanced around the office while Toohey was settling into his gigantic, overstuffed leather throne, legs crossed at the knees. The chair was obviously intended for a larger man, or the king of a small country. The only items on the oak desk were a nameplate with the FDA logo, "*Dr. Toohey, Principal Researcher*," a few dog-eared sheets of paper, and an ashtray with a mound of cigarette butts and ash. The walls were bare, save for an oversized mirror directly behind the two low visitor chairs. No framed medical degrees in sight.

"Mrs. Borsky said that my niece referred you to me. Can you fill me in?" Torrey could smell his minty-fresh breath from across the desk, suggesting that he had just rinsed with mouthwash to erase the tobacco odor.

Torrey locked her eyes on his, but it wasn't easy considering that Toohey didn't look the part of a brilliant physician. With his poufy white shirt and black vest, he had a nineteenth century, Little Lord Fauntleroy look about him. If she hadn't seen him stand up already, she might have wondered if he were wearing leather buckle shoes.

Torrey had memorized her story, so she knew her lines. Now she just had to pour on the emotion. "Doctor, thank you for seeing me without an appointment. After speaking with Sunshine, I was desperate to talk to you." She surprised herself with the ease of the deceptive charade. Even though her words were fabricated, her emotion was deep-seated and real.

"What's going on?" His voice was buttery smooth.

"My daughter, Madeline, is four years old. I have all of her medical records in the car. She was just diagnosed with a type of astrocytoma known as—" Torrey pretended she was struggling to come up with the correct medical terminology. Before she could finish her sentence, Toohey interrupted.

"I don't need the records. I don't care what kind of tumor it is. My treatment is the same. Astrocytoma is a classification of Glioblastoma Multiforme, and that's all I need to know," Toohey said as he raked his bony nicotine-stained fingers through his thin, limp hair.

A wisp of suspicion formed in Torrey's mind. Within seconds, the vague foreboding turned into a full, albeit silent, alarm. A voracious reader of medical studies, with a photographic memory, Torrey was a walking encyclopedia of medical knowledge. She knew that astrocytomas start in cells that support the nerves. And she knew that astrocytomas are grouped by grade, location within the brain, and expressed symptoms in the body. Most importantly, she knew that the treatments for various types of astrocytomas could not possibly be identical. And *no* doctor would treat without a complete medical history. Torrey disliked having to play dumb, but she couldn't let Toohey know that she was skeptical. She had to somehow coax some helpful information out of him.

Torrey leaned forward. "Oh really. What's your treatment?"

Toohey paused a beat and rearranged the few sheets of paper on his desk before answering. "That is proprietary and very technical. But the short answer is that my drug mixture, compared to what you might receive traditionally, more easily crosses the blood-brain barrier. That barrier is highly selective and only allows specific substances and not others, such as toxins, to enter the brain. That is normally a good thing. But that barrier prevents most medicines from getting to where the brain tumors are hiding. But my medicine blend is different. Therefore, I can cure patients without surgery, chemotherapy, or radiation."

"My husband looked you up on the internet. You used to work at the FDA?"

"Right, for many years."

"So, is your work here a part of the FDA program?"

"This is not technically a clinical trial, if that is what you mean to ask, because I'm not comparing my medicine to a placebo. I am comparing my medicine to traditional drugs used by those robotic doctors who do what has always been done, whether it works or not. I'm sure my friends at the FDA will eventually approve my drug combination, but it takes years of jumping through hoops with all the bureaucracy. And how many children will be brain damaged or die in the meantime? I just want to help as many kids as possible."

Torrey wasn't sure if Toohey was shining her on or not. But if he was, an Oscar was in his future. She had once heard a TED talk on how to spot a liar, and although something seemed to be off, Toohey passed every test. He was very convincing. But Toohey wasn't finished with his pitch. "Those physicians, like the ones at the hospital where your daughter is being treated, refuse to acknowledge the obvious—that sawing open the head of a child and following it up with chemotherapy and radiation is old school and not in the best interests of the child or her family."

"They say my daughter needs surgery right away. How can I get her out of the hospital and into your care?"

Dr. Toohey leaned back in his chair and said regretfully, "The problem is, Mrs. Swan, that we are at capacity already. And it is very expensive for me to have my drugs made, especially in intravenous form so that they are tolerated by children. Each course of ten treatments costs over $100,000. Perhaps next month—"

"Dr. Toohey, please! I am begging you. If it's a matter of money, my husband's family comes from wealth. I'm sure they would help us with whatever fees are involved! Money will not be an object."

Toohey came out from behind his desk and put his arm around her shoulders. "Let me see what I can do. I think one of our patients is almost finished with his treatment. I will look at the schedule. Leave your number with Mrs. Borsky, and we'll call you tonight. Can you find your own way out?"

Torrey gave him a grateful smile, and they both stepped towards the door. Dr. Toohey held his office door open for her. Just before he closed it, he patted her arm reassuringly. "I'm going to get you in. Don't worry. So go ahead and talk to your in-laws about the fees."

After the door shut behind her, Torrey stood alone in the long corridor, thinking. In the silence, she heard a muffled voice coming from one of the patient's rooms. She thought of Matthew's admonition, *Get in, talk to Toohey, and get out.* She didn't doubt the wisdom of that advice, but without an escort, she found herself slowly walking down the hallway towards the voice. She paused every few feet, and the voice became louder and more distinct. It sounded like reading.

Once she was directly outside the correct door, she knew for sure that someone was reading, and the book was familiar. She felt her phone vibrate in her pocket. She knew without looking that it was Matthew, wanting to know what was taking so long. Without another thought to Matthew's warning or to the fact that he was waiting for her downstairs, Torrey quickly and quietly opened the door and slipped inside.

She was struck by the scene as she looked at the two faces peering up at her. A young girl, maybe six years old with an IV tube in her left arm, was lying on a hospital bed, and her mother was sitting in a chair next to the bed, reading out loud. Torrey knew the title of the book without looking at the cover—*The Adventures of Tintin.* Like a bad horror movie, Torrey flashed back to reading the *Tintin* books to Leia in the last weeks of her young life. Torrey reached up and ran her fingers over the "Princess" tattoo on her left shoulder, a constant reminder of what she had lost. Seeing this little girl in Toohey's office, with a *Tintin* book, filled her full of steely resolve.

Torrey figured that no one would question her presence if she kept talking and acting like she belonged. As nonchalantly as she could, she said, "Don't mind me, you two. I'm just popping in to check your bag." She walked over to the hanging clear-plastic IV bag, making a mental note of the wording stenciled in block letters. "You know," she continued, "*Tintin* is one of my all-time favorite books. I read the entire series when I was about your age."

Torrey noticed that the youngster, wearing a sparkly American Girl T-shirt, was hugging a white stuffed animal. "Oh! I see you like Tintin's dog, just like I did! Snowy is the best." Torrey bent down and gave Snowy a quick pet. The girl's eyes darted to Snowy as Torrey's fingers rubbed the soft fur.

As she stood, Torrey saw that the girl's shirt had stenciling on the front: Addie B. "What a cute shirt," Torrey remarked.

Without skipping a beat, the girl explained in a serious tone, "There are three Addisons in my grade. Our moms had T-shirts made for each of us with our last name initial on the shirts. So, everyone just calls me Addie B. Me and Addie M wear ours everywhere."

"That's so sweet," exclaimed Torrey.

"Addie M isn't sick like me. But she's still my best friend."

As she was about to leave, Torrey noticed an open cardboard box in the corner filled with IV bags. "I was wondering where I put this box!" exclaimed Torrey. "I just need one of these to get ready for the next patient," she said as she grabbed the top bag. "Well, good luck to you both. And to Snowy, too!" The little girl, who looked surprisingly chipper considering the circumstances, grinned as Torrey opened the door and waved a jaunty goodbye.

Before she could get out of the door, the girl's mother gently touched Torrey's elbow. When Torrey turned, the mother whispered, "I just want to thank you for what you're doing for us. I know Dr. Toohey said there are no guarantees, but Addie says she is feeling better. The pain is way less, and she has more energy. The treatment must be working! And with tomorrow being Thanksgiving, my parents are going to see Addie looking more chipper than usual." Torrey studiously ignored the optimism. She nodded, looked back at Addie, with the IV needle sticking into her hand, and managed a wooden smile.

Out in the hallway, Torrey congratulated herself on her make-believe act, but abandoned the idea of additional phony small talk with Ms. Olympia. She stuffed the IV bag into her oversized purse and then drifted past Mrs. Borsky without stopping, like an invisible wind. As she loped down the stairs, taking two at a time to the first floor, Torrey hoped that she was wrong about Toohey. She hoped that Toohey could actually cure Addie B, the Tintin girl.

• • •

Later that afternoon, Dr. Toohey made the phone call he was dreading. He was nervous, and it reflected in his tentative voice. "I had a visit today from a young woman who said her daughter needed my treatment."

"That's good, right?"

"Well, there might be a problem. She sounded interested, and I told her to leave her number with Borsky. But she didn't. I asked Borsky about it, and she said the young woman just walked out quickly without stopping."

"Sounds like she just had second thoughts. So what?"

"Well, when I was talking to another patient, the mother remarked how much she and her daughter liked my new nurse who had come in to check on them. But there was no nurse in the office. And they certainly weren't talking about Borsky."

"Anything else?"

"One of the IV bags is missing."

"What?! Who was she?"

"She said her name was Bella Swan. But it was probably bogus."

After a long pause and a condescending sigh, "No shit, Sherlock. That's a character from the *Twilight* books. And how could you let anyone walk around unattended?"

Toohey winced at the rebuke, even though it was fully expected. He knew that he sounded like a petulant teenage boy, but he lamely protested, "She seemed so nice. And desperate for the treatment. She just showed up without an appointment, so I wasn't able to do the normal checking. I—"

The voice on the other end of the line was even but vaguely threatening. "Dammit, I'm sick of your impotent whining while the money is coming in hand over fist. You better not screw this up. I set this scam up so that even a moron could run it. And as you well understand, I know where you live." The line went dead.

Chapter 17

The stolen IV bag had to wait. Miraculously, Matthew and Torrey were scheduled to get Thanksgiving off. He had purchased a fifteen-pound turkey and was getting ready to try his hand at making a complete turkey dinner, with all the trimmings, for Torrey to enjoy on their first Thanksgiving as a married couple. But around noon, they were paged to get to the hospital—some sort of an emergency that required all hands on-deck. The half-cooked turkey was going to be a total loss.

On the drive there, Matthew was in a prickly mood because of missing a holiday at home, and he was still upset over Torrey's failure to follow the script when she visited Toohey's office. "I was planning on making stuffing and gravy!" Matthew pouted.

Torrey had never cooked much of anything, so she didn't really get the whole Thanksgiving feast thing. But she tried to sound sympathetic. "Why don't we start over on Saturday? A Thanksgiving feast will be just as tasty then!" she said brightly.

"That's not the same," moped Matthew.

Matthew was drumming his fingers on the steering wheel at a red light. When the light turned green, the car in front of Matthew hesitated for a second too long for his liking. He honked his horn repeatedly. Torrey stared at him in surprise. "What's the matter, Matthew? I've never heard you honk at another driver! This can't be about a turkey dinner."

Matthew glanced at Torrey. "As I told you yesterday, I'm not happy that you went rogue in Toohey's office. This isn't a game. Toohey could be dangerous."

Torrey shrugged, "We needed to know what Toohey is doing, and now, with the saline bag, we can find out."

Matthew sighed. "Setting aside the risk in taking a saline bag, how are we supposed to analyze the medicine? We don't have the authority to order an analysis of the IV bag by the hospital lab."

"I was thinking that you could ask TJ to have his lab do it," remarked Torrey hopefully.

"He's already suspicious of us. What excuse could I use to get him involved?"

Torrey leaned over and kissed him on the cheek. "Last time I checked, you are a brilliant doctor who finished top of your class in medical school—tied with me that is—" she said with a wide grin, "who can charm the socks of a Grinch and who can orchestrate the demise of an incarcerated killer . . . I'm sure you'll figure something out."

Matthew's face went from skeptical, to determined, to confident within seconds. She figured she'd better make sure his ego didn't get too far out of control. "By the way, I saw you flirting with Nurse Williams the other day. She's pretty cute, right?"

"I wasn't flirting. She was coming on to me!" Matthew protested.

"Well, don't get too full of yourself. She was flirting with *me* last week."

• • •

When they arrived at the hospital, the entrance to the emergency room was a hotbed of activity. Paramedics were unloading five ambulances. Torrey and Matthew had assumed the worst—a crane accident, a chain reaction collision on a freeway, or heaven forbid, a mass shooting at a mall or workplace. It was none of the above. Apparently, a fight had broken out at a Turkey Tournament Little League baseball game.

A teenage umpire had called a runner safe on a close play at the plate. The unhappy pitcher then threw the next pitch at the batter, hitting him in the face, just below the left eye. The batter collapsed to the ground. Blood was everywhere. The batter's family went ballistic and charged the field, screaming that they were going to kill the pitcher. One thing led to another, and a brawl developed. The batter's older brother picked up a bat and used it to strike several opposing dads who were trying to restrain him. The batter's mother attacked the umpire, jabbing at him with the blade of a medium-sized Swiss Army knife, while screaming it was all his fault for not keeping the game under control. The batter's father focused his fury on the pitcher's coach, suspecting that the coach had called for the beanball. All in all, six parents were injured, several seriously, not to mention the batter, the coach, and the umpire.

Torrey ran into the ER just as Joey, the eleven-year-old batter, was being rolled in on a gurney. Dr. McKnight was yelling orders as the triage was in full swing. Most of the injured adults were left to the nursing staff while the minors were treated by the doctors. Torrey noticed that one of the injured was a twenty-something man dressed in military fatigues. His own mouth was bloody, but he was trying to comfort a woman who looked like she was in shock.

Matthew was assigned to the young umpire who came in with blade punctures to his chest and stomach. Without being instructed, Torrey went immediately to join senior emergency physician, Dr. Evan Blankenship, who was perceived as a generally ungracious and superficial physician. He was examining the batter who had been hit in the face with the baseball. Besides being in shock, the boy's face was covered with dried blood, and there was a ball-sized crater, indicating a comminuted fracture of the left eye socket. Dr. Blankenship directed Torrey to apply ice packs to reduce the swelling and to call for a pediatric surgeon to repair the bony structures. Then Dr. Blankenship moved on.

"How could this happen?" Torrey grumbled, loud enough for the entire ER to hear.

Matthew called back over the din, "Don't you know? 'Fan' is short for fanatic. I would say these folks qualify!" All of the parents undoubtably heard the exchange. Not one of them said a word.

Every medical resident knows about the imposter syndrome concept—the self-doubt, the mindset that every other doctor actually knows what she is doing, whereas you are a fraud. You were just lucky to get through medical school. Your success to date has been a fluke, totally undeserved. You are less prepared and less competent than everyone around you. You are an imposter with a physician's stethoscope. Torrey had never experienced that sentiment.

So, when Dr. Blankenship issued his directive, Torrey thought back to President Reagan's famous, all-purpose quote: "Trust, but verify." She gently turned Joey's head and saw bright red, fresh blood oozing out of his right ear. As bad as the facial fractures were, Torrey knew that bleeding from the ear after head trauma was a likely sign of bleeding around the brain. If not treated quickly, pooled blood would exert life-threatening pressure on brain tissue.

Dr. Blankenship was behind closed curtains working on another patient, so Torrey paged her surgical residency mentor, Dr. Marissa Bond, and explained her suspicion of a cerebral edema. Within minutes, the boy was whisked into an operating room where Dr. Bond, assisted by Torrey, drilled a burr hole into his skull to relieve the pressure, thereby allowing oxygen paths to be restored. When the procedure was finished, Dr. Bond put her arm around Torrey, saying, "You saved little Joey's life."

Before she did anything else, Torrey returned to the ER to look for Matthew and the man dressed in military fatigues. Neither was there. She found the admitting nurse and asked about the soldier. "Nurse, you know that group of injured Little League parents that were in here earlier?"

"Of course. That was one for the books, right?"

"Yes, I'm trying to find out what happened to the patient who was a military veteran. A Marine, I think." Because Torrey's dad and uncle were Jarheads, Torrey was familiar with the attire.

"I remember him. He was awfully nice. Made sure everyone else was treated before he would consent to an exam." The nurse then lowered her voice, "Don't tell my boyfriend I said so, but he sure was good looking. He looked like one of those 'boy band' backup singers. And I just love a man in uniform, don't you?"

"Yes," said Torrey impatiently. "But—"

"Oh, and I heard them talking while they were all here. Apparently, the soldier was just trying to separate two brawlers, and he got hit in the face with a bat."

"Good to know. Could you check what treatment he received?"

After pulling the paperwork, the nurse replied, "It says his name is Howard Borden. Lives in Las Vegas. According to these notes, he reported headache, eye pain, and blurred vision."

Torrey grimaced. "That's serious. Who treated him? We called in an ophthalmologist, right?"

The nurse kept reading. "He was denied treatment because he said he is a vet, just discharged actually. No private medical insurance. He was transported to the VA hospital over by UC San Diego, the poor guy."

● ● ●

Torrey had just finished cleaning herself up when she was summoned to Dr. Anne Peterson's office. "Uh-oh," said Torrey to herself. "She must have heard that I went over Dr. Blankenship's head." While cooling her heels outside Dr. Peterson's office, Torrey thought up a number of clever justifications, depending on how much trouble she was in.

After twenty minutes, Torrey was summoned. Before she could make herself comfortable in one of Dr. Peterson's visitor chairs, Dr. Peterson started to lecture. "Torrey, I got a call from Dr. Blankenship who said that he gave you a direct treatment order for a boy who was hit with a baseball. He called in to the hospital later and was told by the nurse on duty that you never called the pediatric facial surgeon. He is considering lodging a formal complaint against you. He says you need to be reprimanded. Before I do anything else, I want to hear what you have to say."

Torrey explained the situation and suggested that a call to Dr. Bond would help fill in the blanks. Then Torrey launched into what she thought of as her Dr. Richard Kimble defense. "You should know that I remembered our last meeting regarding Dr. Volkov. I did *not* confront Dr. Blankenship like I did Volkov. He left before I could ask him about the ear bleeding. Didn't you see the movie, *The Fugitive*? Remember Harrison Ford was disguised as an orderly, and he changed the doctor's orders for a young boy so that he got the operation that he needed. Harrison saved the boy's life. And I didn't act alone, like Harrison did. I called Dr. Bond and followed her instructions."

"Torrey, this is real life, not a movie. I'll talk to Dr. Bond and Dr. Blankenship. I'll let you know if disciplinary action will be taken against you."

"Yes, ma'am."

"Off the record, I remember being a young doctor. I remember being brash sometimes. I got in trouble sometimes. But I always put the patients first. I can see that you do, too. Now get out of here."

Torrey, more relieved than thrilled, quickly left the office, this time without any attempt at humor.

• • •

The following day, Joey was resting comfortably in his hospital bed when he had a visit from Matthew. The boy's face was heavily bandaged, including his left eye, but he could see out of a slit with his right eye. Matthew knelt down so that the boy could see him without straining. "Hi there, big guy," said Matthew. "I heard that you've had quite an ordeal. How are you feeling today?"

"I'm okay." He struggled to raise his head to look around. "Where's my mom?"

"She just went down to the cafeteria to get some food. She hasn't left your side since you got out of your last surgery."

After a slight pause, Joey asked, "When can I go home?"

"Depends on when your surgeons release you. Probably a few more days."

Matthew could sense the disappointment through the bandages. "Hey, I was talking to your mom about how much you love baseball. She says you and your dad collect player autographs. Is that right?"

The boy perked up. "Yeah. My dad has a bunch of baseballs signed by old guys, but I like to get signatures from the guys playing now. So far I have twenty-three."

"My dad and I used to do the same thing. We had season tickets to the Dodgers, and he let me hang around the opposing team's dugout. I would pester the players until someone would sign." Matthew smiled at the memory, and he could see the boy's bandages wrinkle as he grinned. "Your mom told me that you like the Dodgers and the Mets. Who are your favorite players?"

Matthew already knew the answer from a prior conversation with Joey's mom, and he had then visited a local sports memorabilia store. Joey said, "I like Clayton Kershaw and Jacob DeGrom."

"Oh, you go for pitchers with great hair!" said Matthew. "Are you a pitcher?" Joey nodded. "I wonder if you would have any interest in these two balls?"

Matthew reached into his backpack and pulled out baseballs signed by the two Cy Young winning pitchers. He placed one into each of the boy's hands. Matthew watched with satisfaction as the boy gleefully held them up to his good eye. "No way!" Joey cried out. "These are great! Thank you! I can't wait to show my parents!"

Matthew slipped out just as the boy's mother returned to the room. As he walked down the corridor, he heard the boy exclaiming over his prized baseballs. He looked back and saw Joey's mother bent over the bed as the two shared a tearful embrace.

Chapter 18

Joe Cook knew, without being told, that Matthew would want him to find out what was in Toohey's storage locker. Joe was curious himself. Why maintain a storage unit for routine office supplies? Or for household items that could be stored in their spacious home? He had never rented a storage unit. Everything he knew about them was based upon watching that TV show where morons bid on abandoned lockers.

Joe wasn't a criminal. Far from it. But he freely admitted, to himself at least, that he was a proponent of situational ethics. If a few rules had to bend in order to do a job, or to catch a bad guy, then so be it. He retired to his home-basement office, sat down at his huge oak desk, and fired up the sophisticated maps application on his computer. He studied the side streets and alleys surrounding the large storage facility to plan out his approach and parking options. The business took up an entire block and was edged with a tall, rusty chain-link fence, topped by barbed wire. The front sliding gate was controlled by private security codes. Toohey's unit was back from the main street, which was helpful, but Joe figured that the unit would be visible from the street, from the right vantage point. The unit was sandwiched in between several separate buildings. Security lights were randomly placed.

Joe walked over to his vintage bank safe, spun the dial to his ex-wife's busty measurements, and swung open the heavy door. He had considered buying one of those high-tech gun safes with fingerprint identification, but he couldn't give up his old Wells Fargo two-ton safe. Plus, he thought of the good times with his former bride every time he opened it. His eyes passed over the heavy artillery until he found what he was looking for. He figured that everything else he needed was already in his car trunk, buried under the flattened third-row seat in a custom-made cavity.

The night was unseasonably cold and windy. Joe donned his usual stake-out gear of black pants, gloves, shirt and windbreaker, which did the trick for nighttime surveillance and borderline illicit conduct. In a nod to the chilly temperature, he shoved a black stocking hat into his coat pocket, to be worn over his long-billed baseball cap, which would obscure his face from any casual witnesses or overhead video cameras. At 2:00 a.m., he climbed the stairs to his kitchen, made himself a large aluminum-travel mug of hot coffee, and headed out the back door to the garage.

He unlocked the side door and gazed at his pride and joy—an almost new, dark gray Range Rover. Joe passed by the rear end full of shiny chrome and reflective wax and instead got into the beat-up Sentra, the most nondescript, and unmemorable model of car ever manufactured. Balancing his coffee on his lap, he backed out of his driveway, off on another glamorous private eye adventure. Jim Rockford and Barnaby Jones would be jealous.

By the time that Joe reached the storage facility and drove the perimeter looking for anything unusual, it was almost 3:00 a.m., his preferred time for breaking and entering. The good citizens of the world were in their deepest sleep, and the few people up and about at that hour— drunkards, criminals, and of course high school hoods and college art history majors who stay out all night smoking pot with their likewise happily unemployed friends and then go home to their moms' basements and sleep all day—were unlikely to notice suspicious behavior and even less likely to act on it. Joe slowly drove through the back alley and stopped adjacent to the most remote section of the chain-link fence. He quietly opened his trunk, and with practiced care, he removed his favorite long-handled bolt cutter, his low-light camera, and his utility knife. He silently placed the items on the ground next to the fence and then covered them with an old rag from his car and a nearby spent piñata that the wind had trapped against a metal post. He then got back in his car and drove two blocks away to a residential cul-de-sac that he had scoped out online. The homes in this area were rundown shacks. Cars in driveways were up on blocks or held together by rust. After parking, he sat in his car for two minutes, watching for the flicker of lights and listening carefully for any sounds. He double-checked that his phone was on silent, and then he put on his gloves and pep-stepped through fractured light back to his tools, being careful not to trip on the cracked and buckled sidewalks.

The chain link was no match for his bolt cutters. He was inside the fence within seconds. He pressed his back against the closest building, partially to listen for movement, but mostly to gain a fractional shield against the stiff wind. As he shivered, he tried to make himself as thin as possible and silently vowed to lose those fifteen pounds that he had gained in the years since his college days. The super moon of a few nights earlier was gone, but the security lights were blinding in the dark of night. Joe crept along the walls to stay in the relative gloom of the shadows. He slowly advanced to the building which encompassed Toohey's unit, along with three others. He squatted in the shadows, put down his heavy bolt cutters, and reached into the inside pocket of his jacket. A bump against his ankle caused Joe to jump up out of his crouch and reflexively kick his foot. He gasped, "Crikey!" as he looked down. A stray cat, with long orange fur and a big belly, which probably lived off handouts and rats at the facility, was rubbing against his leg and starting to meow. On the dog v. cat scale, Joe was ninety-three percent Team Cats. They didn't need to be walked, and they didn't care if you paid any attention to them. Just set out a daily bowl of Kibble, and you were done. Joe picked up the cat, gave it a quick pet on the head, and gently set her down a few feet away. He smiled and affectionately hissed at her, "Scat!" and "Get out of here, you dumb cat!" The cat raised its tail with a twisted air of indignation and huffily complied.

Joe's LAPD firearms training had been perfunctory and specialized, but having grown up on an Iowa farm, he had entered the force with plenty of practice from shooting rodents and small game. And since then, he had kept his sharpshooter's eye with regular visits to the shooting range. He pulled out his favorite boyhood long-barreled pellet pistol, which he had recently equipped with a hand-made suppressor that was whisper quiet compared to any commercially available, or legally obtainable, silencer. With one shot, he knocked out the security lamp shining down on Toohey's unit. The bulb fragments rained down, and the circle of light disappeared. It was pitch dark. Joe again listened long and hard for a response to the sound of the breakage. All he heard was the wind.

A friend of Joe's was known for his safecracking ability. Richard Fobes, a reformed second-story man, was by all accounts a genius when it came to breaking into homes and safes. He had invented a device which somehow allowed him to hear the tumblers inside a combination lock. Within minutes, he could open a safe or padlock. He also had invested in expensive software which could break PIN codes on all sorts of locks. Richard's downfall was his generosity. He gave away the spoils of his crimes to homeless shelters. The police knew just where to look to determine if Richard had been the brains behind any particular robbery.

Richard had been arrested many times, but local law enforcement agencies were always glad to have him in their jails. He was like the friendly, wayward, smiling relative who was always in trouble, but everyone in the family just shook their heads and fondly chuckled. Like everyone's favorite uncle. In fact, Sgt. Rodland at one precinct had dubbed Richard with a nickname that stuck: Uncle Dick.

Uncle Dick's sophisticated tools were great, but Joe preferred old-fashioned, low-tech solutions. For unseating deadbolts, Joe had learned to use a tension wench and hook pick as well as the most seasoned burglar. But old-fashioned keyed padlocks were best handled with brute strength, not nimble fingers. The bolt cutters made short work of Toohey's storage unit lock. Joe rolled up the door, stepped inside, and quickly closed the door behind him. He shifted his weight from one foot to the other to ward off the chill.

It took a few seconds for his eyes to adjust, even with his trusty miniature Maglite. He panned the room and saw the wood tables, boxes, and stacks of papers that he had seen from the street when Toohey had paid his visit. In the back of the unit, he saw two items that immediately caught his attention. In one corner, there was a stainless-steel table topped by two industrial wattage lamps and a large magnifying glass. Under the magnifier was an empty IV bag, with a two-inch strip of white cloth tape attached on which was handwritten, in black permanent marker, the name BERNSTEIN. On the cement floor, next to the desk, was a scattering of cigarette butts. "So that's where that ash smell is coming from," Joe muttered to nobody.

In the other back corner, there was a two-by-four-foot Mosler safe. Joe knew that Mosler safes had been around for decades because they were considered impenetrable. They were a favorite of individuals who had liquid wealth and wanted to keep their cash, gold, and bonds to themselves. Joe spit out a theatrical sigh, "Oh c'mon!" when he noticed that the safe was locked with a shiny brass combination dial. He grimaced, regretting that Uncle Dick had retired and was now living an anonymous life in a secluded cabin in the San Juan Islands.

The next thirty minutes were spent documenting everything in the unit. He used his utility knife to open sealed boxes. Some were filled with bottles of distilled water and others with blocks of powders labelled with chemical names that meant nothing to Joe. Other boxes contained plastic IV bags, tubes, and nondescript medical supplies. The stacks of papers seemed to be medical files and some sort of accounting ledgers. He took so many photos that he wondered if his camera battery was going to last.

What set Joe apart from his gumshoe colleagues was that Joe was an expert in the art of misdirection. When he was finished with Toohey's unit, he cut off the locks on the adjacent units, opened the doors, and rifled through the contents looking for something of value to take. In one of the units, he found a sack of old coins, a 38 revolver, and a box of shells. In another, he found some jewelry. It was probably fake, but he didn't care. He just wanted to create the impression that some teenagers had broken into the units looking for money to buy drugs. Toohey would be upset about the vandalism to his locker, but he would not suspect that he had been targeted. Joe would return the stolen goods, except for the gun and bullets, with an anonymous note of apology, once this assignment was completed.

Chapter 19

Rocco Washington was a smart guy. Not book smart like those professional students with fancy degrees, from fancy schools. He had worked his way up the ladder to his current position of responsibility. And he had big plans for his future. Maybe a desk job where he was calling the shots. The first step was keeping an eye on Dr. Toohey. If things went according to plan, he would be on his way.

Watching for a misstep by Toohey was getting old. His boss had admonished him against any interaction. "Don't ever let the subject know that he is being watched. See, but don't be seen," was the mantra. But when Rocco observed Toohey and his wife entering a small breakfast diner, he had the idea to take some initiative. He wouldn't talk to them, but how could it hurt to go in and watch them up close? Isn't creativity on the job something to be praised? After all, being inside would allow him to keep a better eye on Toohey. And he was hungry.

Rocco entered the eatery carrying a *USA Today* newspaper and stood next to the PLEASE WAIT TO BE SEATED sign. He scanned the narrow, oblong room. Six tight booths lined each wall. Half the booths were occupied. The Tooheys sat in the back left booth, heads buried in their menus. Eventually, a harried sixty-something waitress wearing a grimy half-apron over a dull orange uniform and sporting a 1950s hair bun, glanced his way and instructed in a semi-friendly tone, "Sit anywhere, hon."

Rocco nonchalantly looked around as if deciding on the perfect spot to eat and read. As he walked to the rear of the diner, he noticed that Toohey was wearing a crumpled blue suit and that Mrs. Toohey was dressed in a sheer white blouse, a very short skirt, and red high heels. Her shapely calves and an immodest length of tanned thighs were visible. Rocco slid into the booth adjacent to the Tooheys so that he was back-to-back with Dr. Toohey. The red vinyl bench covering was even more sticky than the fake wood table. It probably had not been wiped with anything other than a dirty rag since the Eisenhower presidency, when the waitress' outfit was in style. Inside of a coffee ring stain were the faded scratched initials *J+R*. He hoped that J and R had gotten married, had two wonderful kids, and were living happily ever after.

Rocco pretended to study the pancake choices while he struggled to overhear the conversation behind him. It didn't help that the young women at the table across the aisle were giggling loudly about some bachelorette show that had aired the night before. Fortunately, the laughter diminished after their egg-white omelets and vegan cinnamon rolls arrived. He still couldn't hear much of what the Tooheys were whispering about, but Rocco caught the distinctive voice of Mrs. Toohey as she expressed her displeasure over something Toohey had said. The louder they argued, the more he could hear.

" . . . but you said we were going to move to the other side of the street. You said we were going to buy a house suitable for a queen. Right now, I feel like the queen's poor second cousin. You need to step it up!"

" . . . so I think we should go on that extended trip we've been talking about," said Dr. Toohey in the raspy voice of a long-time smoker. "I already called, and they said we can have the plane whenever we want it."

"Can we go to Cabo this time?"

"Sure, my love. Anywhere you want."

"Can we get a different pilot this time? That last guy kept telling me to sit down as we were landing."

"Of course. I'll ask for that young man that you seemed to hit it off with when we flew to Key West."

"When would we go?" Mrs. Toohey asked.

"How about next week?"

"Are you out of your mind? Why would we go so soon? You told me just yesterday that things were going well at your office."

"I know, sweetheart," said Dr. Toohey, "but—"

Toohey's voice dropped to a whisper so that Rocco couldn't hear the reply to his wife's question. Suddenly, Toohey looked around the diner and pulled his wife out of the booth. "Let's get out of here and talk at home."

"But I'm not finished!" said Mrs. Toohey. "I'm hungry!" Toohey did not answer. He just threw down a couple of twenty-dollar bills and strong-armed her out of the front door. Mrs. Toohey complained the entire way, unaware that everyone in the place was watching her walk out. Including Big Rocky.

Chapter 20

Matthew wanted to meet with Joe Cook, but nowhere public. He phoned, hoping that Joe would pick up. Joe was in the Bristol Farms produce aisle when his phone buzzed. He saw that Matthew was calling, so he answered while maneuvering his cart around a large woman who was loitering in front of the oranges. "Hey, Matthew, what's up?"

"Joe, I got your text that you've got some information for me. I need to go up to LA to see my uncle. Would it be too much trouble for you to drive up and meet with me at my parents' house? The caretaker won't be there tomorrow, so we'll have the place to ourselves."

"No problem. Up in Pacific Palisades, right? I've got the address in my book. You pick the time."

They set a meeting time of noon. On the way to the house, Matthew stopped at Big Dean's Famous Burgers on the Santa Monica pier and picked up two lunch orders of Dean's giant burgers, with everything on them. Of course, with fries and slaw on the side. Matthew used to go to Dean's often when he was growing up, but he had not been back for several years. As he waited for his order, he glanced around at the customers sitting at the crammed-together café tables. Just as he remembered, the clientele was mostly sun-bleached, rowdy beach kids, sporting tattoos and multiple ear, nose, and eyebrow piercings. A hazard,

Matthew supposed, not for the first time in his life, of growing up with enough family money so that their parents would always rescue them from their poor life choices.

Joe had already pulled into the driveway leading to the motor court when Matthew arrived. After a hearty handshake, Joe saw the take-out bag that Matthew was holding. Joe smiled as he opened the trunk of his Range Rover, opened a cooler full of ice, and pulled out two giant bottles of Kirin beer. "I hope whatever is in that bag goes well with beer!" Joe said.

"What doesn't?" replied Matthew.

Because the weather was warm, Matthew led Joe through the house to a backyard patio. Joe carried the beer and a bulging backpack. They sat at the same table where Matthew and TJ had sat a few days earlier. "Let's eat before we get down to business," Matthew said as he opened the grease-stained, white bag and pushed one lunch order to Joe.

"Suits me," said Joe as he used the lip of the tabletop to pop off the beer caps. He handed a bottle to Matthew. Joe took a huge bite of his burger and drained half his bottle of beer.

"Wow, you really sucked that down," said Matthew.

"What are you, my mom?" countered Joe with a burp.

They ate in silence for a few minutes. "Oh my God," said Joe. "This is the best burger ever! I hope you have a couple more in that bag!"

"Sorry, I only brought one each. They're gigantic."

"What about that pickle?" Joe said as he gestured to Matthew's plate. "You going to eat that?"

"As a matter of fact, I am," replied Matthew as he shooed Joe's hand away.

"More heartless words have never been spoken," moaned Joe as secret sauce dribbled down his chin.

While they ate, Joe listened respectfully as Matthew wistfully reminisced about his childhood in this house. There was a faraway look in Matthew's eyes as he remembered having meals at this very table with his parents. "When you are young and naive," Matthew mused, "you think you'll never die. You think your parents will never die. You just assume they'll always be there."

Joe nodded. He knew that Matthew's father had been murdered in the upstairs master bedroom when Matthew was a boy. He remained silent and waited for a sign that it was time to get down to business. He didn't want to intrude on Matthew's sorrow.

After they had licked and wiped dry their fingers, and Matthew had been quiet for a few minutes, Joe sensed that it was time to begin his report. "Matthew, you asked me to find out about this Toohey guy, so you probably already know this, but he's up to no good." Joe opened his notebook and spoke while reading his own scribbles. "I first used every database known to man to learn his backstory." Joe told Matthew all about Toohey's personal data, employment history, and financial records, but he saved the best for last. "Here's the kicker. Yes, he apparently was a big-deal doctor at the FDA, but he got canned after twenty years for sexual harassment of a young female lab tech. Apparently, late one night, the two of them were caught in a compromising position on top of a lab bench. She didn't want to press charges, so Toohey was simply sacked. The young woman quit soon thereafter. The employee's name was Hillary Flint, the same Hillary who later married Toohey!"

"Wow, still waters run deep, I guess. I had the impression that Toohey was a straight-laced, fuddy-duddy. What is Hillary like?"

"That's another oddity. She looks like a girl-next-door centerfold! I'm telling you. She's gorgeous. No idea how Toohey did it."

"Did you get some photos of the gold digger?"

"This sounds a bit like '*The dog ate my homework*' excuse, but honestly, I fell down on the job there. I saw her come out of their house to greet Toohey, and I was so surprised by her looks that she was back inside before I could get my camera ready. Sorry, rookie mistake."

"No worries. You can get a photo of her later if necessary," said Matthew.

Joe continued, "Another weird thing is that I could tell that someone else had Toohey under surveillance. I don't think he noticed me, but I saw a guy in a Crown Vic just sitting there watching Toohey's house. I got a license number."

After a pause, Matthew inquired, "Do you think he's Toohey's bodyguard?"

"No idea."

"What did the guy in the car look like?"

"Couldn't see his facial features. But I could tell he was big guy. Looked Caucasian from a distance. Why, do you know who he is?"

"No, but we need to find out. There was someone following a friend of mine who fits that description. What else have you got?"

Joe proceeded to tell Matthew about what he had found in Toohey's storage unit. He didn't volunteer how he had gained access, and Matthew didn't ask. Joe pulled a stack of large glossy photographs out of his backpack. As he handed them over, he said, "I also made three duplicate sets for you." Matthew thumbed through the stack, staring at each photo for a few seconds. When he got to the last couple of pictures, Joe volunteered, "See, he's got a safe in there, too. I wonder why he needs a safe."

Matthew replied without looking up. "I have a pretty good idea." He then slowly spread the photographs out on the table, peering intently at each one.

Joe pointed at a few of the photos. He said, "You'll notice there are wrappings and packages bearing labels with weird chemical names. I presume those words mean something to you, being that you're a doctor and all."

Matthew looked at Joe with narrowed eyes and announced gravely, "Those words mean Toohey is worse than up to no good. He's morally bankrupt. He's a cold-blooded killer."

"Say what now?" asked Joe with a furrowed brow.

"I have to make a call. Be right back."

While Joe sat at the table, Matthew disappeared into the house, called Torrey, and asked her to arrange a meeting for later that night with Mrs.

Ed and Hawk. When Matthew returned, Joe was direct. "Matthew, what's going on? What do you mean he's a killer? Don't you think I'm entitled to know who you've gotten me involved with?"

"Yes, Joe, you're right. Let me tell you what's happening."

Because Matthew was meeting with his uncle at TJ's medical office at 3:00 p.m., he gave Joe an abbreviated, white-washed version of the story. When he finished, Joe simply said, "So what can I do to help?"

"I'm not sure. I still have something else to check out. In the meantime, not a word about this to anyone."

Joe said, "Of course," as he crossed his heart.

• • •

When Matthew arrived at TJ's office, he was warmly greeted by longtime office manager, Mavis Zimmerman. Matthew had known her for many years. "Matthew!" Mavis cried out as she hugged him hard. "Let me look at you! How have you been? How's that cute little wife of yours?"

Matthew chuckled as he sought to escape her grip. "We're doing great, Mavis. How are you?"

After a few minutes of catch-up, Matthew was anxious to see TJ. "Is he back there, Mavis?"

"Oh yes. He asked me to clear his afternoon for you. He's in his office."

Matthew didn't need directions. He had worked at his uncle's medical office during summers and had visited many times since then. But he'd only rarely come up from San Diego since starting his residency. He felt guilty about that, but he knew that TJ understood the demands on his time. Ninety-hour work weeks, interrupted sleep when on call at the hospital, and a new wife. Not much time for a social life, even with family.

After hugs and greetings, TJ insisted on hearing all about Matthew's patient load, new doctor experiences, and of course, Torrey. When Matthew complained about the long hours resulting in sleep deprivation,

TJ assured Matthew that this was a time-honored rite of passage for new doctors.

Matthew strongly disagreed with the premise. "Functioning without enough sleep isn't good for the physical or mental health of the residents," said Matthew. "It's more akin to hazing than training. And who could say with a straight face that tired doctors are just as effective and efficient as doctors who have had a good seven or eight hours of sound sleep? And don't give me that 'I had to do it, so you should have to do it, too' argument. It's insane."

TJ looked skeptical. "Isn't it important for doctors to have practiced long hours of work to prepare them for emergencies?" he insisted. "And for long surgeries?"

"I'll grant you that surgeons may be in their own special category. Torrey, for example, thinks nothing of the hours. She feels like she is training for sixteen-hour brain surgeries." Matthew shrugged his shoulders. "But let's not have the exception dictate the rule. When I finish my residency, I'm going to be an advocate for a more humane and healthy work schedule for residents," Matthew vowed. "Surgeons can do what they want." They both laughed.

Having decided to agree to disagree on the subject of resident hours, TJ and Matthew, still smiling, stared at each other lovingly. TJ, like he had done numerous times in his role as a surrogate father, asked, "Matthew, you know I always love to see you. And any reason for you to visit is okay with me. But I can read it on your face. You came here for a reason. What do you need?"

Matthew grinned. "You know me too well. Actually, I do need a favor—but with no questions asked."

TJ hesitated, then nodded silently. Matthew pulled out the small vial of clear liquid that he had drained from the IV bag that Torrey had swiped from Toohey's office. "I wonder if you could have this fluid analyzed by your outside lab. I need to know the precise contents. What substances and how much of each. And I need it yesterday, so I'll pay all expedited fees."

Matthew could see in TJ's eyes that he was uncomfortable. But TJ merely said, "I presume there's a good reason that you can't have your own hospital's lab run the assay?"

"Yes."

"And I presume that you can't tell me the reason?"

"Correct, at least not at this time."

"Let me guess. You, and I imagine Torrey, want to use outside channels in order to check on the work of another doctor. You don't want to falsely accuse anyone. Am I warm?"

"Pretty hot, as a matter of fact."

TJ buzzed Mavis and asked her to come into his office. "Mavis," said TJ while handing the vial to her, "would you do me a favor and run this sample over to the lab? Tell Fred Banks over there that I need this immediately. A matter of life and death. If he gives you any guff, hand him your phone, and have him call me."

"Mr. Banks usually says it takes a day to expedite, is that okay?"

TJ looked at Matthew, who nodded. After Mavis left with the vial, TJ looked at Matthew and said in a serious tone, "Tell Torrey for me, 'I hope you two know what you're doing.'"

Matthew didn't reply to that. Instead, he asked, "Will you text the results to me the second you receive them?"

TJ nodded.

Chapter 21

"So now what?" asked Edwina.

The impromptu meeting called by Matthew was fully attended. Matthew, Torrey, Edwina, and Hawk sat around the dining room table in Matthew and Torrey's condo.

"We're so glad to see you, Hawk. How's Angela doing?" asked Torrey.

"Not too well. Her parents are with her now, so I felt that I could get away and see where we are on everything. Do you have some news?"

"Well," said meticulous planner Matthew as he shot Torrey a look, "we have the IV bag that Torrey took from Toohey's office." They all stared at the innocuous-looking, almost full, clear plastic bag that Matthew had lifted from a box and plopped onto the table.

Edwina stared at Torrey in surprise. "You stole that?"

Torrey flashed defiant eyes. "Do you want to get to the bottom of this or not?" she snapped with a tightness in her throat that Matthew instantly recognized.

Edwina held up her hands in surrender. "I'm not upset. I'm impressed! If I had a hat, I would tip it!" She reached across the table for a fist bump. Torrey lit up and returned the gesture.

"Don't encourage her," Matthew groaned. "She was only supposed to meet Toohey, not commit a felony."

"I bet it was a misdemeanor at most," countered Torrey.

"You all see what I have to put up with?" sighed Matthew.

Torrey blew a kiss towards Matthew, and she countered, "You love it."

Hawk let out a frustrated huff and blurted out, "You guys are cute together. But I'm here to talk about a plan."

Matthew cleared his throat and shot Torrey a "let's get serious" look. "I arranged for the contents of the IV bag to be analyzed. We should know the results tomorrow."

Hawk put his hands flat on the table and said in an irritated tone, "I know you didn't summon us here to tell us that. If you don't have any information yet, why drag us all over here?"

Edwina admonished her brother. "Hawk, Matthew is doing us a favor. Please let's allow him to explain in his own way."

Hawk's head drooped, and the rest of his body went slack. "I'm sorry, man," he said contritely. "I haven't been sleeping and—"

Torrey cut him off. "Hawk, no need to explain. We all understand, me most of all." She reached across the table and gave his forearm a light squeeze. "And I think Matthew has more to tell us. Isn't that right, honey?"

"Actually," Matthew said as he reached under the table, "I have lots more." Matthew brought out four identical stacks of eight by ten photos. As he shoved a pile in front of each person, he shot a look at Torrey that said he was sorry that he hadn't had a chance to talk to her in advance of the meeting. She nodded her understanding, knowing that she had been late to arrive due to complications in a surgery that she had been observing.

Matthew remained still and silent as everyone flipped through their set of photos. Edwina, in an exasperated tone, was the first to speak. "What are we looking at Matthew?"

"Yeah," added Hawk. "And where were these taken?"

Torrey was certain that she had already figured it out.

"The photos were taken by a private eye I hired to discreetly tail and investigate Dr. Toohey. My guy followed Toohey from his office to a storage facility where Toohey mysteriously dropped something off on his way home. The investigator went back to Toohey's locker later that night, broke in, and took these photos. And don't worry, he covered his tracks, so Toohey will not suspect anything," said Matthew.

"Well," said Edwina as she gestured with a puzzled look, "I know an IV bag when I see one. And I see a bunch of them in boxes and one on that steel table. So what?"

Torrey broke in. "I'll tell you so what," she said grimly. "Yes, bags of saline are normally innocuous. But this kind is special." Matthew, realizing that his brilliant wife had instantly come to the same conclusion as he had, nodded at her to continue. "0.9% sodium chloride solution is the common choice in the United States for hydration and electrolyte replacement, even though some research suggests it can cause kidney failure. In Europe and Australia, IV solutions called 'balanced fluids' are widely used. These solutions contain other substances, which cause the fluid to act more like human plasma, a little thicker and a little less transparent than base saline solution."

"That sounds like a good thing," shrugged Edwina.

"In a vacuum, I don't disagree," said Torrey. "But look what else was in the storage unit." She held up one of Joe's photos and pointed. "Look here. See this box labeled 'cannabinoids?' That is soluble marijuana powder. And look here," Torrey said, pointing to a photo, "sugar water." She grabbed another photo. "And see right here? These small plastic bags of pink pills? They are labeled 'Fentanyl.'" Torrey thumbed through the remaining photos. "Notice in this one? See the ceramic mortar and pestle in the foreground?" she said while indicating. "You can see that the mortar, or bowl, has pink residue and remnants showing that Fentanyl pills were crushed in it."

"I've heard of Fentanyl," said Hawk. "But I'm not clear on what it is."

"It's a powerful pain killer, a banned synthetic opioid that is a hundred times more powerful than morphine. Most of it is manufactured outside the country and smuggled in. It can be taken as a pill or dissolved in liquid.

Users become dependent on it and need to take higher and higher doses to get relief. Eventually, overdoses can occur, leading to death."

"Where on earth would he get that much Fentanyl?" asked Edwina.

Matthew blurted out the answer. "After my investigator showed me these photographs, I asked him to do some more research. During the last year of Toohey's tenure at the FDA, a large shipment of Fentanyl was seized at a Los Angeles harbor dock during a raid of a ship from China. A few bags of it disappeared from the FDA evidence lockers shortly before Toohey and the FDA parted company. They were never found."

"Until now, right?" offered Hawk.

Matthew continued, "So why would Toohey go to the trouble of obtaining saline from Europe, with substances already added, and have available two other drugs which can be dissolved in those IV bags with no discernible change in color or viscosity? And why stock liquid sucrose?"

"I presume you're going to tell us?" inquired Hawk.

"Matthew is big on rhetorical questions," replied Torrey. "Medically, no one would ever deliver Fentanyl by IV. And drug dealers would sell it in pill or powder form, not dissolved in IV bags. The only logical conclusion is that Toohey is adding tiny amounts of Fentanyl, and likely cannabinoids also, to the IV bags of his brain cancer patients. He's probably adding sugar to avoid any potential aftertaste or chemical odor."

"Is that mixture a cure?" asked Edwina.

"Not in the least," said Torrey.

"Then why would Toohey do that?"

Torrey took a deep breath. "When I met with Toohey, posing as a prospective client, I ran into one of his current patients, a young girl named Addie B. Addie was hooked up to an IV bag, which allegedly contained Toohey's secret potpourri of curative drugs. Addie's mother told me that since starting the Toohey regimen, Addie had been feeling much better. Less pain. Happier. And guess what? The medical community has long understood that prescription weed can help alleviate pain in certain people with terminal cancer. And we know that

Fentanyl binds to opioid receptors in the parts of the brain that control pain and feelings."

"In English please," said Edwina impatiently.

"Addie's perceived improvements are simply short-term side effects of marijuana and Fentanyl." Torrey could barely contain her anger and disgust.

The room went silent as Hawk and Edwina worked to process that news. "Wait a minute," said Hawk with a raised voice and a mutinous expression, "Are you telling us that Toohey fed these drugs to my daughter? With no intention to make her better?" He sprang up out of his chair, his piercing blue eyes opening wide. "I'm going to—"

Matthew arose, too. "Now wait a minute, Hawk. We don't know that for sure. We have a pretty tight theory but believing something to be true is not the same as knowing."

"Of course we know it!" Hawk yelled. He pointed at Matthew and Torrey, "You two just got through telling us that's the only explanation! He's dead meat!"

"What are you going to do?" said Edwina, her voice raising in pitch.

"Do I have to draw you a picture?" Hawk yelled angrily. "Do I need to sugarcoat it? I'm going to rip his head off! Are you going to try to stop me?" He glared at Edwina, then turned to confront Matthew. "How about you Matthew? Do you want to try?" Although he was 6'2" of muscle and proficient in martial arts, Matthew knew that his brain, not his brawn, was his only chance of keeping Hawk under control.

Torrey got up and grabbed Hawk, who struggled to break her clamp-like grasp. She raised up on her toes so that her 5'3" frame was lifted as high as possible. She looked into Hawk's eyes, "We're trying to help you, Hawk!"

Matthew stepped in to help, holding Hawk's wrist in a vice grip. "C'mon," Matthew calmly urged, "we need to sit down and talk."

Edwina slowly came over and hugged Hawk. "Bro, we all want to get the guy. But Matthew's right. Let's talk this out." Hawk reluctantly sat back down, back ramrod straight, jaw set, upper lip curled. Edwina kept her hand resting lovingly on Hawk's forearm, with just enough pressure exerted to prevent Hawk from making a break for it.

The next thirty minutes were a blur. Everyone was talking at once; no one took control. Torrey eventually slammed a flat hand down on the table. "C'mon, guys, let's take a breath!" The last few murmurs died away. "I know we all have ideas as to how to proceed. Fortunately, I happen to be married to a top-tier planner. Take my word for it. Matthew can help us figure out something that we can all agree with." Matthew said nothing. Just looked at Torrey. So, she added, "Right, honey?"

By this time, Hawk had maneuvered his arm out from under Edwina's grip and sat with arms crossed unnaturally high, still skeptical of any plan involving less than immediate and total annihilation of Toohey. Matthew tried to buy some time to think. He turned on the charisma and announced, "I'm making an executive decision." Three pairs of eyes turned towards him expectantly. "We'll know what's in the IV bag sometime tomorrow. Let's table this until we get the results. If you all agree, let's meet here again tomorrow evening. I promise we won't leave until we have the semblance of a game plan that suits us all." Matthew knew that Torrey would back him up, and he figured Edwina would go along. He stared only at Hawk. "So, what do you say, Hawk?"

Hawk spoke in a way that was both threatening and calm. "On one condition. If the IV bag has in it what we all imagine, don't try to hold me back. Whatever plan you come up with, it had better end with my hands around Toohey's neck." With that, Hawk stood and strode away. He threw open the front door so hard that it bounced and slammed closed.

Edwina murmured, "Sorry," to Matthew and Torrey. "I'd better go after him and make sure he doesn't do anything foolish. Would you mind watching Koa for me while I'm gone?" She hurried to the door, opened it slowly, and softly closed it behind her.

Matthew and Torrey looked at each other and then at Koa who was snoring softly in the corner.

Chapter 22

Once Torrey and Matthew were alone, Matthew collapsed on the couch, hands rubbing his face. "Are you all right?" asked Torrey.

"Actually, no. I was already exhausted from my shift at the hospital, my discussion with Joe, and my meeting with TJ. And now Hawk is giving me grief about things over which I have no control. Maybe we're just fooling ourselves. Maybe we should just walk away from this. Maybe we should let the professionals investigate Toohey. Maybe just call the police."

"You know we can't do that," said Torrey as her face hardened. "We owe it to Edwina. And to Hawk and Angela. We owe it to the other families who Toohey has duped. You didn't see the Tintin girl and her mom. But I did." While she spoke, Torrey gazed up at the large photo of Torrey and Leia on the living room wall taken just before Leia got sick. The photo was a wedding present from her parents. "If Toohey is scamming these folks, any punishment doled out by the government would not be good enough. Can you even wrap your mind around the depth of Toohey's cruelty?" Torrey's eyes flashed ice. "Hawk is right. If Toohey is guilty of what we suspect, we need to be sure there is complete justice."

She crossed her arms and stared at Matthew, daring him to oppose her on this. Then she added, "Look how fortunate we are. God knows we've had our share of hardships and more. But look how lucky we are now to have found each other, which would never have happened without what came before. With Hawk, Angela, and Mrs. Ed, we've been given a chance to do something similar for others. Something beyond ourselves." Matthew was listening hard. Torrey then quoted one of Matthew's favorite sayings, "To whom much is given, much is expected." Matthew leaned back as Torrey ran her fingers through his hair.

Matthew sighed and closed his eyes. "You are preaching to the choir about justice. And about the families' rights to revenge against Toohey. You know I agree with that. But with our work schedules, we've been burning the candle at both ends and in the middle for so long that I am about dead on my feet. Don't you feel the same way?" Matthew said with slumped shoulders.

Torrey could see that he was completely exhausted. "Of course. How about this? Why don't we forget about Toohey for the rest of the night? You'll get the saline bag lab results tomorrow. Then we can meet with the others and decide what to do. Deal?"

"Okay." Matthew gestured to Torrey to come to him. "I sure love you."

Torrey climbed onto the couch and melted into Matthew's strong arms. She whispered, "Why don't we get a good night's sleep, get up super early tomorrow morning, and go for a walk on the beach? We haven't done that for ages, and it always clears our minds."

"That sounds good except for the getting up early part."

"C'mon. It'll do us good. Windansea Beach is steps away. Lots of pelicans flying by."

"Pelicans are my favorite bird!" said Matthew with some enthusiasm in his voice.

"I know. By the way, what do you call a group of pelicans?" Torrey asked in order to keep the mood light.

"It's not fair that you have a photographic mind for such trivia."

"Is that your way of saying you don't know? Even though it is your favorite bird?" Torrey asked with a grin. "C'mon, you can at least guess. I'll give you a hint. There are at least three correct answers."

"Fine," said Matthew with fake annoyance. "One answer has to be 'flock.'"

"That is not only a wrong answer, but also the most boring answer you could possibly give."

"I give up then," replied Matthew. "So, Miss Smarty Pants, what are the three correct answers?"

"Scoop, squadron, and pouch," shouted Torrey with a fist in the air.

"Got it. You win!" Matthew laughed as he squeezed her upper thigh.

"Anyway, let's go to the beach in the morning. And we can take Koa with us!"

"Well, we can't take Koa. Don't you remember all the 'No Dogs Allowed' signs on that beach?"

"Let me get this straight," Torrey laughed, "you spent most of your life plotting how to avenge your father's death, and now you are the mastermind in figuring out how to exact the ultimate punishment against Toohey. Yet you're worried about a ticket for walking a dog on the sand?"

"Since you put it that way," Matthew lazily smiled, "I guess I'll take the risk. Plus, there are always lots of surfers at Windansea. You know how I always wanted to learn to surf. Maybe we'll find someone down there who can teach me."

"I hate to be the bearer of bad news, but you need to learn how to swim first," said Torrey in a mock serious tone. Matthew nodded sheepishly. They both remembered well what happened when Matthew fell out of TJ's small motorboat; Torrey had to come to his rescue. It wasn't pretty.

Just then, Koa waddled out from the bedroom and sat on the rug next to the couch. She barked three times. "I guess someone wants her dinner," moaned Matthew. "By the way, is Edwina coming back tonight?"

"She texted that she's staying over at Hawk's place tonight. She'll be back here tomorrow evening."

"Well, let's feed this darn dog, so we can get to bed." Koa barked her approval.

• • •

The next morning over breakfast, after a walk on the beach, Torrey reached across the small wood table that was situated on their ocean-view deck. She put her hand over Matthew's. "Are you feeling better now after having had a good sleep, a fun walk, and seeing squadrons of pelicans?"

"Much better. Now I have the energy to face the new day," said a beaming Matthew.

"I know this is bad timing," said Torrey, "but I need to ask you something. Remember the day at the hospital when we had all those injuries from a Little League brawl?"

"That's a day that I'll never forget," said Matthew with a chuckle. "What about it?"

"I'm not sure that I mentioned it at the time, but one of the injured guys was a military vet who got hit in the face with a bat when he tried to break up a fight. He had no private insurance, and he said he had no money, so they sent him to the VA for treatment."

"So what? That happens all the time."

"Yes, but in addition to the obvious soft tissue and bone injuries, he was complaining of blurred vision, pain in his left eye, and a terrible headache. I'm worried that the VA doctors might treat only the observable injuries, and not the less obvious ones. If they failed to do a complete evaluation, it could lead to cognitive disabilities and permanent loss of sight."

"I'm guessing that this concern of yours stems from your uncle's poor treatment at the VA in New York after he mustered out of the Marines? But in any event, what can you do about it? You don't work at the VA."

"Of course, my uncle Scott's treatment is the precipitating factor. My father has complained to me many times about what happened to his brother. He survived three tours in the Middle East, goes into the VA for a checkup on his ankle bone that had been shattered by shrapnel, and he comes out with no lower leg, a systemic infection, and terrible bed sores. And to top it all off, they dropped him during physical therapy, which broke both of his wrists. Now he can barely move his fingers."

"I know. I'm sorry all that happened. But maybe that was a one-off. The VA hospitals have improved a lot in recent years. And we know that was at a different VA facility. I imagine that the one here is much better."

"Maybe it is. But I don't know that. And I'm afraid of what might happen to the guy who got sent there from our hospital. So, that leads to my question to you. Would you mind awfully if I did a rotation at the VA so that I can check on that soldier? Not only for my own peace of mind, but I would like to tell my dad that I am doing my part for military vets."

"If that's what you want to do, I'm not going to say a single word."

"No, but your face is," said Torrey, studying Matthew's concerned expression.

"Well, you already have a lot on your plate, but of course I'll support your decision. But I'm not the one you need to convince. You'll have to talk to Dr. Peterson. I'm not sure that she—"

"I already did!" said Torrey triumphantly. "Anne said they always need good doctors over there. She will loan me out for one month."

"When do you start?"

"Today. In fact, I'm going to be late if I don't leave right now!" Matthew snorted. Torrey laughed, "Honey, I knew what you were going to say!" As Matthew raised his eyes and arms to the heavens, Torrey added, "So what does your day look like?"

"I've got clinic duty," said Matthew in a disgusted tone.

"Ha! Too bad, sucker!" Torrey was out the door before Matthew could reply.

Chapter 23

At that very minute, about ten miles away, in the small suburb of North Clairemont, Addie B was lying on her bed, softly crying. "Mommy, I don't feel so good."

"Is it your stomach again?" asked Mrs. Bernstein, fear clouding her face.

"It's everywhere. My head, too." Addie clutched her favorite stuffed animal to her chest. Her tears fell on Snowy.

"Stay right there. I'm going to call the doctor."

Two minutes later, she returned with coats and hats. "Dr. Toohey's phone is busy, so we're going straight to his office." Just as they were about to open the front door, Addie vomited on the hallway runner. "I'm so sorry, Mommy! I didn't mean to throw up right there! It just happened!"

Carol Bernstein was freaking out, but not about the rug. "That's okay, honey. I'll take care of that later. Let's get you to the car. Can you walk?"

"I feel dizzy, but I'll try." The two of them held hands as they shuffled slowly to the street in front of their home where their five-year-old Mazda was parked. Carol's eyes watered, even as she tried to remain strong for her only child.

When they arrived at Toohey's office, Mrs. Bernstein double parked on the street, helped Addie to unbuckle her seatbelt, and then carried her into the building. She didn't even notice the OUT OF ORDER sign on the elevator because she headed straight to the stairs. Bursting into Toohey's office suite with Addie in her arms, she saw Mrs. Borsky behind the counter, looking bored but menacing at the same time. "We need to see Dr. Toohey! My daughter's pain is back, worse than ever. What's happening?"

Mrs. Borsky replied in a flat, unwelcoming voice. "Sorry, Dr. Toohey isn't in today. Would you like to make an appointment? We can get you in next Thursday afternoon." She pulled out her appointment book and readied her pencil. "What's your name again?"

The Bersteins had been in the office six times, but Carol had no time to be offended at Borsky's lack of familiarity. She simply stared at the muscles bulging in Borsky's neck and arms, which were emphasized by her too-tight Beatles T-shirt. Apparently, she dressed casually when Dr. Toohey was absent. "Where is he? My daughter is having a relapse. We need to do something! Now!"

"I'll tell you what," said Borsky with a condescending shrug, "there's a patient in the back right now. I can only work with one family at a time if the doctor isn't here. They should be out of here in about fifteen minutes. Shall I hook your daughter up with another treatment when they leave?" She added with a wooden smile, "No extra charge."

Chapter 24

Matthew left for the hospital at the same time Torrey left for the VA. He had to do one day of clinic every two weeks like every other medical resident at every teaching hospital, and he couldn't be late. The line of patients to get into the clinic waiting room was probably already out the door and into the parking lot.

Matthew had just turned onto the main drag out of La Jolla when his phone beeped. A text from TJ with an attachment. Matthew was a big proponent of not looking at your phone when driving. In this case, he made an exception. He mouthed a "thank you" as the light turned red at the intersection of Torrey Pines Road and La Jolla Shores Drive. He knew from his daily commute that he would be stuck at the light for almost two minutes. He usually cursed that time loss, but today it was perfect.

He opened the text from TJ. It only said, *Test results attached. Say hi to Torrey.* While the attachment was downloading, he glanced at the driver in the beat-up Toyota stopped next to him. Her windows were down, and rap lyrics were screaming to be heard over the pounding base. She had her bare right foot propped up on the dash, painting her toenails. Matthew had to smile—only in SoCal.

The attachment took only a few seconds to download and a few more to open. He scanned the results, reread them more slowly, then turned off his phone. The traffic light turned green. Matthew stepped on the gas, weaved through the rush hour traffic, and walked into the hospital right on time.

Clinic duty is uniformly despised by hospital doctors. An adventure awaited in each examination room, with tales of impossible symptoms, sicknesses caused by the failure to take prescribed medicines as recommended, and requests for medicines that would be unnecessary or harmful. Matthew was sent to Exam Room 3 the moment he walked into the clinic. No time to call or text Torrey. Scheduling the meeting about the test results with Hawk and Edwina was going to have to wait.

Sulla Stanford was Matthew's first patient of the day. Even though Matthew was exhausted, he smiled broadly as soon as he saw Ms. Stanford. A plump woman who looked to be about eighty years old was up on the exam table, blouse off. She was wearing an oversized running bra and sweatpants.

Matthew looked at her intake chart. The nurse had noted a complaint of right shoulder pain. "What can we do for you today?" asked Matthew warmly with a full smile. Sulla leaned in to read the name embroidered on the breast pocket of Matthew's white coat.

"Good morning, Dr. Preston. I hope you can help me." She rubbed her left hand on the top of her right shoulder. "My shoulder hurts."

"On a scale of one to ten, what is the pain level right now?"

"Well, it doesn't hurt at all right now."

Matthew frowned quizzically. "What do you mean? Why did you come in today?"

Sulla raised her right hand up over her head and moved it around in a circular motion. "My shoulder hurts whenever I do this," she said with a pained expression.

Matthew stifled a laugh. "And how often do you do that?"

"Not too often. Maybe once a month or so just to see if it still hurts. What should I do about it?"

Matthew could not help himself. He had to say it. "My first thought is that you should stop doing that. Would that work for you?"

"I suppose I could try that."

"Fair enough. And if it starts to bother you when you are *not* doing that, why don't you come back, and we will send you for an MRI of your shoulder to take a look at your rotator cuff. How does that sound to you?"

"Do you think there's a tear in my rotator cuff?"

"Maybe. Can't really know without more tests."

"Dr. House would know without more tests," she said with a crinkly smile.

"Who?"

"Dr. House! From the TV show!"

"Oh, right. Well, Dr. House had some help. He had screenwriters."

They shared a laugh while Sulla put her top back on. Matthew helped her down from the table.

"Oh, thank you, Dr. Preston. You look so young, but you're so wise! I have a niece that you would like. Shall I give you her phone number, so you could give her a call?"

"Thank you for the sweet offer, but I am already married. And very happily."

● ● ●

Matthew's next patient was not quite so simple. When Matthew walked into Exam Room 4, Andrew Robinson, a good-looking kid, age nineteen, was sitting in the patient's chair in the corner of the room. He was gym fit, wearing a tight white T-shirt. He looked like an amateur bodybuilder from the waist up. However, instead of tight shorts or skinny jeans, he was wearing greenish, baggy dockers, three sizes too big, and bright orange Croc clogs on his feet. He had a newspaper opened on his lap. Matthew glanced at Andrew's sparse chart as he walked over to shake hands. "I see that you told the nurse that you had a heart attack. What were your symptoms?"

"Well, it seemed like my heart was racing last night, but it seems fine now." Andrew was quick to add that he still had a headache and felt lightheaded.

"So, you just want a checkup and a little reassurance? Why don't we take a look? Hop up on the table," said Matthew with a smile.

Andrew stared at the ceiling as though he were counting the holes in the acoustic tiles. "I can't." Matthew looked at Andrew with a puzzled look. Andrew folded up the newspaper and put it on the floor. He pointed at his crotch. "I can barely walk."

Matthew could see the bulge. Any male past the age of puberty knew what it was and probably most adolescent girls. "Hmm, how long have you had that erection?"

"Since last night."

"Is this natural, or did you have some help?" Andrew turned bright red. "While you get undressed, tell me what happened." Andrew hesitated. Matthew said firmly, "Look, Andrew, I can't help you unless you fill me in."

Andrew stood up and slowly started to unbuckle his belt. "I lift weights. Ever since I started taking steroid supplements, things down there haven't seemed to be working very well." Matthew was just starting to say something about the steroid use, but Andrew interrupted, "Yeah, I know. Steroids are dangerous long term, but I just wanted to give them a try. All of a sudden, my muscle mass increased, so I kept taking them. I didn't have a girlfriend back then, so I didn't care that much about the inability to get hard."

Matthew wanted to roll his eyes. Instead, he just said, "Go ahead. So, what happened last night?"

"My girlfriend's parents were out of town for the weekend, and she invited me over. I was nervous about whether I would be able to, you know, *function*, so I stole some of my father's Viagra. I know where he keeps it. The first one didn't do anything, so I took more."

"How many in total?"

"Four, I think. Maybe five."

"What was the dose on each pill? Twenty-five milligrams? Fifty? One hundred?"

Andrew looked blank. "How should I know?" After a few seconds of silent staring at each other, Andrew continued, "Anyway, by the time I got to Sarah's house, I was ready to go. I was happy for the first hour or so, but then it started to hurt. Then I got a headache and felt dizzy. Then my heart started to race. We stopped fooling around, so I could rest."

"How long ago was all this?"

"I got over there at about 10:00 p.m., and we stopped everything by about midnight. For the next eight hours, nothing got better. I just lay there in agony. So, Sarah said we needed to go to the doctor. I couldn't get my pants on, they were too tight, so Sarah let me borrow her brother's pants. As you can see," said Andrew as he held out the waistline of the pants, "he's fat. And I couldn't bend over to lace my Nike lifting boots, so I am wearing these hideous shoes. Sarah drove me here. She's waiting out in the lobby." He started to tear up. "What is going on? Do something please!" He was now up on the table. His penis was rigid and purple.

"Okay, just relax. For right now, I'll spare you the lecture on taking someone else's prescription medication. And we will talk later about the importance of telling the nurse the truth about your history and your complaints."

"I was embarrassed. I thought she would ask to look—"

"I know. We'll table that discussion for now. Lie flat please."

All the while Andrew was talking, Matthew was getting his instruments ready. "Andrew, you have what is called priapism. There are two types, and it looks like you have the most serious kind called ischemic priapism because it is not resolving on its own. The blood in your penis is not able to exit using normal channels. What I'm going to do is drain some blood using a needle and syringe."

"Wait, what?!" exclaimed Andrew with alarm.

"Don't worry. It will be a little uncomfortable for a minute, but you should then get some relief. And then I have some medication for you to use at home which will allow blood flow out of the penis." Andrew struggled to raise his head, so he could see the needle. "Lie back down," instructed Matthew. "And stay still." Andrew lay back down and yelled, "Ow," even before Matthew touched him. "Keep quiet! And don't move."

Because the blood had been deprived of oxygen for so long, Matthew removed three syringes full of black blood. Within minutes, Andrew announced he was feeling better. Matthew draped a cotton dressing gown over Andrew and let him rest. Andrew closed his eyes and breathed evenly while he listened to Matthew lecture about the dangers of steroids, about not taking medicine prescribed for another person, and about the importance of an accurate medical chart. Matthew was no fan of premarital sex, but he figured that horse was already out of that barn. He simply counseled the value of protection.

Matthew allowed himself a smile as he looked forward to seeing Torrey after work. They had a standing bet—loser does the dishes—over which of them had the most interesting patient that day. Somehow, Torrey usually won. But Matthew was pretty sure Torrey would be hard-pressed to top him today.

When Andrew was finally out the door, Matthew texted Torrey, who probably wondered why she was getting such a message: *I'm so lucky to have you. And I'm so glad I don't need any little blue pills.*

• • •

The rest of Matthew's shift was filled with straight-forward and relatively boring patients. That was lucky because Matthew's mind kept wandering to Toohey and what they were going to do about him.

Chapter 25

Parking at the Veterans Administration building was a breeze. The parking structure was wide open and well-marked. Torrey easily found a spot in the covered lot. But the walk to the entrance of the building was another matter. The large concrete plaza in front of the building was meant to be a place of beauty and relaxation. Trees and flowers were everywhere. But so were the homeless. Most sat quietly with handmade signs. Torrey was torn between holding tight to her purse and the temptation to empty her wallet every few steps. Halfway across the plaza, standing by the defunct fountain that was dry because of the years-long California drought, a young man wearing a tattered green jacket bearing an American flag patch, a dingy T-shirt with matching fatigues, and grubby boots addressed Torrey in a polite southern drawl. "Hi, miss, I wonder if you could spare a dollar for a guy down on his luck." Torrey noticed that he had with him a dirty matted dog of indistinguishable breed. The dog looked better fed than the man. As they sized each other up, the man gushed, "Hey, aren't you that actress?"

It was not uncommon for Torrey, with her blonde pixie cut and bright blue eyes, to be mistaken for models and Hollywood actresses. "No," she replied with a chuckle.

"Sure you are. Didn't you used to be that girl who was on that show about that thing?"

Torrey changed the subject. "What kind of dog is that?" she asked.

"I say with great pride, he is an All-American mutt!"

"Are you a vet?" asked Torrey when she noticed he was wearing dog tags.

"No, my older brother was. He was killed in some hellhole on the other side of the world. These tags and this coat are all I have of his."

"If you aren't a veteran, why are you in front of the VA?"

"Well, if I'm honest, I used to panhandle in front of places where rich guys hang out. But frankly, they were cheap. The vets and their families are the most generous givers around."

"Can you work?" asked Torrey.

The man scoffed. "Not according to my last five employers. After a few days, my temper gets the best of me, and I get fired," said the man without much emotion.

"Do you live around here?"

The man pointed to the west. "A lot of us live under that freeway over there."

"What about your parents? Can't you live with them?"

The man lowered his voice. "Both my parents lost it when my brother died. They're still in Mississippi. Still in mourning." He shrugged with upturned palms. "I haven't seen them in years."

Torrey grimaced. "What's your name?"

"Bill Bonner."

Torrey looked at Bill and then around at the fifteen or twenty other men within view. She didn't have much cash on her, but she opened her purse and pulled out the few twenty-dollar bills that she had. Torrey handed the money to Bill. "Share this with the others however you see fit. My prayers are with you." As Torrey slowly walked to the building entrance, she thought about the impact that a death in the family can have. She was grateful that she was able to help Matthew exact justice for his father's death. She had allowed him to move on in life, to be the wonderful doctor and husband he had become.

Without a VA ID badge, Torrey had to wait in the security line with the general public. Once she got inside the building, Torrey was even more taken aback than she had been out in the courtyard. Torrey thought she might be welcomed with open arms by overworked and underpaid doctors and nurses. Instead, her motives were questioned, and she was treated as an interloper with no right to treat patients or even suggest treatment.

She was instructed to check-in with Dr. Bertram Sommerville, who had spent his entire medical career at six different VA branches throughout the country. He was now in charge of all daily medical decisions, and he made sure Torrey knew that during their initial meeting in his office.

Dr. Sommerville sat in his overstuffed office chair while Torrey was relegated to a hard, wooden guest chair that looked and felt like it came out of an 1800s schoolhouse. He was dressed in a three-piece herringbone suit, complete with a visible gold pocket watch chain. Somehow, he had a narrow ferret face; yet he had doughy jowls like Richard Nixon. Dr. Sommerville did not get up from his throne of power or extend his hand in greeting. But that was okay with Torrey who had a finely tuned radar for limp-fish handshakes. Dr. Sommerville simply fixed Torrey with an imperious stare. He tilted his head down, so he could look over his reading glasses at her from across the desk. "So, I received an email last night from some Kaiser administrator telling me that you are going to be doing us a big favor by slumming it here for a few weeks. Is that right?"

"Excuse me?" asked Torrey in disbelief.

"Are you going to be setting us straight? Telling us how to treat our patients?"

"Dr. Sommerville, I'm just trying to help out. My father was in the service and—"

"Oh, I see, one of those do-gooders who thinks dropping in here will shine up the resume. Like those rich kids who go to Africa to build a mud hut for three days and then stay on for another few weeks glamping at a game preserve, right?"

Torrey felt the heat crawl up her back, which she identified as righteous anger. She knew that feeling from when she was in the same exam room with Ted Nash at San Quentin. More recently, she had felt it when confronting Volkov.

Torrey stood, rested both hands on the desk, and leaned forward. Dr. Sommerville involuntarily scooted back and crossed his arms. "Look, sir," declared Torrey, "I'm not sure what your problem is, but I'm not rich, and I don't care about a resume. I'm going to work here for thirty days whether you like it or not. If you have a problem with my being here, I suggest you contact your boss, who happens to be the president of this institution, who talked to my boss, Dr. Anne Peterson. I'm here to work with head trauma patients. I'm training to become a brain surgeon. The VA is on the front lines. Maybe I can learn. Maybe you can teach me something that I can use to help others. And this might sound clichéd to you, but I hope I can do something while I am here that helps a patient." An awkward silence befell the room. Torrey held his gaze until Sommerville looked away to rearrange some papers on his desk. A pyrrhic victory, but Torrey liked winning.

She stood up straight, grabbed her purse, and said, "Now if you would just direct me to Dr. Mathers' office, so I can pick up my credentials and get started."

Out in the hallway after her angry exit, Torrey was taking a few deep breaths when an orderly walked by pushing an empty gurney. She let him run interference for her through the vets using walkers and canes and between their despondent family members, all the way to the elevators. The orderly was very helpful with directions. The VA facility was five stories, shaped like a cross. The first floor of the medical center, Torrey had noted when she walked in, held the most benign treatment departments, like blood draw, occupational therapy, and podiatry. Also located there was a café and the VA police force. She wondered why police were necessary.

By the time she started her visit with Dr. June Mathers on floor three, Torrey was calm and composed. "I just got through seeing Dr. Sommerville. What is *wrong* with that guy?"

"He is a joy, isn't he? Try not to get on his bad side. He's been known to hold a grudge."

"Good to know. But I'm not worried. Besides, grudges work both ways."

• • •

"I was told you intend to be a brain surgeon. Is that correct?" asked Dr. Mathers.

"Yes, and I thought the VA would be a good place to learn. Dr. Sommerville seems less than thrilled about having me here, but as a young aspiring *female* doctor, I am getting used to the cold shoulder from old white male physicians," confessed Torrey with a shrug.

"His attitude towards us 'women folk' is absurd, but frighteningly common," Dr. Mathers responded with a knowing smirk.

Torrey asked, "What has been your experience here? Been here long?"

"I come from a long family history of veterans. My brothers, father, and grandfather all served. I was not keen on becoming active-duty military, so I decided to do my part for my country by working here. After I finished my internal medicine residency in Alaska, I figured San Diego would be a great change of scenery. And this is a remarkable place to work. Very uplifting due to the courage of these veterans. Most of the nurses are great, but they don't have much power around here. Same with most of the wonderful, newer doctors." Then June lowered her voice to a conspiratorial whisper, "The problem is Sommerville and his circle of long-time cronies. Doctors who should have been pushed out long ago. You didn't hear it from me, but I swear there is something weird about Sommerville."

Torrey gave Dr. Mathers a raised eyebrow. "What do you mean?"

"Well, for someone who has spent his career working for the VA, he doesn't seem to care much for soldiers."

"What do you think is going on?"

"I have no idea. Let me know what you think. You will definitely see him around. He is very proprietary about the treatment regimens."

"I can think of lots of words to describe him, and 'weird' is the most flattering. 'Insufferable' might be another descriptive term. Anyway, if it's okay with you, I thought I could spend my first day reading through the charts of your current head trauma cases. Maybe a few patients will stand out as good learning experiences for me. And if I can add something which might help, all the better."

"Sounds like a plan," replied Dr. Mathers. "Let me take you to the Records room and show you how the patient charts are organized. We're in the process of moving everything onto a computer system, but it will be a while before that's up and running."

Dr. Mathers led Torrey into a windowless, interior room the size of basketball court. All four walls were lined with old, dented filing cabinets, and there were cabinets back-to-back down the middle of the room. Some beat-up, heavy oak tables were scattered around. A few medical personnel were going through thick files with pale green cardboard covers. With only an industrial style clock on the wall—the annoying old style that emits a loud tick every second—the area was devoid of any physical comforts that would cause someone to stay in there for a minute longer than required. No plants, no coffee machine, and no contemporary lighting. The flickering overhead fluorescent lights and the hard-as-cement wooden chairs were designed to cause the most discomfort in the least amount of time. Dr. Mathers explained, as she opened the top drawer on the cabinet next to the entry door, that the cabinets were organized alphabetically, with discharged vets taking up the vast majority of the cabinet space. The back wall cabinets were reserved for deceased military vets who had died at the facility during the course of treatment. Torrey and June set a time for the following morning to discuss Torrey's next few days.

As soon as June Mathers was out the door, Torrey ran her hand across the top of the cabinets as she shuffled along, searching for Howard Bordon's file. It was easy enough to find the "B" cabinets, but a young man in light blue scrubs had the middle drawer open while he leafed through the records. Torrey casually kept walking, pulling open a random drawer every so often, to appear occupied, or at least not idle. When she got to the wall of cabinets containing the records of the deceased soldiers, Torrey tugged on a drawer, almost absentmindedly, but it was locked. She tried other drawers with the same result. "That's odd," mumbled Torrey to herself. "Why on earth would these charts be locked up?"

Torrey glanced around and then walked over to a middle-aged woman sitting at a table who was almost hidden behind stacks of frayed documents. The credential hanging around her neck identified her as Dr. Wills. "Excuse me," said Torrey, "I'm Torrey Jamison. I'm here on loan for a few weeks. I wonder if you can tell me who has the keys for those filing cabinets over there," she said, pointing to the back wall of cabinets.

Dr. Wills looked up and said with a smile, "Welcome to the VA. I'm always happy to see doctors who volunteer to come on board." After exchanging pleasantries, Dr. Wills answered Torrey's question with a grimace, "Dr. Sommerville keeps the keys in his office. You would have to talk to him or his minion, Scott Belman."

"Why are they locked?" Torrey asked quizzically.

"Like I said, you'll have to talk to Sommerville or Belman." Then Dr. Wills added, "But good luck getting the keys. I've been here four years and have never seen the charts of any deceased vets."

"Where can I find Scott Belman?"

"He is usually skulking around, making sure that everyone is doing Sommerville's bidding," said Dr. Wills dryly.

"I've met Sommerville. What does Belman look like?"

"He's extremely handsome," said Dr. Wills with a wink.

"Really?"

"No, not really. You'll know him when you see him coming. He's short and round. Has piggy eyes and plump red cheeks. Always carries around one of those aluminum clipboards. He stares at you and then writes stuff down. Oh, and to top it off, he is a condescending twit."

"Wonderful. Can't wait to meet him," said Torrey with a muted laugh.

Just then, a bored voice blandly announced over the public address system, "Today is nurse Davidson's birthday. All medical staff are to report to the doctor's lounge at four o'clock. Cake will be served."

Dr. Wills sighed. "Get used to cake every day at 4:00. Not a day goes by when it isn't *someone's* birthday. And all doctors are required to attend to show the nurses and staff how much we appreciate them."

Torrey looked dubious. "Obviously, we value them. But do we have to eat cake to show it?" Torrey was loath to abide by rules that made no sense. "Is that a Sommerville rule?"

Dr. Wills bobbed her head and snorted. She went back to reading her files, and Torrey took a seat at an empty table, waiting for access to Borden's chart. While she sat, she couldn't help the fact that the locked filing cabinets niggled her. She tried to work out in her mind why the locked filing cabinets bothered her so much. Torrey couldn't put her finger on it, but even as a little girl, things that were nonsensical were bothersome. She got up and walked over to the cabinets again. While she lingered there, she surreptitiously took a photo of the locked cabinets.

• • •

Twenty minutes later, Torrey took her turn with the B filing cabinets. Howard Borden's file was way too thin. She thumbed through the handwritten case notes. It didn't take long. As she feared, Bordon was only being treated for the crushed eye socket bone, despite complaining of headaches and blurred vision.

When Torrey found him in Room 214 on the second floor, he looked like a shell of the vibrant fellow she had seen at Kaiser. Gone was the handsome young man who had the look and demeanor of a boy-band singer. It wasn't the facial bandages. It was the lack of responsiveness, the failure to notice Torrey's entrance, and the obvious inability to focus on her when she sat on the side of his bed. His formerly bright eyes were now dull and blank. "Howard, how are you doing?" She grabbed his hand. "Howard, I am Dr. Jamison from the Kaiser hospital. I remember you from the day that some Little Leaguers came in after a brawl. Do you recall that?"

As Howard turned his head slightly towards the sound of her voice, his jaw quivered. He spoke in the same disinterested monotone that a traffic cop would use when asking for license and insurance information. "I'm sorry. I can't see you very well," he said. Tears glistened in his watery blue eyes. When he turned his head away and closed both eyes, a tear slid down his cheek. Within seconds, he drifted off to sleep.

Torrey felt numb. She looked at the other men in the room and gasped, "My God, what is happening here? Who is this man's doctor? How long has he been like this?"

The patient lying in the bed closest to the door was the first to reply. "Hey, doc, did I hear you say that you're not a VA doctor?"

"That's right."

"Well, if they find out that I complained to you, they'll take it out on me. But you are the first person who seems to care about that guy."

Torrey crossed the room and stood next to the man's bed. Part of his forehead and cheek were missing so that his entire face was off kilter. His false teeth were gathering dust on a side table. "What's your name, soldier?"

"Private First-Class Biggs, ma'am," said Biggs with a gummy lisp.

"I'll protect you, Biggs. Tell me what's been going on."

"Your boy there has been complaining for days about the pain in his head and that he is losing his sight in his right eye. The doctors here ignore him. One just told him yesterday that until he goes to medical school, he should shut his mouth about his treatment." Torrey was stunned. Biggs added, "I tried to stick up for your boy, but the doctor told me to shut up, too. Didn't I try to help the boy?" Biggs looked at the guy in the next bed. "Tell her, Stevens," said Biggs with an air of desperation. "Tell her I tried to help her boy." Torrey glanced over at Stevens who was stretched out on his bed, his artificial lower leg propped up on pillows. Stevens gave a thumbs up.

"I believe you, Biggs," said Torrey. "I'm going to get to the bottom of this. Did you know Borden before seeing him here?"

"No, I never laid eyes on the guy before he was shoved in here with the rest of us. We tried to make friends with him, but he was in a bad way. Not only complaining about his injuries, but he said his girlfriend broke up with him. Said he didn't know if there was any point of going on."

Now Torrey was even more worried about Borden. Physical trauma is bad enough, but emotional injuries can lead to even worse outcomes. As Torrey was leaving the room, she took a closer look at Biggs. "Private Biggs, I see your left shin is puffy and red. How long has that been going on?"

"For a week or so, I guess."

"Are they treating that? It looks like an infection." Torrey lightly touched the shin, and Biggs jumped in pain. "Biggs, I'm sure this is cellulitis which needs to be treated. You could lose this leg. What are they doing about this?"

"Nothing, ma'am. When I mentioned it, the doctor said I was here for this stuff," he said while pointing to his face. "Got hit with some red-hot shrapnel. Doctors in Afghanistan did all they could. Anyway, the doctor here said not to bother him with a bunch of other malarky."

Now it was Torrey who wanted to cry. She knew she was backing herself into a corner with her next words, but she said it anyway. "I'll fix this. I promise," she solemnly vowed.

Chapter 26

Wanting to give Torrey a heads-up before they got home, Matthew texted her that he had the results of the saline solution analysis. He added only that the findings were as predicted. He knew that Edwina would be at their condo tonight, so he left a short voicemail on Edwina's phone to have Hawk meet them there at 9:00 p.m. Within minutes, Edwina replied that Angela had been admitted to the hospital with exhaustion and that Hawk was insisting that the meeting take place at his house. No one objected.

Matthew arrived first. Hawk opened the front door, stared at Matthew, and simply said, "Follow me." Hawk led the way into what looked like a third bedroom, but clearly Hawk was using it as a study, or a man-cave. The walls were filled with photos of his family and of his overseas platoon buddies. There were military artifacts everywhere, including a large tin sign boasting an American flag and the words, YOUR COUNTRY NEEDS YOU. While Matthew gazed around the room, Hawk used his fingerprint to open an oversized gun safe in the corner. It was at least six feet tall and three feet wide. It looked to weigh a thousand pounds. He swung open the steel door and moved out of the way. Matthew took a few steps forward and gawked. Inside there was enough armament to equip a small militia. Besides some sort of machine gun, and several huge rifles, there were at least five handguns, several knives, and a couple of bulletproof vests. Hawk shrugged. "The Second Amendment lives here. You okay with that?"

Matthew looked at Hawk. Their eyes met. Matthew knew what Hawk was thinking before Hawk verbalized it. "If Toohey killed my daughter, he is going down. Understood?" Matthew nodded tentatively just as the doorbell rang. "That must be Torrey," announced Hawk. "Edwina has a key."

After Edwina arrived, all four of them were seated in the living room. Hawk hadn't acknowledged Edwina's arrival. He sat like a statue ready to explode, with a dour expression as he stared at Matthew. No drinks were served. The silence was deafening, punctuated only by the barking of the next-door neighbor's dogs.

"So?" asked Hawk incisively to Matthew. "Are you going to tell us?"

Matthew had been trained how to handle unruly and angry patients. But Hawk was a singular case. There was no point in trying to sugarcoat the situation. So, he calmly announced the test results. "As you know, I had the saline bag that Torrey took from Toohey's office analyzed. As suspected, the bag contained sugar, marijuana, and Fentanyl. There is nothing there that would treat cancer of any kind, much less a brain tumor. Hawk, I'm so sorry."

Surprisingly, Hawk did not leap to his feet or start to yell. He sat without moving or speaking. Edwina eventually whispered, "Hawk, hey man, are you okay?"

Torrey put her hand on Hawk's shoulder, "We're here for you, Hawk."

Matthew saw Torrey's eyes fill. "We need to come up with a plan," he said.

Hawk jerked his head towards Matthew, eyes blazing. "You saw my gun safe, right? You know my plan!"

Torrey and Matthew glanced at each other. He nodded at her to take the lead. "Hawk," said Torrey, "you asked for our help. We want to give it. But we need a plan. You can't go off half-cocked. We need a plan that includes not getting caught and going to prison. Think of Angela. What would happen to her if you're not around?" Torrey could see that bringing Angela into the mix resonated with Hawk. "And take my word for it. Matthew is a world-class planner."

"Hawk," added Edwina, "they're right. We need a foolproof plan."

"I have a foolproof plan. It's called a sniper rifle and a hollow bullet. And let's skip the part where someone tells me that we need to take the high road. That we're better than that." Hawk paused to take a deep breath. "And don't bother playing the religion card. Don't try to tell me that taking a life is a sin. I've taken plenty of lives, in the name of liberty, of course. I haven't prayed since I was in some godforsaken dust bowl in the Middle East, and I saw a land mine blow my buddy, Frank Thompson, to bits. The fact is, we would be working as the hand of God to rid the world of a man like Toohey."

"But, Hawk, setting aside the religious arguments, we cannot afford any collateral damage," urged Edwina.

"Believe me, with me taking the shot, no innocents will be hurt. Toohey won't even see it coming. No muss, no fuss." They all stared at him. "And if you don't like that, I've got a ten-inch serrated Bowie knife. I could take him somewhere deserted. Draw out the pain. That might be better because I could look him in the eyes before I slit his throat," said Hawk roughly.

The air was thick with tension. After a pause, Edwina knew better than to provoke Hawk, but she offered an alternative to the group. "You know, we could just go to the police. No risk to us and Toohey gets arrested and is out of business."

"And what, Toohey gets a slap on the wrist?" asked Hawk, now livid. "A plea bargain to community service? He posts bail and disappears to the wind? Toohey is a dead man walking. The only question is how to do it," Hawk declared. "That is non-negotiable. Everyone okay with that?"

"Can we just consider our options?" Matthew pleaded.

Hawk did not pause a beat. "Look, if you are talking about the *justice system*," said Hawk disdainfully, "I used to believe in that. I put my life on the line for our country, for our justice system. I've grown up now. I see felons get elected to public office. OJ gets acquitted. Rapists get academy awards. Politicians allow looting and even murder, in the name of political correctness. This guy killed my daughter. You can't possibly think I am going to leave Toohey's fate in the hands of such a corrupt system."

Matthew understood, better than the others possibly could, Hawk's obsession for retribution. Matthew had spent years figuring out how to avenge his father's murder, without getting caught. Planning and precise execution were required. Before he could respond to Hawk, Edwina sounded the voice of reason. "Hawk, if Toohey is found shot dead by a sniper's rifle or by one of your other precision military weapons, the first thing the authorities are going to do is look for a motive. That will lead to an investigation of Toohey's patients and of the families of the patients who died under Toohey's care. You'd be arrested within a week."

"You think I'm going to leave a calling card? I could take him out from 500 yards. His head would just vaporize," said Hawk. "Besides, people believe what fits the script in their heads. Truth has nothing to do with it."

Edwina interrupted. "There is no way we can get away with it."

Torrey, who had been largely silent, suddenly announced thoughtfully, "But what if we could?"

• • •

By the time the meeting broke up at midnight, the group had considered and rejected any number of ideas. Matthew, who looked at the issue from the perspective of a doctor, was a proponent of using a lethal dose of an untraceable medicine. He described a case in which a man contracted and died from barking pig syndrome due to exposure to the Nipah virus. Matthew was about to explain how they could expose Toohey to the virus without his knowledge, when Edwina interrupted. "You're joking, right?

You want us to find a barking pig?" Before he could correct the confusion, Matthew was shouted down, even by Torrey, whose eyes crinkled with amusement.

All other proposals were eventually discarded except for one. Although the plan was not fully formulated, and Matthew considered it rudimentary at best, Torrey was confident in its merits. It still needed fine tuning, but if everyone did their part, it might just work. They set a tentative timetable of three days.

The last order of business was to figure out what to do about Mrs. Toohey and the other patient families. Even though everyone agreed that Mrs. Toohey might be peripherally to blame, they also concurred that she was of trifling importance, so there was no reason for her to be caught in the crossfire. "She married the guy," said Hawk, "and she's probably the reason that Toohey is running this scam, but she'll be punished enough by having to spend the rest of her life thinking about the pain caused by her husband when she eventually learns what he's been up to."

Matthew added, "She won't have any trouble finding another meal ticket. She's a real hottie."

Torrey jerked her head around towards Matthew. "You know I'm sitting right here, don't you?" said Torrey with faux outrage.

"Hey, I'm just reporting what Joe said. She's apparently centerfold material."

"I'm still here," chirped Torrey with a wry smile.

"Will you guys knock it off?" said Edwina fondly. "So, we all agree about the wife. What about the families of the other victims? They have to be told. But if we do that, then one of them may go to the authorities, and Toohey will be arrested. We'll lose our opportunity."

Matthew said calmly, "We have the information we need from the photos of the ledger. And we only have to concern ourselves with *current* patients at the moment."

"Agreed," said Torrey. "But we can't morally keep this information from current patients even for three more days. We have to act immediately."

"You're right, of course," admitted Matthew. "I'll go over the ledger information with Joe and have him identify current patients. Couldn't be too many. Joe can think of a way to talk to those families and keep them away from Toohey for a few days."

"That's fine," interjected Torrey. "But I'm going to be the one to talk to the mother that I met when I was in Toohey's office. I want to make sure that she goes back to Lady of the Angels for her daughter's treatment. And that she doesn't call the cops."

Chapter 27

When Matthew and Torrey were back home, alone at last in the privacy of their bedroom, Matthew's calm and collected veneer finally cracked. He looked and felt deflated as he pinched the bridge of his nose with his right hand and rubbed the center of his forehead with his left. As Torrey ran the tips of her fingers against Matthew's stubble, the scraping noise was the only sound in the room.

"Matthew, honey, what is it? What's wrong?"

"What's wrong?" exclaimed Matthew, his voice tinny. "How about everything? Don't you think this has gotten out of hand?"

"What do you mean?"

"What do I *mean*?" Matthew opened his eyes and stared at Torrey.

Torrey flashed a smile, "If you're just going to parrot everything I say, we won't get anywhere!"

"This isn't a joke, Torrey. The four of us just sat around a table and planned a murder. With four people involved, do you understand how many things could go wrong? How dangerous it is to be relying on Hawk and Edwina? I didn't detail the risks and problems with our plan tonight because I didn't want Hawk to go off the deep end."

"Well, go ahead and tell me. What are the odds that we can get away with this?"

Matthew moaned, "If we're lucky and everything goes smooth as silk, a million to one."

"Then you're saying there's a chance!" Torrey said with a bright expression.

"Hey, I'm serious," insisted Matthew. "And where are we going with this, Torrey? It was one thing to plot the demise of the man who murdered my father and to seek revenge against your high school rapist, but now we've been dragged into this mess with Hawk and Edwina. How many times can we tempt fate and expect to not get caught?"

Torrey's playful demeanor changed on a dime to deadly serious. "Wait a minute. You spent most of your life figuring out how to kill Ted Nash."

"That's a non sequitur."

"No, it's not. Ted Nash was without a soul and so is Toohey. Both caused immeasurable pain. And for what? Money. Both deserve to burn in hell everlasting."

Matthew cringed. On one hand, Torrey's words dismayed Matthew. This was his wife, his lover, his everything. It bothered him that she talked so freely about murder. Even if the killing was morally justifiable. On the other hand, no one knew better than Matthew how a theoretical desire for vengeance could turn into an overpowering obsession. He tried again to express his unease. "If I'm honest, I felt like a huge weight was lifted off my shoulders when Ted Nash and George Rincon were eliminated. Those guys were our personal burdens. Now the weight of vengeance is back. I'm not sure that I have the life force to expend on another bad guy. And what's next after Toohey? There are an unlimited number of bad guys. We can't save the entire world by ourselves."

"We don't have to save the whole world," said Torrey reassuringly. "Right now, we're simply saving the world from Toohey. And this does feel personal to me after what happened to Leia. I couldn't save her, but I can save other kids by getting rid of Toohey."

"Are we really going to go around killing every bad guy on the planet? That doesn't leave much time for our jobs. Our patients. Our marriage."

"What's that supposed to mean, Matthew?" said Torrey slowly as she sat up.

Matthew pushed out his lips, blew out a long breath, and looked up at the ceiling while he pondered how to answer the question. "Let me ask you: are we going to have kids?"

"What? Why would you ask that right now?"

"Can you just answer?"

"You know I want children. But we agreed to table the discussion of when to start a family until after we both finish our residency programs, and you know that mine is seven years long. So why bring that up in this conversation?"

"Because I'm afraid."

"You? Since when are you afraid of anything?"

Matthew pulled Torrey close and gazed into her eyes. "Ever since I married you, I'm afraid of losing you."

"Losing me? What are you talking about? You will never lose me," exclaimed Torrey.

"How many risks are you willing to take to help Hawk? How much will you risk when you run across another villain? Will you risk it all when we have kids who will suffer if we're caught?"

Torrey relaxed her body and snuggled against Matthew. She whispered, "Look, honey, I'm afraid of becoming an avenger, too. I'm terrified that things will go wrong, and we will end up in prison. But right now, I'm more frightened by the idea of doing nothing. I couldn't live with myself if we just sat on our hands. Toohey is evil. He preys on the most vulnerable—sick kids and their parents. Matthew, in different circumstances, it could have been my family that he preyed upon. I'm scared of not ending the suffering that Toohey has caused and will cause in the future if he's not stopped with certainty."

Matthew lay still, silent. Torrey added, "I know you like to plan things to the nth degree. You want to control the future. That's an admirable trait, and I love that you want to ensure that our future together is as solid as a rock. But, honey, we can't plan for every contingency. I can't bear to walk away from Hawk, Angela, and Edwina. And I know you can't either. We have a moral obligation. Every child who Toohey has murdered is someone's son or daughter. Someone's brother or sister. It was bad enough to lose my little sister, but how much worse would it have been if a doctor had intentionally caused Leia's death? When we have the means to stop evil, aren't we obligated to do so? We have to help them kill Toohey."

Matthew's forehead scrunched as he considered Torrey's line of reasoning. "Are you trying to convince me, or yourself?" Matthew didn't expect a reply, and he was not disappointed. She pressed her head into his shoulder. He hugged her as tightly as he could while giving a sluggish nod. He loved the smell of her. Not perfume. She wore none. Just her essence.

"I remember a time when you didn't believe in vengeance," said Matthew.

"I remember a time when you did," replied Torrey.

He touched her cheek gently with his fingertips as he whispered in her ear, "I wouldn't want to get on your bad side."

"No," replied Torrey. "You wouldn't."

Torrey decided that this was not the right time to tell Matthew that she suspected wrongdoing at the VA.

Chapter 28

When Matthew called Joe Cook and told him it was a matter of life and death, the investigator dropped everything. That was a big ask because he was in his basement office fine-tuning his huge model train layout. He had received a small gift set for Christmas when he was ten years old, and he'd been adding to it ever since. Most collectors like the larger scale Lionel trains, but Joe was partial to vintage Marx locomotives and accessories. He purchased collections on eBay from widows who were selling off their husbands' possessions. He now ran multiple trains on multi-level tracks. He had been planning to spend the evening cleaning track and lubricating his rolling stock when Matthew contacted him. The only actual assignment he would have to postpone was late-night spying on the cheating owner of Fred's Tires. Fred's wife was certain that Fred was having an affair with the pretty new receptionist. That stakeout would have to wait.

He laid out in front of him his photographs of Toohey's storage unit contents, including the patient ledger that he'd found. Joe quickly determined that Toohey had only four current clients, and Matthew had reported that Torrey was going to talk to Carol Bernstein, one of the four.

Matthew had not told Joe *why* these Toohey patients were to be prevented from going to Toohey's office again at any cost, but Matthew had concocted a believable script that Joe was to use—that Toohey had to leave the country to be with his dying brother in Europe and that he wanted all of his patients to return to the hospital for traditional treatment until his return.

Torrey was going to use a variation on the same theme with Carol Bernstein, the mom of the Tintin girl. She decided to go to the Bernstein house on the way to work at the VA. Despite the fact that it would be an early morning visit, Torrey decided not to call ahead. She didn't want to alarm Carol. She did, however, place two other calls.

The first was to Matthew's uncle TJ. He had always said that Torrey could call at any time. And that he was always available to help in any way he could. She decided to take advantage of the invitation. TJ answered his cell phone on the second ring. He was thrilled to hear from Torrey, and he started to chit chat. But Torrey was short on time and had to get right to the point. After stating what she needed and the timetable, TJ agreed. He didn't ask for details or for a medical explanation. Torrey was family.

The second call was to her boss at the hospital, Dr. Anne Peterson. Torrey knew that Dr. Peterson was in her office every day by 6:00 a.m. to have uninterrupted time to do paperwork. After apologizing for the interruption, Torrey explained her plan. Anne was on board when Torrey promised that all the hospital costs and expenses would be covered.

Torrey knew from Matthew's investigator that Carol lived in a rental house in the working-class neighborhood of National City. Back in the day, the housing development had been irrigated orange orchards surrounded by desert. In the 1950s, low-income housing was needed, and this along with similar developments sprang up all over Southern California. Most of the orange groves disappeared. Some of the homes on Carol's street were low-end flips, but most looked like they had not been touched for half of a century.

Torrey, a big proponent of Waze, had no trouble locating the Bernstein address. The house was a tan single-story bungalow with peeling white trim paint. The house was within walking distance to several strip malls and an off-brand coffee shop. The cars in the driveways were uniformly old and boxy.

For shade against the early morning sun, Torrey parked a few doors down under a huge Magnolia tree whose branches were overhanging the street. Walking back to the Bernstein house, Torrey almost tripped on a piece of raised sidewalk.

Carol's home had seen better days. The little gate on the white picket fence was pulled from its hinges and resting on some brown grass. Torrey stepped carefully around the cracks in the concrete path leading to the front doorsteps. She took a deep breath as if readying herself for a performance on the stage. She knocked softly on the aluminum screen doorframe. While waiting, she saw a little girl's pink bike tucked away in the corner of the porch. Torrey suspected that it hadn't been ridden in a while. Mrs. Bernstein answered, wearing pajamas and a robe. Her hair had not been brushed. She obviously had not been up long, but nevertheless her expression brightened right away when she saw Torrey.

"Good morning, Mrs. Bernstein. You probably don't remember me, but I—"

"Of course, I remember you. You were so nice to my daughter at Dr. Toohey's office," she said with a smile. Her face then shifted to a look of concern. "But why are you here? What's wrong? Is it something about Addie's blood work?"

"No, no. Nothing like that," said Torrey quickly. "I was just wanting to talk to you about—"

"Oh, I'm so sorry. I didn't mean to leave you outside. Please come in! And call me Carol."

Before Torrey could explain her visit and her desire to speak privately, Carol called to her daughter, "Addie! Come out here please. We have company!"

For someone in the terminal stage of brain cancer, Addie looked pretty good. She came out in a floral flannel nightie, holding a *Tintin* book in one hand and her Snowy stuffed animal in the other. She walked right up to Torrey and gave her a heartfelt hug.

"Well! That's quite a greeting!" said Torrey. "Hello to you too!"

145

Torrey, with a quizzical look on her face, glanced over at Carol, who just nodded with a broad smile.

When Addie wouldn't let go, Carol explained that Addie was frightened of Toohey's nurse, Mrs. Borsky. Torrey wasn't the least bit surprised to hear that. "And when you showed up at our last visit, Addie talked of nothing else all the way home," said Carol.

Torrey and Addie sat on the worn couch and chatted about Addie's favorite activities while Carol made coffee. A dimly lit, ten-gallon, fresh-water aquarium holding a few guppies was on the end table. It was in need of a good cleaning and a new water filter. On the living room coffee table was a stack of jigsaw puzzles and children's books, including a dog-eared storybook from Torrey's childhood—*The Adventures of Frog and Toad*, the one with the story about ice cream melting all over Toad. Torrey felt herself becoming irrevocably attached to and protective of Addie B and her mother.

Addie was currently reading a *Tintin* book titled *Explorers on the Moon*. "I'm going to be an astronaut when I grow up," declared Addie.

Torrey saw the parallel to her sister. Until the very end, Leia, too, could not grasp the concept of her own death. Torrey smiled sadly at Addie, "What a courageous dream! Astronauts are very brave!" said Torrey in a soothing voice.

After the coffee was served, Carol asked her daughter to get going on her homework.

"Mom, do I *have* to?" Addie cried in mock protest.

"Yes, you have to," said Carol with a smile. "Off you go."

When they were alone, Carol explained, "She hasn't been going to school since she got sick. Her teacher emails homework to her every day, so she won't be too far behind her classmates when she returns." Carol paused a beat and then asked the million-dollar question with trepidation, "*Is* she going to return?"

Torrey noticed that Carol had not touched her coffee. Torrey had practiced what she was going to say to Carol but seeing the pain in Carol's eyes caused her to hesitate. Carol took the delay in Torrey's reply as a bad sign. Her lower lip protruded as she fought to hold back a flood of tears.

"Carol," began Torrey, "Dr. Toohey has asked me to come talk to you and to his other patients, to let you know that he had to leave the country to deal with a family emergency. His brother was in a bad car accident, and they aren't sure if he is going to pull through. Mrs. Borsky went with him, so there is no one in Dr. Toohey's office to provide treatments. Dr. Toohey is not sure how long his office will be closed, so in the meantime, he wants you to return to the hospital and to resume the original treatment plan outlined by the hospital neurologists and surgeons."

Carol's face dropped, and her shoulders visibly sagged. "But Dr. Toohey said that the traditional treatments were worthless. Why would he want us to go back to that?" Carol looked a little embarrassed and lowered her voice. "And what about all the money we paid to Dr. Toohey? My husband passed away several years ago, and my father-in-law mortgaged his house to pay for the treatments. If Toohey abandons us, will my in-laws at least get their money back?" Torrey noticed that Carol had begun twirling her wedding ring around her finger as soon as she mentioned her late husband.

"It's just temporary." Torrey almost choked on the next sentence. "Dr. Toohey cares so much for you and Addie that he doesn't want to you to lose the gains you've been seeing. He thinks that the traditional treatments will maintain the status quo until he returns."

Carol looked unconvinced. "And," added Torrey, "he was going to surprise you with this at your next visit, but he thinks he has figured out a way to make his IV treatment protocol even more effective." Torrey shocked herself and felt guilty about how easily the lies slid off her tongue, even knowing that the fabrications were in Addie's best interests. She was a hundred percent against lying, except when the circumstances warranted it. The first order of business was to get Addie back to the hospital without raising suspicions. At least there, Addie had a chance. Everything else had to take a back seat for now. Carol would find out about Toohey's death soon enough.

Chapter 29

While Torrey was meeting with Addie and her mom, Matthew was starting a two-week stint in the hospital's cardiology department, one of his many required rotations. Like every well-rounded doctor, he had to know about exercise stress tests, electrocardiograms, and the symptoms of heart disease and heart attacks. He arrived a few minutes before the 7:00 a.m. shift change, when there was a scheduled handover between the incoming and the outgoing group of medical personnel. His minimum twelve-hour shift had begun.

As a first-year resident, called an intern in a teaching hospital, Matthew was required to attend weekly Grand Rounds where an experienced doctor lectures in an auditorium or conference room on a particular medical problem and how to treat it. Grand Rounds is also where it is drilled into the newbies that if a doctor makes a technical error in treatment, like a surgeon nicking an artery during a routine procedure, or an error in judgment, like an ER doctor confusing brain trauma with intoxication in a drunk homeless man, they must immediately confess, so the mistake can be addressed and not be repeated by others.

During daily rounds, training continues as the residents accompany an attending physician during visits to individual patients. The attending will often use the Socratic method to quiz the residents on diagnoses and treatments.

One of the most important jobs of an attending is to provide "consults" when asked to do so by doctors in the emergency room to help determine whether a patient should be admitted into the hospital for more extensive or permanent treatment. Today, Matthew's attending, cardiologist Dr. Linda Best, was paged by Dr. McKnight in the ER when Matthew's group was almost finished with rounds. Dr. Best and her entourage, including Matthew, hurried to the emergency room to find a husky gentleman clutching his chest. His breathing was shallow, and his face was the color of tomato juice. The man was surrounded by a group of family members, all dressed in outdoor barbecue attire, insisting that their father had had a heart attack, and the doctors needed to *do something*. An adult child opined that his father needed open-heart surgery *now*. Dr. Best shooed the family out, so she could hear herself think, not to mention, so she could listen to the man's heart. She checked over the vitals that had been taken and then addressed the patient. "Sir, my name is Dr. Best. What's your name?"

"Oscar."

"Okay, Oscar, what is going on with you?"

Oscar grimaced. "My chest hurts."

"When did your chest start to hurt?" Dr. Best calmly asked.

"After lunch," he groaned in pain. "And I need water! I can't swallow!

"Hmm," said Dr. Best. She looked around at the residents. "Anyone want to chime in here?"

Matthew offered, "We should send him home."

Dr. Best suppressed a smile and asked, "Doesn't he warrant some testing, or at least some monitoring? You heard his family say he had a heart attack."

"What he had was too much to eat," said Matthew with a confident grin.

"Explain, please."

"Acid reflux. Chest pain and difficulty swallowing are classic symptoms, not just of a heart attack, but more commonly of AR. I suspect, and this can be easily confirmed, that he had a big meal of fatty red meat followed by a stint on the couch. Let's just rule out a dysfunctional valve between the stomach and the esophagus and then give him a couple of antacids."

Dr. Best said to Dr. McKnight with a smile, "You heard the man. Let's scope him and get him out of here. There is a waiting room full of people out there that need real attention." Then Dr. Best said to Matthew, "Good job, doctor. Now you get the fun of going out there and telling Oscar's family members what's going on. And directing them to the cashier's office to pay the mighty big bill for our treatment of indigestion."

• • •

Torrey hoped but did not expect that her second day at the VA would be less confrontational than her first. She flashed her credential as she entered the building and scurried to the elevator, hoping a quick visit to Room 214 would go undetected. When she arrived, the four patients looked exactly the same as the day before, except that Howard Bordon looked even more hollow and unresponsive. "Hey, you came back!" exclaimed Private Biggs.

"Of course I did," replied Torrey. "I told you I was going to fix your leg! Just hold on a second while I check on him," she said as she gestured to Bordon. She knelt beside Bordon's bed, took his pulse, listened to his heart, and felt his forehead. "Has any doctor been in this morning?"

"You're joking, right? The only one who comes in here before noon is the old vet from the Vietnam War who delivers our food. He's nice enough, but he ain't no doctor."

"I'm going to have Borden transferred to my civilian hospital. That's where he was taken the day of his injury. He should never have been moved. Don't tell anyone before it happens."

Torrey moved over to Biggs and looked at his leg. "Anything change with this red patch since yesterday?"

"It hurts more. Is there anything you can do to make it feel better?"

"Yes. I'll be back later this morning with some medicine that should take care of it. Can we agree to keep this between us for now?

"Yes, ma'am. And thank you!"

"I should be the one thanking you for your service to our country. And your buddies here, too," said Torrey as she smiled and made eye contact with the other roommates. Torrey was particularly touched by the fact that Private Stevens was missing his right leg, but he sported a large USA tattoo on his right arm.

Torrey spent the next couple of hours in the medical records room studying the charts of Bordon and Biggs. She satisfied herself that neither patient was getting the necessary treatment and that she was justified in her plan to fix things.

At 10:45 a.m., right on time, the Uber that TJ had sent arrived in front of the VA hospital. Torrey was there to greet the driver and take possession of a small, unmarked box. She lifted the lid and peeked inside. As expected, TJ had come through with flying colors. She hurried back inside, utilizing her credentials to use the doctors' entrance.

Back in Room 214, Biggs gave her a thumbs up and said, "No one has been here since you left." Torrey glanced at the other roommates. They nodded.

Biggs had a sheet over his legs. "Uncover your lower leg," ordered Torrey. She examined the red patch and opened the box she had received from TJ. She removed one of the five syringes, told Biggs to hold still, and demonstrated how to inject the skin under the infection. She showed Biggs the remaining syringes and instructed him to inject himself with one of them every four to six hours. "We would normally deliver this antibiotic through an IV, but this will work just as well," said Torrey. "Keep the box hidden from hospital staff," she added.

Before she left the room, Torrey asked each roommate whether they needed anything. Private Stevens waved her off. "We're fine, ma'am. But we know who to call now if we need a fixer," he said with a smile.

Torrey spoke quietly from the doorway, "I'll be back here with help for Bordon at noon."

● ● ●

At 11:45, Torrey was standing on the curb in front of the VA again. A few minutes before noon, an ambulance arrived, and Torrey breathed a sigh of relief. She knew that Dr. Peterson had agreed to the unorthodox plan yesterday, but sometimes things change. One of the two paramedics jumped out. "Are you Dr. Jamison?" he asked.

"Yes, thank you for being here so promptly. Are we clear on how this is going to work?"

"Sure, doc. But usually, we go in through the back entrance and do all the transfer paperwork before taking a patient from one facility to another."

"I know. But as I'm sure Dr. Peterson explained, this is a special situation. You've got the release forms ready to go?"

"Right here," he said, patting his breast pocket.

"Okay, follow me."

The two paramedics turned on the flashing lights, opened the back of the ambulance, and removed a gurney. The ambulance was double-parked, but with its proximity to the VA hospital, no one seemed to notice or care. Torrey led the way towards the entrance with relaxed confident strides. As they crossed the plaza, she glanced around at the homeless men milling around, who were trying not to look too desperate. She spotted Bill Bonner and his All-American mutt over by the fountain. Torrey and Bill made eye contact, and Bill gave her a barely perceptible wave. Torrey and the paramedics stormed into the building, past the startled guard, and up to Room 214. She shouted, *"Emergency, coming through!"* every few seconds, and the seas parted for them.

As the paramedics worked to transfer Borden onto the gurney, an ancient-looking doctor by the name of Pitman and two nurses walked into the room. "What's going on here?" demanded Pitman. He had the largest forehead that Torrey had ever seen, a look that was emphasized by a severely receding hairline. A huge purple vein was throbbing at his left temple.

Torrey signaled for the paramedics to keep working. "Emergency transfer, doctor. His parents want him taken back to the hospital that saw him originally for this injury."

Pitman stammered, "This is my patient. I wasn't notified of this! I haven't signed off on his transfer."

"I've got the release form right here," said Torrey as the astute paramedic handed the form to her. "Just sign right here," instructed Torrey as she pointed to the signature line.

"No!" said Pitman exclaimed.

"No problem," said Torrey. "I'll just write in that you refused." Torrey began scribbling on the form.

"Hey, you can't do that!" Pitman said, his voice rising.

"Already done, doctor. Problem solved."

Pitman's face fell. He looked defeated and confused. "You wait right here," he commanded. "I'm going to get Dr. Sommerville." He and the nurses marched out in formation.

"Knock yourself out. I'll be waiting right here," Torrey called after them with a demure smile.

As soon as they were gone, Torrey whispered to the paramedics. "Can you hurry it up? It would be better if you were gone when they come back."

The medics didn't need to be told twice. After confirming that the straps were tight and that Bordon, who appeared to be in a trance, would not fall off the gurney, the paramedics double-timed it to the elevators. A minute later, Torrey observed from the window as the gurney was wheeled across the plaza to the waiting ambulance. Torrey continued to watch until she saw the paramedics hoist the gurney into the back of the ambulance. She breathed a sigh of relief. Just as the ambulance raced away, with lights and a siren, Dr. Pitman reappeared, followed closely by Dr. Sommerville's minion, Scott Belman. Torrey needed no introduction. The combination of the sniveling face, the doughboy physique, and the aluminum clipboard was a dead giveaway. Like a true self-important administrator, Belman came into the room wearing the officious expression that seemed to be mandatory for all bureaucrats. He was dressed in a black three-piece suit usually reserved for undertakers, with a crisp white shirt and a coordinating bold red tie. His shiny black shoes almost glowed. He didn't have a dangling pocket watch, but he wore a lapel pin that Torrey deduced was some sort of years-of-service award.

Pitman pointed at Torrey with the rimless eyeglasses that hung from his neck chain. "There she is, Scott," he said with a scowl. His soft features scrunched up. "She's the one who defied me. She had a patient transferred over my objections and contrary to protocol." Pitman stepped off to the side, so he could witness Belman's attack on Torrey. Other staff gathered in the hallway outside the door expecting fireworks. But Torrey could see in Belman's eyes that the minion was more frightened than furious. It didn't take Torrey long to discern that Belman was afraid that *he* was going to get into trouble. That *he* would be blamed for an emergency patient transfer that occurred on his watch. That *he* would incur Sommerville's wrath because some outside doctor had the nerve to challenge the treatment protocol prescribed for Borden.

Torrey, fueled by a surge of adrenaline, quickly went on the offense. "I understand you are Dr. Sommerville's assistant. Dr. Pitman," she calmly declared, "has demonstrated gross incompetence in diagnosis and treatment. The man who was just transferred back to my hospital likely has a brain injury requiring an immediate fluid drain procedure. And if that isn't bad enough, he is losing sight in his left eye because Dr. Pitman failed to have his eye examined by a surgical ophthalmologist. I will be filing a report with the Board of Medical Examiners."

Pitman fired back, his voice thick with venom. "Scott, this is outrageous. Tell her!" Belman, thinking things over, was silent, so Pitman tried to defend himself. "Listen here, missy," stammered Pitman while fingering his tie with his left hand and jabbing his right-hand pointer finger at Torrey, "I was treating soldiers at this facility before you were dreaming of a training bra. I started as a resident. Worked my way up to Senior Attending Physician. You have no idea what it takes to come up through the ranks."

Torrey quipped without thinking, "You kissed a lot of butt, did you?" After a stunned silence, Torrey added, "You miss the old days, right? When you could be a misogynist. I ran into another good old boy when I worked at San Quentin prison. Like you, this guy was older than dirt and wished he had lived in the 1950s, or better yet, the 1800s. Newsflash: sorry to be the bearer of bad news, but those days are over. Missy? Really? That's quite a vocabulary you have there. Missies like me are not only going to change medicine, but we are also going to change the world. So, get on board, or get out of the way."

Torrey only mildly surprised herself with her brazen comments to Dr. Pitman. It had taken years of condescending remarks by older males in positions of authority to ignite her fire to respond without fear of the consequences. She had hoped that the equality she craved would be evident in medical school. Her hopes were dashed early. It was absurd, but male professors and doctors, especially those who had been teaching and practicing for decades, were almost uniformly patronizing.

Torrey and fellow medical student, Barbara, who was both gorgeous and brilliant, had discussed the subject on numerous occasions. Barbara's theory, which Torrey was inclined to agree with, was simple. These days the competition is so intense that only the most outstanding and committed applicants are admitted to medical school. But forty years ago, anyone with money and privilege could get in, so jerks, misogynists, and guys who just weren't very bright became doctors. Many of them were still practicing and were still frat boys at heart. They still believed that they ruled the world.

She had been asked by these bozos on numerous occasions why in the world she wanted to be a doctor—specifically a brain surgeon—even though she had started Stanford Medical School with the highest grade-point average and MCAT score in the entering class. "Surely nursing or pediatrics would be more appropriate," they would say. Experience had taught Torrey that she had to ignore the unwritten rule that senior doctors are not to be challenged. She learned the necessity of standing up for herself and her gender. It was nerve-racking at times, but afterwards she always felt vindicated and liberated.

Pitman's breath caught, and his eyes flicked to Belman as he cried plaintively, "Scott! Say something! I did nothing wrong! I talked to that patient every day!" His face darkened as specks of spittle sprayed everywhere.

Biggs snorted. Torrey asked, "Dr. Pitman, what's the name of the soldier that you talked to every day?" Silence. "What caused his injury?" Silence. "What was the next step in his treatment?" Silence. "When is the last time that you thought of these soldiers as actual people, with spouses and children who are relying on you to provide proper care and treatment?" Pitman wiped his brow and then wiped his hands on his pants. Torrey continued, "How long did you think you could get away with ignoring the treatment needs of these American heroes without anyone finding out?"

Every eye in the room went to Scott Belman, who stood stiffly without emotion. His piggy eyes did not blink. He turned to Pitman with a somber expression and coldly said, "Dr. Pitman, meet me in Dr. Sommerville's office in five minutes, please." Pitman's defeated eyes registered the rebuke. He nodded dutifully, but Belman didn't see. The minion had already turned on his heel and marched out. The crowd outside the office quickly dispersed among soft murmurs.

Pitman glowered bitterly at Torrey. His mouth was moving, but no sound came out. Torrey walked up to Pitman, put her hand on his shoulder, and said in a low solicitous voice, "You know, I don't like the look of that vein popping out on your forehead. It could be a carotid artery problem. You really should have that looked at."

Pitman audibly swallowed and seethed something undecipherable. Crestfallen, he shuffled, head down, slowly out of the room. When Pitman was out of earshot, Biggs and his roommates broke into cheers and applause. Biggs doubled over with laughter as he kept yelling, "*Kissed a lot of butt, did you?*" Biggs was so caught up in the moment that he knocked his lunch plate onto the floor. Splashes of spaghetti sauce were everywhere.

"The *butt* comment was for you, Biggs."

Once things quieted down, and her knees stopped shaking, Torrey reflected on the results of the day and assessed her situation. Biggs would recover from the cellulitis infection. Howard would get the best treatment money could buy because she had promised Anne Peterson that all of Howard's bills would be paid—a perk of having a rich husband. Matthew would be surprised, but not upset, at her promise. Finally, she knew she would be a marked woman for the rest of her time at the VA.

Chapter 30

Torrey bid goodbye to Biggs and his compadres, then slipped out of the building to allow tempers to cool. She consciously opted to avoid the stare of the hospital police officer who was standing at the exit doors. She wanted to disappear before Sommerville, or his minion, came looking for her. She didn't want to be trapped in the records room or collared in a maze-like, narrow corridor with no graceful escape available. Besides, she figured that Matthew would be more likely to pardon her faux pas of spending a ton of his money without even discussing it with him if she got home early and prepared a feast. That she wasn't much of a cook did not deter her in the least. She would pick up the steaks, but she planned to ask Edwina, a chef in training, to cook them. Torrey would serve the wine. And she had to make a stop on the way home.

Joe Cook was surprised to get Torrey's call. He was unaccustomed to being contacted by the spouse of a client. Joe had learned a lot about Torrey from Matthew, but he hadn't ever met her. And now she wanted to meet at an office equipment store near UC San Diego. As usual, Joe didn't ask *why*. He just obligingly exchanged information about their cars and where in the giant parking lot they would find each other.

Joe arrived first. He watched Torrey drive her bright red Jeep into a parking spot a few feet away. Matthew had offered to gift her a shiny new pearl-white, gull-wing Tesla after they were married, but Torrey insisted on something less showy and more practical. "Just think," she had said to Matthew, "when we buy a house together, we can use the Jeep to haul fence boards and tools from the Home Depot!" Matthew had given his signature shrug. The next day, the red Jeep arrived. Torrey had loved it immediately.

She jumped out of the Jeep, walked around to Joe's passenger door, and climbed in. "Hi, Joe. I'm Torrey."

"I figured." But Joe hadn't really figured. Matthew had always talked about Torrey's intelligence and bravery and how she had received some kind of courage award in medical school, but he had somehow neglected to share how pretty and petite she was. Joe realized he was staring at her. When Torrey didn't start talking, Joe finally found his voice, "So, what's up?"

"Joe, we don't know each other, but Matthew has told me he has complete faith and trust in you. I'd like to hire you for thirty minutes, starting now."

"Say what?"

"I'll take that as a binding agreement. So now anything we say and do is confidential, just between you and me, right?"

"Torrey, what's this about?" asked Joe with a puzzled look.

"Matthew also told me that in your line of work you sometimes have to pick locks. Is that true?"

Taken aback, Joe stammered, "Well, yes."

"Great, I need you to teach me how to pick a filing cabinet lock." Torrey airily smiled her sweetest smile and showed him a photo of the VA cabinets.

Joe grabbed Torrey's phone and zoomed in on the locks. "These are not standard locks. These are oversized aftermarket locks. The kind of lock that would be on an office payroll safe." Joe looked sideways at Torrey. "What's all this about? Does Matthew know about this?" questioned Joe with a cocked eyebrow.

"Matthew is my husband, not my minder. Besides, I'm going to surprise him with this new skill. So, you'll have to give me the proper tool and show me how to use it." She stuck out her hand to shake. "Deal?"

With a silent laugh, Joe shook Torrey's hand. *She's really something,* he thought.

• • •

Torrey arrived at her condo at about 6:00 p.m. with a bag of groceries in her arms and Joe's miniature lock pick set in her pocket. She was a happy camper. Until, that is, she approached her front door and saw Toohey's enforcer and Edwina sitting on the steps, waiting for her.

• • •

Matthew was relieved to be finished at the hospital a little before 7:00 p.m. After helping Dr. Best with various cardiac tests and procedures, he was famished. Torrey had texted that they were having steak, so he was in a jolly mood as he burst through the front door, calling out, "Torreeeey, I'm hoooome!" As he raced up the inside stairs, he continued to shout, "You wouldn't believe what happened today! I was—" Matthew reached the top of the stairs and turned into the living room. He stopped mid-sentence. Neither Torrey nor Edwina was there. Instead, a huge mass of a man in a sharkskin suit, Toohey's enforcer, was sitting on the couch, with a half-full glass of beer. Koa was draped across his lap. Along with surprise and alarm, Matthew's brain thought, *Some watchdog.*

Chapter 31

Matthew blinked hard and stopped short. "Torrey!" Matthew, in near panic mode, yelled again as he glowered at the man.

"She's in the kitchen with Edwina," said the man evenly. "I'm not sure she heard you come in." Matthew's blood pressure dropped a few points with that comment, and then he focused on the dog. Koa routinely ignored Torrey and ran away from Matthew. Yet there she was, snuggled up against a total stranger.

Matthew's eyes darted in the direction of the kitchen and then back to the man. "Torrey! Edwina!" He strode towards the voices coming from the kitchen. He and Torrey almost collided as they made a beeline to each other. Edwina, hesitating behind Torrey, stood a safe distance back.

"Hi, honey. We've all been waiting for you!" said Torrey with raised eyebrows and a shrug of her shoulders. She embraced Matthew and whispered in his ear, "You do the talking." She gestured towards the man on the couch. "Matthew, we have company." Torrey pulled Matthew by the arm over to the couch. The man gently pushed Koa aside, stood, and offered his hand to Matthew.

"Dr. Preston, good to meet you. Torrey has been telling me how you two met. What a wonderful story."

Matthew shot a baffled look at Torrey but then took the man's extended hand. "Who are you?"

"Oh, I'm sorry. I should have introduced myself." The man fingered a business card to Matthew and said, "My name is Rocco Washington. I'm an investigator for the Medical Board of California. I'm investigating a doctor by the name of Albert Toohey. I'm hoping you and Dr. Jamison can help me."

Matthew read the card, did a double-take, and laughed out loud. "Ha! You were following Edwina! We saw you at the café the other day. We thought you were a thug!"

"I get that a lot," deadpanned Rocco in a mild and self-deprecating manner. For such a big man, Rocco's voice was amazingly soft. Up close, he didn't look much like an underworld kingpin.

"Mr. Washington," said Torrey, remembering her manners, "please sit back down. You said you wanted to talk to us and Edwina, too. What's this about?" she asked innocently. The four of them sat down. Edwina sat the farthest away from Washington, looking like she was ready to spring up at the first sign of trouble and help to subdue him.

"First of all, call me Big Rocky. Everyone does." Rocco reached across the side table and grabbed one of the Stanford tree-embossed coasters before putting down his beer. He pulled out his notepad from his suit coat pocket. He was just about to speak when Matthew interrupted, "Rocco, before we get into the specifics of Dr. Toohey and why you want to talk to us, could you fill us in about the Medical Board and what exactly you do?"

"Sure," said Rocco. "I should have led off with that. Even though you are doctors, most in the medical profession are oblivious to our existence. But when doctors get into trouble, the Board can take over their lives." Rocco leaned back on the couch and rubbed Koa's bulging stomach, causing Koa's back leg to move back and forth. "By the way," said Rocco, "this dog needs to get on some low-carb dog food." Torrey exchanged a meaningful glance with Edwina, whose surly voice trailed off as she mumbled something about big bones.

"Anyway," continued Rocco, "the Medical Board's mission is simply to protect, through licensing and regulations, the consumers of medical services. One of its key functions—and this is where I come in—is to investigate complaints against doctors. Those complaints could be for sexual misconduct, mental or physical impairment, or simply because of conduct that falls below the standard of medical care. We determine whether the conduct warrants administrative or disciplinary action, revocation of license, or referral to the DA for criminal sanctions."

Matthew crossed his legs and leaned back in his armchair. He asked in an even voice, "Okay, that makes sense. But why were you following Edwina? And why do you want to talk to us?"

Rocco half-smiled and opened his notepad. "That's a fair question. A mother of one of Dr. Toohey's patients filed a confidential complaint against him. The mother's five-year-old son died while in Dr. Toohey's care. According to the mother, Dr. Toohey had promised a complete recovery from cancer and charged her an arm and a leg for the treatment."

"When was this complaint lodged?"

"A couple of weeks ago. Obviously, the Board takes these charges very seriously, no matter how outlandish the complaint appears at first glance. I was assigned to the case.

"Before I formally confront Dr. Toohey, I want to find out everything I can about Toohey's other patients and whether this was a one-off grievance or if there was some sort of pattern. I've been trying to identify and talk to Toohey's other patients. He apparently has only a few, so it has been difficult and time-consuming. It didn't do any good to surveil the building because I couldn't tell if someone coming out was a Toohey patient. I finally decided to stand at the end of the hallway for hours, pretending to read a magazine or wait for the elevator, until someone came out of Toohey's office. But that had its own set of problems, especially in light of the other kinds of tenants on the floor.

"The other day I saw you," Rocco said as he pointed at Edwina in a non-threatening manner, "come out looking upset. I followed you home.

But when I pulled up your identity, I could see you had no kids." Edwina shifted uncomfortably in her seat, hoping that her brother, Hawk, was not going to be mentioned. "So, I followed you some more to see how you were related to this situation. Then I saw you talking to these two doctors," gesturing with his head to Torrey and Matthew, "and I figured the three of you might be able to shed some light on what is going on with Dr. Toohey." Rocco spread his arms wide. "So, can you?"

Matthew rubbed his jaw and swallowed hard. "I don't know, Rocco. After all, we're just a couple of neophyte medical residents pretending to be private eyes in our non-existent spare time."

Rocco kept looking at Matthew, waiting for him to continue. Matthew, stalling for time to organize a proper answer to that pointed inquiry, asked his own question. "Have you been able to talk to any of Toohey's other patients?"

"I did observe a woman and her young child leaving Toohey's office. Followed them all the way to El Cajon. Knocked on their door. When I identified myself and said I wanted to ask some questions about Dr. Toohey, the mother said to leave the good doctor alone. That he was saving her daughter. She all but slammed the door in my face." Rocco spread his arms to express his puzzlement. "I know she," gesturing to Edwina, "has been avoiding me, but you two," said Rocco while addressing Matthew and Torrey, "didn't slam the door in my face. You even invited me in. So, I'm hoping you'll tell me what you know about Dr. Toohey."

A long moment of awkward silence was punctuated by Koa's blissful snoring as she pawed the air. Torrey locked eyes with Matthew for a split second. "Matthew," said Torrey with a sly grin, "why don't you tell Rocco what we know about Dr. Toohey?"

Chapter 32

Matthew needed to organize his thoughts. "Honey," said Matthew pointedly to Torrey, "Let's all sit down at the table and talk over dinner. I'm starving."

Torrey made eye contact with Edwina who was shaking her head while mouthing her disagreement. "Sure," said Torrey. "Edwina and I will see if everything's ready." She took Edwina's hand and led her into the kitchen. As she was leaving the room, Torrey half-turned and called out to Matthew, "Why don't you ask Rocco to tell you more about Dr. Toohey's practice?"

"Why did you invite him to stay for dinner?" whispered Edwina with jangled nerves when they were out of hearing range. "I don't believe anything he says. For all we know, he's working with Toohey."

Torrey hushed Edwina, so she could listen hard to the living room conversation. But from the kitchen all she could hear were indistinct murmurs. "Don't worry," said Torrey softly. "Matthew can handle that guy, and he'll find out if we can trust him."

Matthew was well aware of Toohey's background and practice, but he was hesitant to disclose what he knew. He let Rocco drone on while he figured out how much he should divulge. "Do you think Toohey has committed some sort of crime?" Matthew asked.

"That's exactly what we're trying to find out. There is something fishy about the lack of patients compared to his standard of living. I've seen his house and cars. And his wife—let me tell you—a woman like that wants the finer things in life. Where is Toohey getting the money to support her?"

"I'm not a lawyer," said Matthew. "But it sounds like you have nothing specific on Toohey. Just broad suspicions. Is that correct?"

"Yes, that's why I need your help. Your friend there," said Rocco while looking towards the kitchen, "has some sort of tie to Toohey. And I need to know what it is. And how you and your wife are involved."

Torrey, now eavesdropping from the hallway, took this as her cue to ring the dinner bell. "C'mon, men," she called, "dinner is served!"

• • •

After some polite, but meaningless, small talk, Matthew knew he had to give Rocco something that would throw him off the scent for a day or two. Something that Rocco could investigate. Something with some teeth. "Well," said Matthew, "I hesitate to say anything without proof. But we'd like to help you, especially if Dr. Toohey is running a criminal enterprise of some sort."

Torrey jumped in. "Rocco, we don't know anything for sure. We're just looking into an allegation. And of course, we can't divulge any patient information without a court order."

"Naturally," agreed Matthew. "Rocco knows that. But I think we can tell him the basis of our interest. Is that what you're looking for, Big Rocky?"

"Yes, yes, that's it. Just tell me what you can without violating any doctor-patient privilege."

Neither Torrey nor Edwina had any idea what Matthew was going to say. But they knew they had to play along. "We heard from a woman that while she was at Dr. Toohey's office doing some cleaning, she overheard an animated conversation between Toohey and another man. She heard something about Fentanyl." Edwina's head jerked toward Torrey, but Torrey was nonchalantly sipping her coffee, as if she wasn't even listening. Matthew continued, "The woman mentioned the conversation to our friend, Edwina. Per Edwina's request, I agreed to see the woman about a painful medical issue she was having so that she would be an official patient of mine. She knew I couldn't prescribe Fentanyl."

Matthew gave a knowing look at Edwina. "Mrs. Ed, you talked to her friend-to-friend. Did she say why she told you about the Fentanyl?"

All eyes turned to Edwina. "Well," said Edwina as she scrambled to reach back to her college improv days, "she had just seen a *60 Minutes* piece on the dangers and illegality of Fentanyl, and she thought it was weird that her doctor was discussing it in the office. She wondered if Toohey was selling it because it sounded like he and the other man were arguing about how much Fentanyl was available. Toohey kept telling him to keep his voice down."

Torrey knew she was enjoying the farce a little too much under the circumstances. But she still decided to chime in with a glint in her eye. "So, Rocco, we did a little amateur sleuthing and found out that Toohey had been employed at the FDA when some confiscated Fentanyl disappeared from a seized China-flagged ship. We figured that, as members of the medical profession, we had a duty to look into Toohey's practice a little more deeply. We're so happy that you are now involved to get to the bottom of this question. We didn't want to make any unfounded accusations without proof. Don't you have some sort of subpoena power to get access to his medical and financial records?"

Rocco's eyes lit up. "So, it's your working theory that his medical practice is just a front for selling illegal drugs?"

"Well, that's a possibility that occurred to us," said Matthew in a mock serious tone.

Before Rocco left the condo, it was decided that he would take over the investigation and that Torrey, Matthew, and Edwina would bow out. Rocco would look into the missing Fentanyl and would then seek legal authority to search Toohey's home and office. Things were going to move fast.

They all waved goodbye as they watched Rocco get into his Crown Vic. When the front door closed, the three of them went upstairs, collapsed on the couch, and breathed sighs of relief and satisfaction. Only Koa was upset because her warm pillow was gone. She let out a brief whine before settling back down on Edwina's lap. Matthew spoke first. "We have to call Hawk and move up our timetable if we want to get Toohey before he's arrested. We need to meet as soon as possible. Torrey, what's your schedule tomorrow?"

"I can't meet until the evening," said Torrey. "In the morning, I'm helping out with a brain surgery at the hospital. The lead surgeon said I could operate the saw to cut open the skull! I can't change that."

"Seriously?" cried Edwina. "TMI!" Edwina's shock was feigned. She secretly idolized Torrey for her fearless attitude.

Torrey suppressed a smile and continued, "And at 1:00 p.m., I have to go see Howard Borden. He's being discharged from the hospital, and I promised to visit him. Then after that, I have to go to the VA for a few hours."

"Why do you have to go back there?" Matthew asked. "I thought you accomplished your goal of getting Borden transferred out. Plus, you said they hate you over there now."

"That's all true, but I need to check on something. It shouldn't take too long. I expect to be home by 6:00 p.m. What about you, Matthew? Are you still doing that ER rotation?"

"Yes, all week. I'm hoping to have an early day tomorrow. Mrs. Ed, can you call Hawk and arrange a meeting for tomorrow at six o'clock?"

• • •

In the privacy of their bedroom, while lounging on their bed, Torrey filled Matthew in on her adventure at the VA. Matthew shared Torrey's admiration for the veteran patients. She asked him, "Do you admire them enough to have a little skin in the game?"

"Uh-oh! What do you mean?" asked Matthew.

"Well," said Torrey with a mischievous look, "remember I told you about the homeless vets in front of the VA? And that one guy I talked to, Bill Bonner, whose brother was a vet?"

"Sure, I remember," said Matthew.

"I was thinking about what a shame it is that so many veterans are homeless, right under our noses in San Diego. What if we did something about it?"

"Like what?" asked Matthew slowly.

"You know that old hotel we pass by on our way to work every day? The one that's a few miles from the hospital? It's run down now, and it might even be closed. But I bet it was a jewel back in the day before all the redevelopment money was directed elsewhere in San Diego. What if your family foundation purchased the hotel and renovated it to become a home for veterans? We could get them off the streets. I'd guess the hotel has about sixty rooms. It could be a sanctuary run by and for vets and their families. Anyone living there would work there—no handouts. And I bet Bill Bonner, though not a vet himself, would be great as one of the first employees."

"Torrey, ever since my mother passed away, the Board of Directors decides which projects to underwrite. Not me."

Torrey stood up, put her hands on her hips, and looked hard at Matthew with raised eyebrows. As she knew he would, Matthew melted under the pressure. "Okay! Okay! I'll make it happen. Just don't give me that look!" Torrey lay back down on the bed with a contented smile.

Chapter 33

"Stand tall, soldier!" barked Torrey as she entered Howard Borden's room. Howard's eyes shifted from his half-packed suitcase to a saluting 5'3" Dr. Torrey Jamison. As promised, Torrey had made it to Howard Borden's room just as he was getting ready to check out. She felt just fine after having sawn open the head of a brain aneurysm patient. As always, she had brought her trusty scalpel with her, but the surgeon hadn't let her do any cutting.

"Wow, you scared me there for a minute, doc! You sounded just like a drill sergeant I had during basic training. But she was taller than me and built like a tank."

"Hello, Howard, I hear that your surgery was successful and that you're doing great. How do you feel? Well enough to go home?"

"Yes, ma'am. And thank you so much for having me transferred here. Private Biggs phoned and told me everything you did. I can never repay you."

"No need, Howard. I'm just glad I could help in some small way. Where will you go now?"

"My parents live in Las Vegas. They are downstairs right now waiting for me. I'm going to stay with them for a few months while I recuperate. Then I'll decide what to do."

"I already know what you should do," said Torrey. "Get a dog!" Torrey had recently read a study that had detailed the benefits of four-legged therapy.

"Excuse me, ma'am?"

"Parents are nice. But you need companionship—now and when you move out of your parents' house. You need a dog. Studies show that having a dog around helps us better cope with a crisis, and I understand that you have suffered several, both physical and emotional. It even helps with cognitive recovery. Moreover, a dog makes us more social and makes us generally happier people. From what I hear from Biggs, you are going through a rough patch and could use that kind of help."

"Hmm, I'm not really much of a dog guy. Got bit once by the neighbor's vicious French Bulldog when I was little. And to make matters worse, after it bit me, it let out this ear-shattering screech. As if I bit him! The experience scarred me."

"Forget about Frenchies. They're trouble. Get a dog that you can play with. Maybe even one of those agility dogs!"

Just then, a nurse came in to check Howard's vitals one last time. Torrey busied herself by texting a progress note to Matthew. When the nurse left, Howard took a deep breath and said, "How about this? I'll get a dog if you go on a date with me."

Torrey gasped and felt for her wedding ring. She realized she had taken it off when she gloved up for the surgery and had failed to put it back on. She self-consciously brushed back the short bangs on her pixie-cut hair and said truthfully, "Howard, you are just the kind of guy I would date, if not for the fact that my heart is already taken." She pulled her wedding ring out of her pocket, slipped it on her ring finger, and held up her hand for Howard to see. "Happily married, I should add."

"Oh, I'm sorry. I didn't know," he blushed. After an awkward silence during which Howard folded a T-shirt into his luggage, he came back with, "Okay, how about this. I'll get a dog if you can solve this license plate mnemonic." Howard grabbed his release orders and tore off a small corner.

He turned his back to Torrey and carefully wrote the following: FLNDFFC. In smaller letters, he wrote his cell phone number. Just for fun, he folded the scrap in half then turned and handed it to Torrey.

"Should I open it now?" said Torrey with a laugh.

"That's entirely up to you," grinned Howard.

"I think I'll save it for later," said Torrey as she slowly put the paper in her pocket.

"Even though you're married, may I give you a hug?" asked Howard.

"I would be crushed if you didn't," she smiled, returning his embrace warmly. She hoped her voice didn't crack.

• • •

There was heavy traffic between Kaiser and the Veterans Administration hospital, so Torrey had to violate even more traffic regulations than normal. She had to be in place and ready to go by 4:00 p.m. She made it with thirty minutes to spare.

She scanned the crowd in the plaza outside the building, wondering if Bill Bonner was at his usual spot with his All-American dog. She had a wad of small bills at the ready in case she saw him. She saw lots of men with canes, walkers, and artificial limbs, but no Bonner.

Torrey kept a lookout for Dr. Sommerville and his minion, Scott Belman, as she made her way to the records room. Dr. Wills was sitting at the same table that she was when Torrey was last there. Dr. Wills looked more like the head librarian, with her hair in a bun and half-glasses on a chain, than a renowned thoracic surgeon. "You're back!" Dr. Wills exclaimed when she saw Torrey. "I heard you pulled some strings and got one of your friends transferred. Everyone on the floor could hear Dr. Sommerville yelling at Pitman and Belman about it. The word around the water cooler is that Pitman resigned later that night. Watch your back. Sommerville is nothing if not vindictive."

"Well, the patient wasn't really a friend. He just—"

172

"Look, I don't need to know what really happened or why you came back, but if I were you, I'd lie low."

Torrey glanced at the wall clock. It was 3:35. "So you don't think I should go to this afternoon's birthday cake celebration?" asked Torrey with a sarcastic smile.

Dr. Wells laughed and returned to her paperwork. Torrey found an unoccupied table and sat with her back to the door, so her face couldn't be seen by passersby. And so that she could keep an eye on the locked filing cabinets on the far wall.

Torrey opened her notepad, grabbed a couple of case files from a nearby cabinet, and spread the papers out on the table to look productive. She watched the clock tick down to 3:50 p.m. Then, her heart skipped a beat when she heard over her shoulder the last thing she wanted to hear. "What the hell are you doing here?" the minion bellowed.

Torrey knew that voice and felt the heat crawl up her back. She didn't answer or turn around. She stayed rooted in her seat, studying her notes. Scott Belman, in his black undertaker suit and polished old-school Florsheims, walked with heavy steps around the table and stood looking down at Torrey. Only then did she look up, and she sweetly exclaimed, "Oh hi, Scott. I didn't see you there. How are you today?" Torrey offered her hand to shake, as if Belman were a casual friend.

Belman ignored the hand and the pleasantries. He repeated his question. "I said, what the hell are you doing here?"

"Oh, don't mind me," said Torrey with an impassive face and a fake yawn. "I'm just reviewing some old files. Just routine. Want to give me a hand?"

"Look, you," said Belman roughly as he looked, literally, down his nose at Torrey and the files on the table, "I don't think you know who you're dealing with here."

"Oh, I think I have a pretty good idea, but do you want to go ahead and mansplain it to me?" asked Torrey while staring straight into his eyes. Belman gasped and reached up to loosen his Windsor knot. During the pause, Torrey asked politely, "By the way, why are the filing cabinets along that back wall locked? None of the others are."

Belman flinched. Torrey knew that she had struck a nerve. But like any experienced, pencil-pushing administrator, he tried to fake indifference to the question. He quickly composed himself and changed the subject like a seasoned bureaucrat. "If it's any of your business, which it's not, we just needed some more cabinets, and those that were equipped with locks happened to be on sale. There's nothing special about them," he announced in his voice of authority. "Now, doctor, let me ask you a question, have you ever heard the expression, 'Go along to get along?'"

Torrey, who had an uncanny knack for cutting to the quick, groaned dramatically. "As a matter of fact, I have. Isn't that the motto of meek sheep?"

Belman shifted his weight, then bent down so that his face was inches from Torrey's. He lowered his voice to a muffled threat, "Dr. Sommerville has a lot of friends in the medical community, including in the AMA and at the California Board of Licensing. If you value your career, you'd do well to follow that piece of advice."

"What are you insinuating? Is that a threat?"

"You're the smartass. You figure it out."

"Dr. Sommerville sounds like a prince among men," Torrey snapped.

Belman switched tactics. "He could help you get ahead."

"Could he now? How magnanimous," said Torrey with fake eagerness.

"He is a big picture guy. Doesn't get bogged down with details. He has a vision for the VA, which I share. Your little stunt—maybe you think of it as some grand gesture—of getting that soldier transferred out of here is not in line with our plans for this institution. I again caution you to—"

"Sorry," Torrey butted in, "ask around! I'm not really into letting things go. Especially improper care by uncaring medical providers." After a brief pause, Torrey added, her tone filled with accusation, "If you're trying to scare me, you're failing miserably."

174

"You have a pretty high opinion of yourself."

"Just in comparison to my opinion of you," said Torrey without a trace of trepidation. The quick rejoinder caught Belman off guard. His mouth pinched closed.

Before he could reply, a bored-sounding voice announced over the loudspeaker, "Today is Nurse Johnson's birthday. Please join us in the large conference room to celebrate."

Torrey shrugged at Belman. She looked over at Dr. Wills who was red with suppressed laughter. Then she looked at the clock. It was 4:00 p.m. exactly.

• • •

The snappy banter with Torrey was too much for the minion. Belman gave her one last hard look. Then he abruptly turned and wordlessly stalked out of the room. Dr. Wills and a few other tired-looking employees gave Torrey a thumbs up, cleaned up their tables, and sauntered out into the hallway, on their way to be stuffed full of Costco cake and punch.

The moment she was alone, Torrey quickly went to the doorway and checked the corridor. Belman was nowhere in sight. She rushed to the locked cabinets and pulled out Joe Cook's lock pick set from her pocket. Joe must have been a very good teacher because she was able to pick the lock on the first cabinet within seconds. All four cabinet drawers clicked open. The drawers were jam packed with original patient files. Not knowing where to start, or even what she was looking for, Torrey pulled out an armful of charts and spread them out on her worktable.

Most of the charts were thick, indicating long and extensive VA treatment. Skimming the first few voluminous files, she saw nothing out of the ordinary in the original treatment notes or surgery records. She figured she must be missing something, so she went back to the first file and examined it more carefully. She was just about to move on to the next file when she saw it. There were two death certificates, an original and a photocopy, except they were different. They described different causes of death—one benign and expected and one suggesting malpractice or worse. Filled with adrenaline, she skipped to the death certificates in the next few files. Discovery turned to dismay and then to anger. It only took looking at five or six charts to see what was going on. She frowned and pinched her eyebrows together as she considered the ramifications. No wonder these files were locked up. Bad administrators directing a systematic cover up of bad outcomes, from bad treatments, by bad doctors. She wondered how many doctors were involved.

She reasoned that the families of the deceased soldiers, entitled to original death certificates, received fake originals, from which photocopies were made and put in the charts. She took photographs of the two certificates in each chart, returned the files to the cabinets, closed the drawers, and reset the lock. She picked up her purse and papers, walked into the hallway, and paused. In the far distance, she heard singing—the last lines of the "Happy Birthday" song.

Chapter 34

Rocco wasted no time in investigating the idea that Dr. Toohey years ago had stolen FDA- seized Fentanyl. Dr. Jamison and Dr. Preston had suggested that Toohey might be selling the valuable illegal pills on the black market. It took several hours of digging and a phone call from a California Medical Board lawyer to a key FDA staffer in Washington D.C., but Rocco learned that Toohey was, back in the day, one of only three FDA employees with unfettered access to the confiscated drug. All three had been investigated in the theft. The other two had decent but not foolproof alibis. Toohey had claimed that he was, at the time of the drug's disappearance, with another employee by the name of Hillary Flint. She had confirmed Toohey's story. So, no action was ever taken against any of the suspects, and the Fentanyl was never recovered.

Rocco knew that Hillary Flint was now known as Mrs. Albert Toohey, and this raised all kinds of suspicions in his mind. Rocco's immediate supervisor thought it was a long shot, but he agreed to sign off on a subpoena to search Toohey's home and office. They hoped the D.A. would issue an arrest warrant the following day. Rocco planned to serve it as soon as the paperwork was delivered, using a ruse he had perfected during his time with the agency.

Rocco first called Toohey's office. Mrs. Borsky answered in her usual disinterested way, "Offices of Dr. Toohey. Mrs. Borsky speaking." Not even a "Good morning."

"Hello," said Rocco, "this is Harry Solomon from building maintenance, calling for Dr. Toohey."

"He's not in."

"When will he be back?"

"I don't know."

"Can I get a cell number for him?"

"What's this about, Mr. Solomon?" asked a suspicious Mrs. Borsky.

Before Borsky could inquire further, Rocco quickly stated before hanging up, "I'll try again later." Borsky put down the receiver and lit another cigarette. She brushed protein bar crumbs from her desk and went back to reading the latest issue of *Muscle Mania Magazine*.

Even though it was the middle of a workday, Rocco took a chance and called Toohey's home number. Toohey answered on the first ring. "Hello, Dr. Toohey, this is Rocco Washington of the California Medical Board." Toohey swallowed hard and held his breath. "I'm calling because one of your patients has filed a complaint with us that your office billed her for a missed appointment even though she says she was merely late due to a flat tire. She says a person by the name of Borsky refused to erase the charge. I need to meet with you to discuss the issue."

"Look, Mr. Washington, there must be some mistake. My office doesn't bill like that. Who is the patient?"

"I can't divulge that information over the phone. But when we meet, I'll show you the written complaint. Then you'll have thirty days to resolve the matter."

"I don't have time for this right now. Just tell me who the patient is," sighed Toohey. "I'll reimburse her."

"I wish it could be resolved that easily," replied Rocco. "But I'm required to get your signature on the complaint in order to do that. When can we meet so I can close the file? It should just take a minute. We can meet at your office or your home, whichever you'd like."

Dr. Toohey didn't want someone from the Medical Board in his office, so he said, "Today won't work. And tomorrow I'm booked all day with patients. How about tomorrow evening at my house? I should be home from work tomorrow by 7:00 p.m. Will eight o'clock work?"

"Sure. See you then. I have the address from your file." Rocco hung up, very pleased with himself. Busting a doctor on a Fentanyl charge could be the big break he needed to move up the ladder at the Medical Board.

• • •

While Rocco was congratulating himself over his good work, he dialed Matthew's cell phone to give him an update. It was the least he could do, considering Matthew and Torrey had given him the lead on Toohey. He expected to leave a voicemail, but Matthew picked up. "This is Dr. Preston."

"Hello, Dr. Preston, this is Rocco."

"Oh, hi, Big Rocky. I've only got a minute. I'm between patients in the clinic. What's up?"

"Just wanted to let you know that you were likely right about Toohey. He was one of the very few FDA employees with access to the seized Fentanyl. And his alibi was his current wife."

"So, what are you going to do?" asked Matthew cautiously.

"Nail him, of course," said Rocco with a satisfied laugh. "I'm meeting with him at his house tomorrow night at eight o'clock. He thinks it's about some minor administrative matter. But I'm going to serve him with a subpoena. The D.A. might even issue an arrest warrant by then. Thanks again for the tip. I owe you one."

Matthew realized with a jolt that everything had suddenly sped up to warp speed. "No need for thanks. He deserves whatever he gets. But," Matthew warned, "you be careful when you go over there. He could be dangerous."

"Seriously?" Rocco snorted. "That old fart?"

• • •

While Rocco was talking to Matthew, Toohey had his own calls to make. He didn't believe for a minute that a representative of the Medical Board needed to meet with him about a billing issue. How gullible did they think he was? He suspected that Bella Swan, the fake patient's mom who had stolen one of the saline bags, was behind this sudden interest by the Board. It was time to leave the country.

His first call was to Mrs. Borsky. "Mrs. Borsky, how is everything at the office today? Sorry I couldn't make it in."

"I've got the place to myself. I cancelled all patient appointments after you called earlier that you wouldn't be here. Are you going to be in tomorrow?"

"Actually, something's come up. I'm not sure how long I'll be gone. So, we'll have to close the office until further notice. I'll continue to pay you, of course. So, go on a trip. Have some fun. Oh, and call Sunshine to give her the news. We don't want her referring patients to us if we're not open for business."

"But, doctor, you've told these families that your treatment is their only chance. What am I supposed to say to them?" asked Borsky suspiciously.

Toohey had no logical answer to that question. He hesitated for a moment, cleared his throat, and said, "Mrs. Borsky, you're an expert at deflection at that front desk. I've heard you. You'll think of something. Goodbye now!" With that, Toohey hung up, and Borsky was left staring at the disconnected receiver. Rather than deal with the families, Borsky gathered up her things, put the CLOSED sign on the door, and left the building.

Toohey's second call was to his wife, who he knew was at her standing weekly hair appointment at the salon. He was not at all surprised that the call went straight to voicemail. He tried to sound upbeat as he left a message. "Hi, hon, I'll explain later, but we have to go on that trip sooner than I thought. We have to leave tomorrow early evening. I've reserved the plane. We couldn't get your favorite pilot, but they said we'll get somebody really good. So, start packing!"

Chapter 35

At 6:00 p.m., Matthew, Torrey, and Hawk were seated in the living room. "Where's Edwina?" asked Matthew.

"She's always been late, even as a kid," said Hawk.

"I'm sure she'll be here any second," Torrey said.

Just then, the front door opened, and Edwina came bounding up the stairs, pulling a lagging Koa who was tangled in her leash. "Sorry I'm late," said Edwina as she tried to catch her breath. "Koa needed to go out, and then I got to talking with the good-looking dog-walker down the street who was—"

"We don't care about your love life, little brother. Let's get going."

Edwina stopped in her tracks. "Sister," she said pointedly.

As Edwina walked over to the living room, Torrey noticed her new shoes. "Love those shoes!" Torrey whispered.

"I know," replied Edwina, "Aren't they fabulous? They spark joy in me."

Hawk and Matthew looked at each other. No words were required. "Oh wait," exclaimed Edwina. "I almost forgot." She got up and ran into the kitchen. As she walked back into the living room, she held up a giant package of beef jerky for all to see. "See what I bought today at the store? You two," she said while gesturing at Matthew and Torrey, "eat like rabbits with your green smoothies for breakfast and all your supplements. I noticed that neither one of you has eaten any of the Lucky Charms that I got for everyone." As she tore into the jerky package, she announced as she bit off a mouthful, "I need real food. Everybody help yourself." Hawk thought about it, but he had had his fill of jerky when he was in the army. Matthew and Torrey politely declined.

While Edwina was getting comfortable on the couch, Koa waddled over to Hawk and rubbed against his leg. Hawk reached down and let out a groan when he picked Koa up. "This is one fat dog," said Hawk without a wit of humor. Edwina frowned and silently mouthed "big bones" to herself.

Matthew was reluctant to break the frivolous mood, but he knew that time was of the essence. "All right. We've established there is a cute dog-walker down the street, that Mrs. Ed has great shoes, and Koa is the fattest dog in town. Now if you don't mind, can we get down to business?" He used his most serious tone to get their complete attention.

Matthew knew there was a gamble in what he was going to say next, that it would set Hawk off, but he felt it had to be said. His initial enthusiasm for his own plan was waning. "Before we get started, this is our last chance to pump the brakes on this whole thing. This isn't just an academic exercise. Do we really want to do this?"

Hawk snarled at Matthew, "Is this your idea of a joke?"

Edwina burst out, "Toohey's going down, Matthew!"

Matthew looked at Torrey for support. Instead, Torrey stared at him, her blue eyes unblinking and said nothing.

Matthew tried another approach. "I'm just saying that once we start down this rabbit hole, there is no return. We have to weigh the consequences of possible failure against the punishment that Toohey would likely receive from society's laws. He may not get the death sentence, but he'll spend time in prison. Do the benefits of this path outweigh the huge risks to us?"

Hawk, though agitated, answered evenly, "Society's rules and conventions are just that—rules for the upper class who never have to deal with real life. Toohey killed my daughter in real life. I am going to settle the issue with real-life punishment. And like it or not, as a member of the human race, revenge is in my DNA. That may be an inconvenient truth for some, but it's a fact. And frankly, for a man like Toohey who kills innocent children for money, death is not even a sufficient remedy."

"Hear, hear," said Edwina solemnly while raising her fist in the air.

"Hawk," replied Matthew. "Torrey and I are taking a huge risk, both personally and professionally in this venture, so—"

Hawk interrupted. "Matthew, no offense, but a risk is not really a risk if you have a big safety net. Now I don't know anything about Torrey's background, but from what I hear from Edwina, you came from money and will always be fine, no matter what. You'll have money to defend the charges if the whole thing blows up. Edwina, Angela, and I have all come from nothing. We have nothing to lose. If you want to bow out, I completely understand. No hard feelings." Edwina turned red from embarrassment.

Matthew knew in his heart that Hawk was right. And who was he to say that the risk was too big? He had risked everything to avenge his father's death. "I'm just trying to start a conversation here," said Matthew.

Hawk replied with a penetrating stare, "What you're saying is a conversation ender. So, are you in or out?"

Torrey licked her lips and started to say something. But she didn't. Unlike Matthew, she was not typically into choosing her words carefully. Instead, she usually opened her mouth, and what she was thinking came out. But on this occasion, she just stared at Matthew with a questioning look and welling eyes. Matthew saw the look on her face. "Honey, what are you thinking?" he asked gently.

She hesitated for a moment, but then said, "Matthew, you say he will go to prison. That's a false narrative. First, there's no guarantee of that. People get killed on the streets every day, and no one goes to jail. Murderers walk free on technicalities or based on politics. I just saw on the news that government officials placed illegal wiretaps on American citizens, and no one went to jail. The officials didn't even get fired. So, you can't know that Toohey will go to prison. Odds are that even if some low-level district attorney tries to convict Toohey, some slick lawyer will subvert the justice system. He will claim that the saline bag that I took from Toohey's office is inadmissible because it was stolen—fruit of the poisonous tree doctrine. And Toohey will surely destroy the rest of the evidence.

"What Hawk said about wealth is unfortunately true in today's criminal justice system. Look how Ted Nash was on the verge of getting released because his family could pull strings. Because they were rich! And we know Toohey has tons of blood money to finance his defense. He will probably get off, and no one will care except for the families of the children he killed."

Torrey looked hard at Matthew. Tears were streaming down her cheeks. "Second, even if the justice system puts him in prison, justice without peace is illusory. You, better than anyone, know this. Hawk will have no peace until Toohey is dead. And just so you know, neither will I." Torrey raised her arm and reached across the table to hold hands with Matthew. He stared at the outstretched hand, then reached across to grab it.

Matthew exhaled. His face registered first defeat and then resolve. He owed his wife literally everything. He looked around the room at the faces of his partners. He nodded his head reluctantly. "Okay then, looks like we're all in agreement. Just thought I'd check one last time."

Before anyone could comment further, Matthew segued back to the plan. "Now since our last meeting, I've made some minor changes to our blueprint. So, let's start from the top."

"Hold on a minute," said Hawk testily. "I thought we already had a plan. And it started and ended with me tearing Toohey's head off. Now if you want to make a change where I shoot him from 500 yards, that's okay. I don't mind turning his head into vapor."

"Well, that's an intriguing option," mused Matthew, trying not to sound sarcastic. "But I was thinking of something a little more subtle and a little less public. I was thinking of a plan where Toohey gets what's coming to him, with no one the wiser, and then we can all go back to our lives."

"Except Emily," said Hawk solemnly. "My daughter is gone, Matthew. Edwina's niece is gone. Angela, Edwina, and I are never going back to our old lives. Those lives are never coming back."

Matthew felt terrible about the way he had phrased his comment. He averted his eyes by staring down at the grounds in the bottom of his coffee cup. Torrey felt a lump in her throat and again had to blink back tears. She absentmindedly began to gently rub the miniature *Star Wars* charms that were dangling from her silver bracelet. Her mind wandered back to the death of her younger sister, Leia, whom the family called "Princess" because Leia was enamored with Princess Leia from the first *Star Wars* movie and had collected charms of all the *Star Wars* characters. That's all she wanted on birthdays and at Christmas. The day before she passed away, she took off the bracelet and put it in Torrey's hand. By that gesture, Leia had signaled that she knew the end was imminent. Torrey remembered that, even as a fifteen-year-old, all she wanted to do was to strike out at someone—anyone—who had caused Leia's pain, suffering, and ugly death.

Edwina brought the group back to reality. "Look, Hawk, Matthew is a meticulous planner and is only trying to help us. Same with Torrey."

Hawk limited his reply to a dismissive wave.

Matthew added, "Hawk, no one's sorrier than I am about the real and devastating loss of Emily. But part of the deal is that no one tears anyone's head off until we learn all the details of Toohey's scheme and who else might be involved. We all agreed that if anyone is working with Toohey, that person also needs to answer."

All eyes turned to Hawk. With an almost imperceptible noncommittal shrug, he simply stated, "Let's hear your new plan."

Matthew took a breath. "Okay then. The basic structure is unchanged. You and I grab Toohey and take him to the cabin cruiser I've arranged to borrow from an old high school friend. We all head out to open sea and then question him. Once we know the full extent of who and what was involved in his plot, then we can deal with Toohey." Torrey gave him a funny look. "And before you ask," continued Matthew, "yes, I said earlier I was going to use my Uncle TJ's boat. But the more I thought about it, I decided not to involve him or the hassle of hiring a boat captain to sail it down here from LA. And I threw out the idea of renting a boat because of the paper trail. My high school friend lives abroad. He'll be oblivious to anything that happens."

Edwina wanted to revisit the question of who might be working with Toohey. "Maybe that guy who was arguing with Toohey in his office is Toohey's partner. The one who's calling the shots."

"Wait a minute. You told me you guys made that up!" exclaimed Hawk.

"Oh, right you are," mumbled Edwina. In an effort to change the subject, Edwina turned the focus back to Matthew, "So what other modifications to the plan have you come up with?"

Matthew continued, "Just some fine-tuning. First of all, we have to change the timetable. We originally planned for next Saturday when we could be more certain that Toohey would be home. And we were going to hit his house after dark, around 10:00 p.m. We not only have to move this up to tomorrow, but we have to move up the time to 7:00 p.m."

"The sun will barely have set! We need total darkness," said Hawk.

"Sorry," said Matthew, "an agent from the California Medical Board is going to be knocking on Toohey's door at 8:00 p.m. to confront him. He might even show up with the police to serve an arrest warrant. After that, all hell is going to break loose. We'll lose our chance."

"And you know that how?" asked Hawk.

"Long story, but you can count on it."

"Then 7:00 p.m. it is," confirmed Hawk. "What else?"

"I've enlisted the help of my private investigator to watch Toohey's house all day to monitor anyone arriving or leaving the home."

Edwina winced. "Is it wise to have another person involved? Can we trust him?"

"I would trust Joe Cook with my life. But for his own protection, he has no idea about our plan. He's just doing surveillance and reporting to me about any comings and goings," said Matthew.

"Next, we had previously planned that Torrey would hang around Toohey's office starting late afternoon when she's finished with her shift at the hospital. And we said Edwina would be at the marina making sure the boat is ready to go. But let's switch that around. I don't want Torrey to be seen and recognized by Toohey or his receptionist. So, Torrey will take care of the boat, and Mrs. Ed will keep watch of Toohey's office. Matthew pulled out his phone and began to text. "Torrey, I'm sending you the name of the boat, the slip, and where you can find the keys." Torrey gave one of her patented mock salutes.

Edwina was pleased with her new role. "Should I wear a disguise? I think I should. Remember, I was in their office, too."

"Sure," said Hawk without missing a beat. "Wear whatever you want." Hawk looked at Matthew. "Edwina has always loved to play dress-up."

"Maybe a camo shirt and one of your old army hats. What do you think?"

"You're a real rebel, you know that?" said Hawk derisively.

"I know, right?" said Edwina.

"That's settled then," smiled Matthew. "Now, if the wife is at home when we arrive, which we'll know from Joe Cook, I like the idea of staging a home robbery. We can wear baseball caps and bandanas pulled up over our faces. Hawk and I will grab and incapacitate Toohey, while shouting about cash and jewelry. I'll scream at Toohey something like, 'Where's the safe!' We can tie up the wife, trash the place as if looking for loot, and then, when we are safely away, we can call the police and let them know to come free the wife."

Torrey added mischievously, "Speaking of the wife, I hear that she's a smokin' hottie. Isn't that right, Matthew?"

"Hey," said Matthew with a grin, "I was just reporting what Joe said. I personally am deeply offended by such language." Torrey rolled her eyes.

"Matthew," said Hawk, "no offense, but as I said before, I really don't need your help to subdue Toohey."

"I know, but an extra pair of hands might come in handy if the wife is there and who knows what might happen. For all we know, Toohey might be armed."

Hawk slapped his forehead with on open palm and scoffed, "Wow, I never thought of that. Whatever will I do if Toohey has a gun?"

"Point taken," said Matthew.

Hawk subconsciously puffed out his chest. "Look, I don't care if Toohey has a tank and a bazooka, he won't be a problem. But you come along if you must."

• • •

After the meeting, Torrey and Matthew retired to the sanctity and privacy of their bedroom.

"I think that went well," said Torrey.

"I don't know. This plan has been cobbled together more with emotion than common sense. I've been over the plan a hundred times in my head, but it still seems like a stretch."

Torrey waved her hand back and forth. "There, now that I've scattered some pixie dust over the plan, nothing can go wrong." Matthew smiled reluctantly. Torrey added, "Don't overthink it. Plans can change. Sometimes the best plan is no plan at all."

"I don't want to underthink it," said Matthew.

"That's not a thing. You sounded confident when we were sitting there with Mrs. Ed and Hawk. If you're worried that the plan is not foolproof, no plan is. You lost your father, and I lost my sister to random events. Plans change. Just accept it. Then you're never disappointed. And don't forget, your plan to eliminate Ted Nash, your father's killer, was foolproof. But then it wasn't. Yet everything still worked out okay." After a long embrace, Torrey asked, "Bottom line, what are the odds of this all going according to plan?"

"You asked me that before, and I said about a million to one. With Hawk being such a wild card, I would now recalculate that to ten million to one," replied Matthew in a deflated tone.

"So, you still think there's a chance!" said Torrey with a grin.

"You are really something, you know that?" said Matthew while fondly giving Torrey a squeeze.

"And don't you ever forget it," replied Torrey with a kiss.

Chapter 36

The planning session had lasted well into the night, but Matthew was scheduled to be at the ER at 7:00 a.m. The attending physician that morning was Dr. Clinton, who had headed up the emergency room for more than fifteen years. He was a semi-famous surgeon back in the day, but that all ended when he shattered his ankle in a skiing accident and was no longer able to stand in the operating room for hours on end. Now when he walked, his ankle made an awful cracking sound with each step. Matthew, like most of the younger male residents, had little contact with Dr. Clinton. It was well known that Clinton preferred the female doctors and nurses.

The morning hours were mercifully slow, which allowed Matthew to mull over the Toohey plans to be sure nothing was left to chance. At about 10:30, a fit-looking, middle-aged man came in complaining that he was about to die from a blood clot in his brain. "Why do you think that?" asked Matthew skeptically.

The distraught man said that he had been watching a doctor on TV who said a gentleman with the same symptoms had died of a blood clot. Matthew said, "I'll send in a nurse to take your vitals. Then we'll see where we are. Just sit tight."

"But I could die before you come back."

"No, you can't."

Matthew went over to the nurses' station to talk to Nurse Cleaver. "Another nocebo effect in Room 12."

"Oh for heaven's sake," said Nurse Cleaver. "That's the third one this week!"

A nurse trainee standing nearby spoke up, "A what in Room 12?"

"A nocebo effect," said Nurse Cleaver. "It's the opposite of a placebo effect. You know what a placebo effect is—when a patient is given a sugar pill, but she is told that the pill is a drug that can cure her symptoms. The patient's belief in what the doctor said can be a powerful factor in making the patient feel better.

"Conversely, a nocebo response can be triggered when someone, usually a doctor, tells a patient that a medication—or even a pill that is actually an inert substance—has debilitating side effects. The patient then imagines she has those side effects, causing actual, measurable symptoms."

Matthew continued, "So there's this doctor who was a guest on one of those morning talk shows a few days ago who said that anyone who takes a particular diabetes medication is at risk for a fatal heart attack or brain aneurism. I've heard that he actually said that the increased risk was miniscule, but the viewing audience who were taking that drug only heard the part about sudden death."

"I've never heard of the nocebo effect," said the trainee with some hesitation.

"Why don't you go help Nurse Cleaver take the man's vitals?" suggested Matthew. "I've got a nickel that says all his vitals are normal. And I'll bet he's diabetic. Write in his chart what medications he takes. We can give him an EKG to be sure he is healthy. Try to assure him he won't die, at least not from this. Come get me if he needs to hear it from me."

• • •

When Matthew walked out, he saw paramedics, nurses, and doctors gathered around a motorcycle accident victim. Despite the fact that he had worked on formaldehyde-soaked cadavers in Stanford's medical school basement, aka The Dungeon, and had seen some gruesome injuries since then, Matthew was not quite prepared for the sight that greeted him. On the gurney was a young motorcycle accident victim who had lost control of his bike on the freeway, had smashed into the center divider, and was thrown into oncoming traffic. He had been wearing a helmet, so his head was somewhat protected, but no other part of his body was quite so lucky. Maybe in this case it wasn't such a blessing that his brain was able to comprehend and register the scope of his other injuries. Matthew remembered back to his first anatomy class during which the professor said that a more descriptive word for motorcycles was *donorcycles* because so many bodies and organs were donated to medical science as a result of motorcycle accidents.

The victim was somehow still alive, but every bone appeared broken, and every internal organ looked mangled. A breathing tube was sticking from his throat. Morphine had been given to stop the pain, so the passing would be peaceful. The young man, probably in his early twenties, looked shrunken and about ten years old. Matthew wondered if the motorcyclist knew the end was inevitable. Matthew hoped the boy didn't realize he was about to become another senseless fatality. He had opted out of religion after his father had been murdered, but he gently touched the boy's cheek and whispered, "God be with you." The soulful look of gratitude in the boy's eyes gave Matthew some comfort.

• • •

Matthew's first patient after lunch was a middle-aged woman who had sliced open her hand while attempting to remove an avocado pit. Until working in the ER, Matthew had no idea how common avocado accidents were. In medical literature, such an injury is termed "avocado hand" and can involve anything from soft tissue injuries to permanent damage to tendons or nerves. Fortunately for Matthew's patient, there was a lot of blood, but some stitches and bandages were all she needed. The run-of-the-mill injury didn't require Matthew to devote his full attention to her treatment, so he started to worry about the boat he had arranged to borrow and whether it would be complicated to maneuver the old relic out of the marina. He hoped Torrey wouldn't have any trouble with it.

• • •

At 1:34 p.m., a tap on the shoulder by a nurse brought him back to the present. "Doctor, I'll finish that up for you. Dr. Clinton would like you to help him in Exam Room 11." Matthew knew Dr. Clinton by sight, but the two had never spoken. What Matthew found curious about Dr. Clinton was that Matthew could tell, even from a distance, that Dr. Clinton was a vain man. His hair, colored black to conceal his natural gray, was styled with too much gel. His face, unnaturally tight from too much plastic surgery, made his eyes look like bulging marbles.

Matthew was surprised by the request to join Dr. Clinton, but he didn't question the directive. He simply reassured his avocado-hand patient, "You're going to be just fine. Nurse Cleaver will take good care of you. And please buy store-bought guacamole from now on." The woman mustered a weak smile.

Matthew was greeted by an unusual sight in Room 11. A very pregnant young woman, in full labor, was panting through a contraction. As an internal medicine resident, Matthew was scheduled to do a rotation in the obstetric department. But that rotation had not yet occurred. "Why is this woman here rather than in obstetrics?" asked Matthew.

Dr. Clinton replied, "Obstetrics has no beds, and every pregnant woman anywhere near her due date and this hospital are here. And the obstetrics unit is short-staffed today, so they sent Ms. Johnson here. I'm turning her over to you."

Matthew introduced himself to the young mother-to-be and checked her vitals. They were a little abnormal. Then he began to notice the non-medical banter between Dr. Clinton and the two first-year female interns, Dr. Fredericks and Dr. Swanson. The three of them were standing unusually close to each other. In the few seconds it took for Matthew to focus on the conversation, he figured out that Dr. Clinton was telling a risqué joke. Matthew missed the joke's set-up, but he could tell that Dr. Clinton was just about to deliver a suggestive punchline. Matthew jerked his head around to look daggers at Dr. Clinton. "Uh-oh," taunted Dr. Clinton, "looks like we have a killjoy in our midst. I'd better whisper the end of this joke to you ladies." He leaned in close to the young women doctors and uttered something that Matthew couldn't hear. Dr. Clinton and Dr. Fredericks laughed heartily, but Dr. Swanson managed only a small nervous laugh. "When we get up to the lounge," said Dr. Clinton rowdily, "I'll tell you the one about a woman, a giraffe, and a hippo that—oops! Better stop right there. Don't want to offend Dr. Preston, do we ladies?"

Dr. Fredericks did not seem bothered by the boorish behavior, or maybe she was playing along as part of a considered career decision. Dr. Swanson, however, crossed her arms and shrank away from Dr. Clinton. She shuffled backwards until she pressed up against the wall. She said quietly, "I don't think I'll have time to go up to the lounge, Dr. Clinton."

"Sure, you will," replied Dr. Clinton. "Dr. Preston will hold down the fort here." He gestured at Matthew with a sweep of his hand. "Won't you?"

Matthew realized that he was gritting his teeth and clenching his fists as he pictured Torrey having to work with Clinton. Torrey had had a surgical rotation with Dr. Clinton, and she simply had reported to Matthew that Clinton was arrogant, like all surgeons. Now Matthew wondered if Torrey had been subject to verbal abuse, or worse. She was not at all voluptuous or flirty and was practiced at ignoring wolf whistles and unwanted advances, but this was different. This was harassment by a superior. And of course, Matthew's anger was magnified due to the setting of having a young pregnant mother in front of them.

He had studied martial arts when he was younger, and he ached to give Dr. Clinton a swift leg kick to the chest. A shadow of disgust crossed his face, but Matthew settled for a more socially acceptable approach. "Dr. Clinton," said Matthew with faux respect, "I don't think Dr. Swanson appreciates your undignified language, or your invitation to go upstairs to hear more of the same. May I suggest that we focus on this patient?"

The mood in the room changed in a heartbeat. The two women gaped at Matthew, but he could see relief in Dr. Swanson's eyes. Dr. Clinton was unaccustomed to any sort of rebuke in his domain. Because Matthew was 6'2" and Clinton was short and squat, Matthew could see the bald spot on the top of Clinton's head turn red. "Well, well," said Clinton with a wooden smile, "I'd heard you had a Sir Lancelot reputation among the staff. Protecting your queen, are you? Are you going to come tackle me like you tackled that prisoner at San Quentin? Oh yes, we've heard all about that. I wonder how that cute little wife of yours would feel about your gallantry on behalf of Dr. Swanson?"

"Don't forget," replied Matthew slowly, "the Black Knight always loses in the end." Dr. Clinton laughed bitterly to cover his growing insecurity.

The air was thick with tension as the two men glared at each other as if playing a game of "chicken." Matthew's heart was racing but he had a good poker face. Dr. Clinton cracked first and broke the silence, "Dr. Preston, I was going to put you in charge of this patient. I was going to take these young ladies with me to the Doctor's Lounge and have you handle the labor and delivery of the baby alone, in between your other duties. But in light of your interest in Dr. Swanson, I will leave you and Dr. Swanson here. You will both stay here until the baby is born. Then you, Dr. Preston, will fill out the paperwork showing the time of birth and the baby's vitals." With a brusque tone he added, "Understood?"

Matthew found himself reflecting on what Torrey would do in this situation. He smiled and replied with his trademark easy confidence, "I can say with certainty that the Chief of Staff, if asked, would demand that you treat the female doctors and nurses with the respect that they deserve. Understood?"

Dr. Clinton tried to look indifferent. He didn't respond. He merely turned on his heels and scurried away like a cockroach when the lights are turned on. Matthew heard his ankle bones crackling as he marched out the door and down the hallway. Dr. Fredericks slowly followed with her shoulders drooped, but she stopped at the doorway and glanced back at Dr. Swanson. Neither spoke. "You can stay here with us," Matthew said. Dr. Fredericks shook her head almost imperceptibly, and then, with a withering stare and a long exhale, she was gone.

Matthew was sure he did the right thing to stand up for the two women, but saving Dr. Swanson for a day was, he knew, a short-lived victory. And now the plans for Dr. Toohey were in jeopardy. The timetable required Matthew to meet up with Hawk at six o'clock to synchronize their plans and equipment. They needed to be on Toohey's doorstep at 7 p.m. He despised the fact that he was somehow now rooting for immediate dilation to ten centimeters, even if it was more painful for the mother, rather than a slow, easy, natural birth.

After Dr. Fredericks left, Dr. Swanson went over to Ms. Johnson and placed a cool compress on her forehead. Matthew came over to help by telling Ms. Johnson what a good job she was doing. He glanced at her identification bracelet. Her first name was Mary. "I see your name is Mary. That was my mother's name. I'll take good care of you." He held her hand, timed her contractions, and monitored the baby's heartbeat with a fetal heart monitor. "How are you doing, Mary?" Matthew repeatedly asked. He continued to talk to her to distract her from her pain. Every so often Mary forced a nod of her head.

"You didn't have to stand up to Dr. Clinton for me," said Dr. Swanson in a faint quivering voice as she carefully wiped the mother's face after a particularly strong contraction.

Matthew, knowing that Torrey would expect nothing less from him, replied crisply, "Yes, I did."

Chapter 37

Joe Cook glanced at his watch at three o'clock, as he had been doing every five minutes since 5:00 a.m. when he had parked down the street from Toohey's house to begin his surveillance. He had been on countless stakeouts as a former cop and as a private investigator. But this job was particularly boring, partially because the street was quiet, but mostly because he had no idea why Matthew wanted him to monitor Toohey's movements. He had learned over the years that most clients don't want their motivations questioned but waiting and watching were much more interesting when you knew the backstory.

Dr. Toohey had left the house in his Camry at 6:21 a.m. and had returned at 12:31 p.m. The highlight of Joe's day had been watching Mrs. Toohey come outside in a short robe to collect the newspaper at 8:00 a.m. sharp. No one else came or left. The Tooheys were inside alone.

• • •

Edwina parked her car near Dr. Toohey's office building at 2:34 p.m. Matthew had asked her to start her watch at 2:00 p.m., but she was a little late because she had been talking to that cute dog-walker down the street from Torrey's condo.

Because it looked like it might rain, Edwina's disguise consisted of items she had pulled out of an old trunk of clothes that she had saved, just for fun, from her days as male—dark blue jeans, an oversized UC Santa Barbara sweatshirt, and a worn Dodgers cap. She thought about wearing a pair of thick reading glasses that she had used one Halloween, but she hated to over accessorize. Besides, when she tried them on, her distance vision was impaired. She stuck the glasses in her purse.

She sat on a park bench across the street from Toohey's building, from where she had a view of the front door and the entrance to the street level parking lot exit. Within fifteen minutes, Edwina was regretting accepting this assignment. She had to sit there like a stump, and her clothing was frumpy. Time passed slowly. But she stuck it out. As of 4:36 p.m., there weren't any Toohey sightings.

• • •

Torrey had left the hospital at 4:00 p.m. with the blessing of the Chief Resident. Dr. McKnight, like most of the more senior doctors at the hospital, thought of Torrey as a little sister. And younger siblings always get what they want.

Torrey knew that the plan required her to be at the boat by 5:00 p.m., but she wanted to leave work a little earlier to be sure she could find the boat in the huge marina. She found the correct pier within minutes, but when she got to the boat slip, she figured there was some sort of miscommunication with Matthew. The boat in Slip 73A was a piece of junk. With its all-wood construction and peeling green and white paint, it looked like it was built in a 1940s high school woodshop class. The name on the bow, barely visible, was *The San Diego Queen*. She couldn't believe it could float.

Torrey double-checked Matthew's text, confirmed the slip number, and climbed aboard. Matthew said that the keys would be on the captain's chair. No one said to wear gloves to obscure fingerprints, but she was glad that she had a pair of surgical gloves in her purse—to protect against slivers and germs.

After an initial walk-around, she found the bridge and what passed as a captain's chair. Matthew said the keys would be on the chair, but the only thing she saw was an old, torn, grimy chair cushion from the Seattle World's Fair of 1962. Now she was doubly glad for the gloves. She lifted up the thick pad, and there was a single discolored key. She held her breath as she inserted and turned the key. The motor, startlingly loud, roared to life. The gas gauge read "full," and no red lights appeared on the console. She concluded that the boat was seaworthy, so she turned off the engine and went down below.

In the cabin was a narrow bed in one corner and a small table with two chairs on the other side of the room. She imagined Toohey tied to one of chairs while being questioned. She thought of Hawk trying to tear Toohey's head off before the interrogation was finished. And she imagined what she herself would want to do to Toohey.

She climbed back up the stairs to the deck to search for some rope or twine. She glanced at her phone and saw she had a missed call from Matthew.

• • •

By 4:45 p.m., with the laboring mother only dilated to seven centimeters, Matthew knew he would never be able to meet up with Hawk at six o'clock at the 7-Eleven convenience store, which was a couple of miles from Toohey's house. Matthew was supposed to park his car in the surrounding neighborhood, walk to the 7-Eleven, and then ride with Hawk to Toohey's house. The timetable was impossible. They would have to abort.

He stepped out into the corridor where Dr. Swanson couldn't hear. He called Torrey, but there was no answer. He called Hawk who picked up immediately. "Hawk," said Matthew, "I'm so sorry, but I'm stuck here at the hospital. Not sure when I can leave. We'll have to call everything off and reschedule. Or think of something else."

There was silence for several seconds before Hawk replied. "No."

"Listen, Hawk, I know how you feel but—"

"Let me stop you right there. I'm locked and loaded," said Hawk defiantly. "I'm going forward whether you're there or not. Frankly, Matthew, you were just going to be in the way. I'm going to get Toohey just as we agreed. I will then head to the boat just as we agreed. Torrey and Edwina will be there as we agreed. Hopefully, you can make it there before we leave the marina, but Toohey's going to be shark bait whether you're there or not." Hawk hung up. He was not altogether bothered that Matthew was out of the picture. And the more he thought about it, the more he concluded that Matthew was right. Tearing Toohey's head off wasn't the best idea. That would cause Toohey to die without sufficient suffering. Hawk decided a better plan was to tear off Toohey's arms, use them for chum, and then push Toohey overboard when the sharks appeared.

When Matthew got off the phone, he could hear from the hallway screaming coming from just inside the ER entrance. He could tell instantly that the cries were coming from the mother of the motorcyclist. "I told him a hundred times—stay off that motorcycle! I begged him. Threatened him. But he said it made him happy. What could I do?" she sobbed. Matthew couldn't hear the responses of the medical personnel, but he could only assume that the doctors and nurses, having witnessed this scene countless times, were giving sympathetic nods and hugs.

When Matthew reentered Room 11, Mary was insisting to Dr. Swanson that something wasn't right. "I'm telling you," Mary was saying, "something is wrong. My baby has stopped moving!"

Matthew immediately looked at the fetal heart rate monitor readings from the ultrasound probe. The heart rate had been borderline low when he first looked at it a few minutes ago. Now it was even lower. Matthew was no obstetrician, but he knew from medical school that decreased fetal movement and decelerating heart rate indicates that the baby's umbilical cord is compressed.

The umbilical cord delivers nutrients and oxygen from the mother's placenta to the baby. If the cord is kinked and cannot perform its function, oxygen is cut off from the baby's brain, resulting in all levels of brain damage. Mary was right. The cord was likely wrapped around the baby's neck.

Matthew turned Mary's head towards him and looked her in the eyes. "Mary, we have to get the baby out now. I've asked Dr. Swanson to call the obstetrics surgeon to get you prepped for an emergency cesarean section."

"No!" Mary cried. "No C-section! I'm having natural childbirth! And no drugs!"

"Mary, there's no choice. Your baby is not getting enough oxygen. We need to get the baby out to save it."

"Do something else. You're a doctor! There must be something else you can do!" Mary grabbed Matthew's hand and started to cry.

Just then, Dr. Swanson reappeared with a surgeon, Laurel Hartman, in tow. Matthew tried to move out of the way, so Dr. Hartman could take over, but Mary wouldn't let go of him. Dr. Hartman checked the baby's vitals. The baby's heart rate was almost nonexistent. She went to the other side of Mary's bed to talk to her. "Ms. Johnson, I'm Dr. Hartman. I'm going to be performing the C-section. We're going to move you into surgery right now." Mary didn't reply. She just continued to writhe around and shake her head from side to side.

An orderly and two nurses appeared out of nowhere and started unhooking the monitors from Mary's body, so she could be transported. "I'll explain what we'll be doing as we head towards the operating room," said Dr. Hartman, who was walking alongside the bed as it was being pushed out of Room 11.

"Wait!" Mary yelled as she pointed at Matthew. "I want him to come!"

A shocked Matthew asked, "What?"

Dr. Hartman had no time for drama. "C'mon then, doctor. You heard the patient."

Matthew started to protest. "But—"

"No time for buts, doctor. Let's go!" ordered Dr. Hartman.

Dr. Swanson called out to Dr. Hartman, "Me, too?"

Dr. Hartman waved for her to come. The entourage disappeared out into the hallway. Matthew followed behind, not sure what had just happened.

In the operating room, Matthew and Dr. Swanson were more in the way than helpful. The surgical team insisted Dr. Swanson stand back so as not to interfere, but Matthew got a place of honor around the table because Mary insisted. The surgical team was a well-oiled machine.

Within minutes of arriving in the operating room, an anesthesiologist had given Mary a nerve block, nurses had hooked her up to an IV with antibiotics and fluids, and Dr. Hartman had made her first incision into the abdomen. Sixty seconds later, Dr. Hartman made an incision into the uterus, through which the baby was delivered. The umbilical cord was unraveled, and the baby boy turned a life-affirming, gorgeous shade of pink.

To an experienced obstetrician like Dr. Hartman, it was just another day at the office. To Matthew and Dr. Swanson, it was a miracle.

Mary thanked Dr. Hartman and her team profusely, but most of her praise was directed to

Matthew. As the baby rested on her chest, Mary lifted her head and read out loud the name on Matthew's name tag in a considering tone. "Matthew Preston, M.D.," she mused. "I don't have a name picked out yet for my baby. I'm going with 'Preston!'" Matthew grinned and gave Mary a kiss on the cheek. "Send me a picture of baby Preston when you get a chance," he whispered. "I'll treasure it forever."

With the mother and baby doing fine, Matthew looked at Dr. Swanson and gave a thumbs up. She grinned back. Matthew asked, "Would you mind finishing up the administrative details of this birth for Dr. Clinton? I've got a pressing engagement." Without waiting for a reply, Matthew hurried out of the room and out of the hospital. Once outside, he glanced at his watch, reached for his phone, and began dialing.

Chapter 38

Matthew tried Hawk's phone at 6:20. As he expected, Hawk didn't pick up. *Why should he?* Matthew thought. Nothing was going to change.

At 6:21, Matthew called Torrey. She picked up and asked, "Matthew, are you and Hawk ready to go?"

"No, I haven't even left the hospital parking lot yet."

"What? You were supposed to meet Hawk at six! What happened?"

"Short answer—bad day at work. Will tell you all about it later. Right now, I need you to call Hawk. I talked to him earlier and told him we'd have to abort, but he refused. Said he is going ahead with the plan whether I'm there or not. Then he hung up on me. I just tried him again, but my call went straight to voicemail. I've already missed the six o'clock rendezvous, and I doubt, with rush hour traffic, that I can even get to Toohey's by 7:00. If you call him, maybe you'll have better luck."

"But what should I tell him? We both know he's going to show up at Toohey's at seven o'clock sharp. He's going to grab Toohey and bring him to the boat. Why not just let him? Then you can come directly to the boat."

Matthew gritted his teeth. "I don't like it. You know what? I'm now in my car, and I'm heading to Toohey's. Maybe Hawk will come to his senses and decide not to go it alone. Call him. Tell him to wait until I get there." Matthew tore out of the lot and headed for Del Mar.

By 6:44, he was still miles away from Toohey's house. He called Torrey. "Well, were you able to reach Hawk?"

"Nope. Went to voicemail. I left a message that you were coming, but I don't know if he's going to wait."

Matthew's phone buzzed, and he saw that Joe Cook was calling in. "Torrey, Joe is calling. Let me see what he wants. I'll call you back."

"Hey, Joe, what's up?" asked Matthew.

"You said to call if Toohey gets any visitors."

"Oh, right. Is it the police?"

"No, why would the police come? Remember I told you about that big guy who was surveilling Toohey's house a few days ago? It's him. He just pulled up to the curb in front of the house. He's just sitting there," said Joe.

Matthew felt numb. He knew it was Rocco. He wasn't supposed to arrive until 8:00 p.m. Matthew deduced that Rocco was too excited to wait. Or maybe an assistant district attorney and the cops were right behind. "Is anyone with him?" asked Matthew in a rushed voice.

"No, he's alone."

"Do you see any police presence on the street? Any government issue vehicles?"

"Nope." Joe rarely raised his voice, but he did now. "Matthew, what's going on?"

Matthew wondered if Hawk was close enough to see what was happening, maybe watching from some bushes.

"Matthew," said Joe, "the big guy is now getting out of the car."

Matthew knew the game was over. Rocco was going to confront Toohey and take him down on the Fentanyl charge. The crimes against humanity would not be addressed. Toohey might lose his medical license and might do some jail time, but real justice would have to wait until Toohey was free. "Joe," said Matthew, "that guy is a Medical Board investigator. His name is Rocco Washington."

"What? I thought he was a bad guy."

"I should've told you about him. He's one of the good guys. I promise

I'll tell you everything soon. Just stay put for now. Call me back if anyone else arrives. I'm in my car headed your way. I'll look for your car."

Matthew signed off and called Torrey back. "Big Rocky came early. He's walking up to Toohey's door right now," said Matthew.

"Oh great!" said Torrey. "What else could go wrong? He said eight o'clock!"

"I know. I just hope Hawk figures out what's happening. We can't have him barging in with the home invasion ruse while Rocco is in there," said Matthew, his voice rising in alarm. "Call Hawk again and tell him about Rocco."

• • •

Joe sat quietly in his car, watching Rocco Washington step up on Toohey's porch. Rocco knocked and took a step back from the door. No one answered. Rocco moved forward and knocked again—this time louder. No answer. Then Rocco used his fist to pound on the door. Joe rolled down his window in time to hear Rocco yell at the door, "Dr. Toohey, this is Mr. Washington from the Medical Board. I see your car in the driveway. Your wife's, too. Open up please!"

Toohey cracked open the door and spoke to Rocco, although Joe couldn't hear the conversation. After thirty seconds of polite arguing, Toohey let Rocco in and closed the door.

As Toohey and Rocco stood in the foyer, Mrs. Toohey came out of a hallway. "What's going on, Albert? Who's he?" she asked while staring at Rocco.

"Honey, this is Mr. Washington from the Medical Board. He has a few questions for me about the practice. I'll take care of it. You go ahead with your packing." Mrs. Toohey nodded and disappeared down the hall.

When she was out of earshot, Toohey told Rocco that they were getting ready to leave on vacation. He crossly suggested that Mr. Washington should have come at the appointed time. "You need to leave and come back at eight o'clock," said Toohey, knowing that he and his wife would be long gone by then. "And really? You need to meet with me over some billing misunderstanding? You don't have something better to do?" asked Toohey with more than a trace of disgust.

Now it was Rocco's turn to apply some pressure. "I think you know that's not why I'm here." Rocco reached into his breast pocket and pulled out a subpoena. He held it out to Toohey. "You've been served. And a search warrant is on the way."

Rocco saw movement behind Toohey as Mrs. Toohey poked her head out from the hallway. She was eavesdropping.

Toohey backed away from the subpoena and feigned surprise, "What are you talking about?"

"In an hour, the local district attorney and a crew from my office will be here to search your home. Another crew is already at your office."

"Oh, c'mon! What on earth are you looking for? I haven't done anything wrong!"

"We know you stole the Fentanyl from a drug bust back when you were with the FDA. We have reason to believe you still have it, or at least some of it."

"That's what you are searching for? That's ludicrous! They asked me all about that back then. They concluded that I wasn't involved. Go ask them!"

"We did. They just said they couldn't prove you took it. But we can."

"What? How?"

Rocco just stared at Toohey. Then he gestured at the couch and said, "I think I'll just get comfortable while we wait for the police to arrive. You can answer the District Attorney's questions from your jail cell."

Toohey started to sweat. "Look, we can make a deal. I can tell you about the Fent—"

Mrs. Toohey stepped into the living room. "Will you shut up!" she yelled at her husband. "You think all this is about a few pills of Fentanyl from years ago? This is all because you let some bimbo steal that IV bag, you idiot!"

Rocco scrunched up his face in confusion. "Huh?" he said.

• • •

Joe had just started to punch in Matthew's number again to give him an update. A split second later, he heard three loud muffled explosions coming from inside Toohey's house. Joe didn't have the highest IQ in his police academy class, and he wasn't the most well-read guy who ever lived, but he knew the sound of gunfire when he heard it. *Oh my God*, thought Joe. *Toohey shot Washington!* He pocketed his phone before Matthew could answer.

Joe reached down and pulled out his loaded Glock 17 which was securely fastened to the underside of the driver's seat. It held seventeen 9 mm bullets, but in an abundance of caution, he also pocketed an extra magazine of ammunition. Keeping low, he ran across the street and up Toohey's driveway. With his gun in his right hand, Joe spider-crawled from the driveway to the front door, keeping himself below the window line. When he got to the closed front door, he put his ear to the wood and listened hard. He heard nothing. He tried the door handle and saw that it wasn't locked. He internally debated whether to open the door slowly and quietly, or to charge in with the gun blazing. Neither sounded quite right, so he wiped his brow with the back of his hand, threw open the door, and charged inside with the gun drawn. The room was bathed in filtered sunset light. He saw the unmistakable, busty silhouette of Mrs. Toohey across the room. He could tell she was wearing one of her trademark short skirts. Joe looked down at his feet and saw the bodies of Dr. Albert Toohey and Rocco Washington.

He squinted at Mrs. Toohey. Her face was in the shadows, but he could clearly see her right arm raised, a revolver in her hand, pointed at his chest. He slowly stepped backwards; his eyes locked on her gun. Mrs. Toohey seethed, "I told him not to screw it up! I told him I knew where he lived!"

As ridiculous as it sounds, all Joe could think of was, *Matthew has some explaining to do.* He dove left, seeking cover behind the couch as Mrs. Toohey got off two quick shots.

Chapter 39

With his Glock at the ready, Joe yelled out from behind the couch. "Put it down, Mrs. Toohey! I'm armed!" He fired a shot into the ceiling to prove his claim. His ears rang from the gunshots inside the house. He was trying to clear his head when he thought he heard the backdoor slam shut. "Mrs. Toohey! You there? Throw out your gun! I don't want to shoot you!"

While he waited in the silence, Joe's heart was pounding. He felt beads of sweat running down his temples. He took in deep breaths, trying to calm himself, so he could think straight about what was happening. With his own eyes, he saw Mrs. Toohey shoot at him. He saw the bodies on the floor. But his brain was having trouble processing the data.

He heard a faint, "Help!" coming from close by to his right. He peeked out from behind the couch. Mrs. Toohey was nowhere to be seen. He heard the cry for help again. He crawled over to the two bodies on the floor. He reached Toohey first. Joe felt in vain for a pulse. There was a bloody hole in Toohey's neck. He then moved to Washington. There was lots of blood on the finely tailored, sharkskin suit, but the big man was alive.

"Hang in there, buddy. I'm going to help you," said Joe, as he saw pools of blood coming from Rocco's left shoulder and right thigh. Mrs. Toohey obviously wasn't an expert marksman, so her shot hitting Toohey's neck was providential. While he was trying to decide what to do next, Joe heard a car squeal out of the driveway. He stood for a second, so he could see out the living room window. He wanted to know which direction she was headed.

Rocco looked at Joe through hooded and confused eyes, but he quickly reoriented. "Who are you?" he asked weakly.

Joe was practiced at anonymity. "I live nearby. I was driving down the street and heard shots. Don't worry, I've got a first aid kit in the car. I'll go get it."

"Wait! She shot her husband! Is he okay?"

"I'm afraid he's dead. Let me get the kit." The shoulder wound didn't look too bad, but Joe was worried about the thigh injury. "I think a bullet may have nicked an artery," said Joe while he placed Rocco's right hand over the spreading red stain on his trousers. "Keep your hand here and press down as hard as you can. I've got a tourniquet in the car."

"No! I'll live. I've been shot before, worse than this. She killed Dr. Toohey and tried to kill me! Don't let her get away!"

"She's not important now. Getting you help is what matters. Just keep pressure on this wound." Joe began to stand. "Besides, she's long gone by now."

Rocco grabbed Joe by the wrist. "You don't understand. I know where she's going. You have to call the police!"

When Rocco suddenly moved, his suit coat flopped open, and Joe noticed Rocco's shoulder holster and gun for the first time. "You've got a gun?"

An embarrassed but honest Rocco lamented, "Yeah, she got the drop on me."

"But why are you carrying a gun?"

"I'm an investigator for the California Medical Board," said Rocco.

Joe pulled out the weapon and studied it. "This gun wasn't issued by the state. It's not even legal in California."

"So sue me," said Rocco. "Are you going to help get that woman or not?"

Joe was torn. He should leave Rocco, run to the car to fetch the first aid kit, and call the police. On the other hand, he wanted to hear what

Rocco knew. And he didn't want to call the police and have to answer a bunch of questions about Toohey's murder. Most important of all, discretion required that he not let his client be involved when the threads were unwound. From a personal perspective, he didn't want Mrs. Toohey to escape. And he had a feeling that Matthew would thank him for finding out where the wife was going—ahead of the police.

Joe stripped off his wide leather belt, sat back down beside Rocco, and fastened the belt around the bleeding thigh. "Okay, you've got thirty seconds. Then I'm going to get the first aid kit."

Rocco explained that he had been eavesdropping on Toohey and his wife in a diner. They were talking about leaving town in a small, rented aircraft. "They were supposed to go together, but I guess she had other plans. She must be on the way to an airport!"

"Sit tight," said Joe as he rose and opened the front door. He looked cautiously around before stepping outside. The fact that no one came out into the street to investigate the shots and that no one had called the police was only moderately surprising. The folks in this neighborhood were used to hearing loud gardening equipment with backfiring motors at all hours of the day. He stuck his gun in his waistband, covered by his now sweat-soaked Grateful Dead T-shirt. He quickly walked out to the street and looked, without success, for Matthew's car. Joe called Matthew as he pep-stepped to his car. "Where are you?" asked Joe.

"I'm just around the corner. I'm on the other line with Torrey. Can't talk now."

"Yes, you can!" replied Joe. "Toohey is dead, and Rocco Washington is shot badly. He's bleeding all over the place. He needs a doctor."

Matthew was dumbstruck. All he could think was, *What a dumpster fire; why did we ever get involved in this?* It wasn't the first time today that he wished for a normal life, to be a normal doctor, and to be a normal husband—devoid of any vigilante drama. Matthew turned onto Toohey's street. "Are you inside the house?" he asked Joe.

"I'm at my car on the street. I'm going to get my first aid kit. Rocco's inside the house. I used my belt for a tourniquet on his leg, which should hold him for a while, and he is also bleeding from the shoulder."

Just as Matthew was pulling up behind Joe's car, he said, "Wait a minute. Did they shoot each other?"

"Nope," said Joe. "The wife did it."

• • •

Matthew got out of his vehicle while motioning for Joe to stay put in his car. Matthew got in the passenger side. "The wife? How do you know?"

"Because she tried to kill me, too," said Joe vehemently. "Then she drove thataway." He gestured down the street. "Rocco believes she's got a private plane reserved for her getaway."

"Joe, I'm so sorry for dragging you into this! I swear that I'll explain everything later. Right now, we need to help Rocco. And we need to do something about the wife."

While they were talking, Joe pulled out his first aid kit and showed the contents to Matthew. "Jeez, you're better stocked than most urgent care centers," said Matthew.

"So, what do you want to do now?" asked Joe.

"Only one way to go at this point. I'm the doctor. I'll stay here and tend to Rocco. I got him into this mess. I have to stay and treat him. He's not going to die on my watch. Any idea which airport she would be going to?"

"Only one possibility. The only airport within range that allows small private planes to take off at this time in the evening is Braxton Airfield. Back in the day, it really bustled. It is pretty rundown now, but they still have lots of private aircrafts and tiny commercial planes hangered there. They do lots of rentals. A friend of mine took flying lessons there. Freelance pilots hang out there for weekend gigs to take semi-rich guys and their families up to places like Mammoth, Vegas, and Napa."

"Joe, if you are willing—"

"Sure, I'll go to the airport and—"

"No," said Matthew, whose brain was working overtime to figure out a new plan, "I'm pretty sure that she's not going straight to the airport. I need you to go back to Toohey's storage unit. I'm betting you'll find her there. If she is, just watch her and report what you see."

"She's had a big head start."

"You've bragged about your driving skills and that souped-up engine. Time to show them off. So, get going."

"Oh, one more thing," Matthew continued. "After she leaves, I need you to go into the unit and clean the place out. Other than furniture and the safe, which I suspect will be open and empty, take everything. The ledgers, the chemicals, the hand tools, everything." Matthew paused for a second, then changed one detail. "Actually, take all the chemicals except the Fentanyl. Leave that. Then just go home and wait for my call. In the next few days, I'll want you to drive it all up to my house in the Palisades so that I can go through it all."

"You don't want me to follow her from the storage unit?"

"No, we know where she's going. And I need you to secure all the stuff in that unit before the police get there. And sorry, one more thing. After the unit is cleared, and you're on the way home, use one of your burner phones and make an anonymous call to the police about the shooting here. Tell them one man is down, and another is being treated by a doctor just inside the front door. I don't want them coming in with hair-trigger fingers." Joe started to pull away. Matthew grabbed Joe's shoulder and pulled him back. "And don't let the wife see you!" warned Matthew.

"Sure, Matthew. No problem. I'm like the wind," said Joe. They shook hands. Matthew took the first aid kit and started running to the house. Joe sped away towards the Toohey storage unit.

• • •

Matthew strode quickly to the house. He had gotten halfway across the street when Hawk appeared from behind a neighbor's hedge. "Matthew!" he shouted.

Matthew stopped in his tracks. They talked quickly. "There you are," said Matthew. "I had a feeling you were around here somewhere."

"I saw two men go inside. Then I heard gunshots. Is Toohey dead?"

"Yes, the wife shot Toohey and Rocco Washington, the Medical Board guy. Rocco's still alive. I'm going in to treat him." Matthew knew he had to add, "You, Edwina, and Torrey—go after the wife. We're pretty sure she's headed to the Braxton Field airport where there's a rented private plane waiting to take her to who knows where. You guys intercept her."

"What about your PI? Where's he going?"

"To Toohey's storage unit. It sounds like the wife was the mastermind. I'm betting that she is stopping there to collect the money that I believe is in the safe. Joe Cook couldn't open the safe, but I'll wager that she can. She won't leave without the money. Joe is going to confirm my suspicions and will then clean out the unit for us."

"Sounds like a plan, Matthew." They gave each other a hug. "I'm sorry you're not coming with us. We'll get the wife, and I'll call when we can."

Matthew's last words before he ran into the house were the words of a concerned spouse. "Torrey's safety comes first!"

"Got it. I'll pick up Edwina on the way to the airport. And I'll call Torrey and let her know to meet us at the airport." Hawk flashed a peace sign and ran to where he had hidden his car.

Chapter 40

Rocco's eyes were closed, and his breathing was labored but even. Before tending to Rocco, Matthew went over to Toohey, whose neck was torn open. The pool of blood under Toohey extended several feet in every direction. Knowing it was pointless, Matthew's training still kicked in. He knew it was futile, but he checked for a pulse.

Then Matthew bent down over Rocco, surveyed his injuries, and gently removed the belt tourniquet from his thigh. The bleeding had stopped. Matthew pawed through the first aid kit and pulled out what he needed. He gave Rocco a morphine injection and slapped on a clean bandage. Rocco's eyes popped open. "What are you doing here?" he asked.

"How're you doing, Big Rocky? I decided to meet you here to see if you needed any help with Toohey. I told you he might be dangerous."

"He didn't shoot me! His wife did! And she shot Toohey, too!"

Matthew feigned surprise. "What? Are you sure?"

"Of course, I'm sure. And she tried to kill that neighbor who was in here helping me. He said he was going to his car to get a first aid kit."

"Yes," said Matthew. "I saw him carrying a bag across the street that I recognized as a hospital first aid kit. I told him I'm a doctor and asked if someone was hurt. He said there was a shooting victim inside the house. I took the bag and said I'd take care of it. I told him to go call the police."

Matthew knew there would be no police until Joe cleaned out the storage unit. He needed to stall everything with Rocco so that Hawk had enough time to abduct Mrs. Toohey.

"Don't let that woman get away!" Rocco was weak and angry. But he was also embarrassed that he had let Mrs. Toohey get the better of him. Rocco prided himself on his situational awareness, but she had taken him completely by surprise.

"She won't. You can count on it."

• • •

Hawk drove to Toohey's medical building to pick up Edwina. When he arrived, Edwina was nowhere to be seen. An unhappy Hawk called Edwina on her cell phone. "Where the hell are you?" barked Hawk when Edwina answered.

"I'm changing my clothes. I couldn't wear that baggy stuff anymore. I'm in a restroom right around the corner. Be right there!"

Hawk hung up and tried hard to keep in mind that he and Edwina were blood related.

He texted Torrey that he and Edwina would be there a little later than expected. When Edwina got in Hawk's truck carrying a paper bag, full of her disguise clothes, Hawk couldn't resist. "You and your clothes!"

Edwina shot back, "You and your guns!"

They looked at each other and burst out laughing.

• • •

Torrey had no regrets about leaving the boat. After having spent less than an hour breathing moldy air, she was relieved that the boat part of the plan had been apparently scrapped. But Hawk, unsurprisingly, had been vague about what was next. Matthew was not answering his phone, so she only knew that Mrs. Toohey had shot and killed her husband, that Big Rocky

215

was injured, and Matthew was staying behind to take care of him. She was to report to the Braxton Field airport, wherever that was, and to look for Hawk's car. Hawk said the airport was in Northern San Diego County, so Torrey again used Waze for directions. Somehow Hawk was convinced that Mrs. Toohey was headed there and that they could intercept her. She didn't like that Matthew was not going to be around for whatever came next, but she knew that he felt a moral obligation to ensure that no good guys died because of him.

Chapter 41

Joe was not normally a fast driver on public roads. He obeyed most traffic signs and signals. He wasn't one for weaving in and out of traffic to save thirty seconds. But setting all that aside, he was very capable of getting from point A to point B as quickly as anyone.

He had paid handsomely to have his old Nissan Sentra modified to give him plenty of horsepower to outrun bad guys—or even good guys if necessary—in order to protect a client. The awful, maroon-colored car was sold originally in 1990 with a 1.6-liter engine and almost no power. The mechanic swapped out the tiny engine for a 3.5-liter powertrain from a Nissan Maxima. He added oversized brakes and shocks. So now the dirty car with faded paint and rust spots could outrun many current police cars. Joe had taken racing lessons in the car from a retired NASCAR driver to be sure he could handle the power. On a private course, he had revved it up to a 125 miles per hour. It was exhilarating.

In the four years since the modifications, he'd only been able to make full use of the horsepower one time when he had witnessed a speeding Porsche 911 whose college-aged driver hit a little boy in a crosswalk and then took off. Joe had followed, racing at speeds over a hundred miles per hour until the Porsche finally went off the road and into a cement culvert. Joe had stopped long enough to observe the driver's head on the wrong side of the windshield. As Joe found himself speeding to the storage facility, he couldn't decide who was a worse human—Mrs. Toohey or the hit-and-run driver.

Driving the speed limit and staying on the main drag to the storage unit, Joe would have made it to the storage facility in about twenty minutes. By taking back roads and putting the pedal to the metal, Joe figured he could make it in under ten minutes. He actually made it in nine.

When he got to the storage unit, he half expected the unit door to be rolled up, the safe empty, and no sign of Mrs. Toohey. The sun was now down, and darkness was falling. Joe pulled up to the curb across from the storage facility. He parked in the same spot from which he had observed Dr. Toohey at the unit. Ignoring all speed and safety laws had paid off. Mrs. Toohey was still there.

Her car was stopped directly in front of the Toohey unit. Joe snickered to himself when he noticed that the security light that he had previously shot out with his BB gun still had not been replaced. From his position forty yards away, he could see that the unit's large door was rolled up and open. A desk lamp was on inside, but it didn't illuminate the entire interior. Joe could see Mrs. Toohey inside with a flashlight, but he couldn't tell what she was doing. He grabbed his low-light binoculars that were hanging on the backside of the passenger seat. He didn't have a great angle from inside the car. He moved the dome light switch to the "off" position, so it wouldn't light when he opened his door. When he was outside, he made sure no one was nearby. Then he tiptoed down into the thick bushes beside the road where he was shielded from random street traffic. He got into a comfortable crouch, next to a discarded Happy Meal bag, and trained his binoculars on Mrs. Toohey.

Mrs. Toohey was kneeling like a stone statue in front of the safe, her back to Joe. Matthew was right; she was after whatever was in the safe. The first movement inside the unit was the friendly orange cat that Joe had seen when he had broken into the unit. The cat was approaching Mrs. Toohey. Even from his distanced position, Joe could hear the loud, persistent "meows" coming from the cat. Mrs. Toohey stood and took a few steps towards the door. The cat met her and rubbed against her leg. Without a word, she kicked the cat and sent it flying out of the unit. The kick had the desired effect—the cat let out a yowl and ran off. Joe's assignment was just to watch and report. But seeing Mrs. Toohey's animal abuse tempted Joe to abandon his client duties and give Mrs. Toohey a taste of her own medicine. Except that she wouldn't be able to run off after Joe's kick.

Mrs. Toohey went back to the safe and resumed her attempt to open it.

• • •

Joe knew that Matthew wouldn't be able to talk, so Joe texted that he was at the storage unit, and Mrs. Toohey was there. He didn't expect a reply, and he didn't get one.

While watching through his binoculars from his hiding place, Joe reflected that he had been a private eye for more than ten years, and somehow, when working for Matthew for only a few weeks, he had witnessed more killings than in all of the other years combined. Assignments from Matthew were like the weekly episodes of television shows with characters like Jim Rockford, Jessica Fletcher, and Barnaby Jones—murder and mayhem everywhere they turn.

Joe watched Mrs. Toohey through the binoculars, which wasn't bad duty, if he ignored the fact that she had tried to kill him less than an hour ago. She eventually stood up, turned around so that she was facing Joe's direction, and leaned over with her hands on her hips; Joe guessed she was catching her breath from her busy night. Joe zoomed in on the low-cut blouse. The light wasn't that good, but he kept looking anyway. He wasn't surprised when he noticed a small tattoo of a dollar sign inside a heart symbol at the top of her left breast. *How fitting*, thought Joe.

Mrs. Toohey went over to the table where Joe had found the mortar and pestle. She picked up an olive-drab canvas duffle bag, very similar in style, but slightly smaller than what an army private might use. Using the duffle straps, she carried it across the unit and placed it on the cement floor in front of the safe.

Mrs. Toohey knelt again in front of the safe, but this time her body was angled differently so that Joe could see exactly what she was doing. Using both hands, she shoveled banded bundles of money into the duffle. It took her several minutes to empty the safe. She struggled to lift the now heavy bag up onto a table. She stood, facing Joe's direction. She looked around the unit, as if trying to decide whether she needed to take anything else with her.

Suddenly, the binoculars' field of vision was filled with movement. Puzzled, Joe lowered the binoculars and looked with his own unaided vision. A large man wearing a black trench coat came out of the shadows and with his back to Joe, stood in the opening of the storage unit. He was blocking Mrs. Toohey's exit. Then he began to advance towards her.

Chapter 42

Mrs. Toohey, clearly startled, almost jumped out of her Jimmy Choo flats. "Mrs. Borsky, you scared me! What are you doing here?" exclaimed Mrs. Toohey with an icy edge in her voice.

"Oh, so you do know my name," said Borsky caustically.

"Of course I do," said Mrs. Toohey. "I've been to the office many times!"

"Yes, I know. And you barely acknowledged me. Never once did you address me by name."

"I'm sure I did. But why in the world are you here? Do you have a storage unit here?"

"No. I see that the safe is empty. What's in the bag, Mrs. Toohey?" asked Borsky as she moved menacingly closer.

• • •

Joe couldn't hear any of the conversation, but he deduced that Mrs. Toohey was about to be robbed, or worse. He suspected that she had left her gun in her car; otherwise, she would have brandished it by now. The man's back was still to Joe. Mrs. Toohey was in full view, and Joe could see fear in her wide eyes and open mouth.

• • •

Mrs. Toohey didn't answer. She just dragged the duffle closer to herself. Borsky stared at her and asked another question. "Where's Dr. Toohey?"

"He's at home," replied Mrs. Toohey meekly.

Borsky looked again at the duffle bag. It was still unzipped, and bundles of bills were visible. She took another step forward. "He's dead, isn't he?"

"What?"

"You really think I'm stupid, don't you? Just like your husband did. He thought I was too dumb to see what was going on in the office because I'm not model material and don't wear fancy designer clothes."

"What was going on? See what?" asked Mrs. Toohey as she swallowed hard and tried to smile casually.

Borsky kept edging closer to Mrs. Toohey and the duffle bag of money. "I don't know what medicine Dr. Toohey was giving the patients, but if it were a legitimate treatment, he would have taken insurance payments. And he wouldn't have charged tens of thousands of dollars."

Mrs. Toohey backed up from the table, pulling the bag closer. "You're crazy! My husband was helping those kids. Whatever the parents paid, I'm sure it was reasonable."

"See, I was right. You do think I'm stupid. But frankly, it didn't take an Einstein to see that something criminal was happening. That husband of yours asked me to rent this storage unit for him. He said it was to store some of your personal belongings. Sounded fishy but whatever. Then I noticed all of these families were paying him by cashier's checks, often in unsealed envelopes. They'd drop them at the front desk. I peeked. The amounts were shocking, so I started to follow him. Every time a check was delivered, he would leave the office and go to his bank. He would then drive to this storage unit, go inside for two minutes, and then come out. He had to be negotiating the cashier's checks at the bank and then hiding the money here.

"And when he called me today and said he was leaving the country, I knew he was never coming back. I'd be left holding the bag, with nothing in my pocket—after all I did for him. I figured he was going to come here to collect the money. I closed up the office and came here to wait for him. I didn't really expect you to show up, but it makes no difference to me."

Mrs. Toohey needed time to think. "Were you going to kill my husband?"

"I really hadn't decided. But you being here instead of him makes it easy," said Borsky as she spread her arms widely.

Mrs. Toohey couldn't back up any further. She pulled the duffle bag up against her waist.

Her gun was in the glovebox of her car. She had to get to it. "Mrs. Borsky, you're right about my husband. He's dead. He never understood the potential of what I had created. I had to tell him what to do every step of the way. He was about to crack, and the authorities would have been all over us, and you, too. He was going to blow the whole thing because he was a weak man. A glorified pencil pusher. He was not willing to put up a fight." Mrs. Toohey opened the bag wide, so Borsky could see in. "Look, I agree you shouldn't go away empty handed. You helped my husband a lot. You deserve a cut. There's plenty of cash in this bag. I'll split it with you. How much do you want?"

"All of it." Borsky flexed her muscle-bound arms and stepped forward so that the table was the only thing between her and Mrs. Toohey.

• • •

Throughout her life, Mrs. Toohey had relied upon her looks and her ability to influence men. Even as a tween, she had noticed that the male species was susceptible to her exploitation. The boys at school gave her their ice cream at lunch. The male teachers let her homework slide. As she grew older and more mature, her influence increased as did her confidence in her ability to manipulate. Albert Toohey was her crowning achievement.

He was an easy seduction, and he was more than willing to do her bidding. After she convinced him to steal the FDA Fentanyl, it was all too simple to gain his cooperation in the lucrative cancer cure scheme. He balked for a nanosecond but came around when she modeled her new lingerie.

To seal the deal, she kept repeating that the cancer kids were doomed anyway, so why not make their last days more bearable with the pain medications. And as an added benefit, the Tooheys could make enough money to live on the ocean-view side of the street.

However, Borsky wasn't a man. She seemed entirely uninterested in Mrs. Toohey's good looks. She was clearly only interested in the bag of money that rested between the two women. Mrs. Toohey would have to try another approach.

"No way am I giving up all the money. I earned my share. I masterminded the whole thing. Have you any idea what I had to put up with being married to him? He was a feeble old man! Look at me! I could have had any man in the world. Think of what I missed out on being married to him. Yes, you could use force to take all of the money, but then what? You need me."

Borsky had been slowly edging around the table. She stopped just out of grabbing distance, sneering at Mrs. Toohey. Borsky was enjoying the fact that the timbre of Mrs. Toohey's voice had changed dramatically from the low confident tone used in the office to a high-pitched nervous babble. The Barbie doll face, with the plastic smile and the perfect white teeth, was gone. The bright eyes were now flat and black. The more Borsky looked at Mrs. Toohey, the more Borsky despised her. The sight of Mrs. Toohey aroused deep-seated anger, if not outright hate. "Is that a fact?" asked Borsky with suspicious eyes. "Why in the world shouldn't I take all of the money? Why shouldn't I tie you up, gag you, close the door, and leave town? No one would ever find you."

"Because," cried Mrs. Toohey, "my husband is dead in our house. And a man from the Medical Board is also there, either dead or severely injured. Another man heard the shots and busted in through the front door. I ran.

I'm sure the police are there right now. They will certainly be looking for me. And you, too, as his only employee. When they see you've disappeared, they'll hunt you down. You need me to help you escape. I can get us both out of the country. Tonight! Right now!"

"How?" inquired Borsky suspiciously. Just then, another car drove into the facility and past the Toohey unit. Borsky half turned towards the car and waved. The car drove on to another building.

Mrs. Toohey said, "At this moment, there is a small plane waiting to take me and my husband to Cabo San Lucas. I could get you on the plane instead of my husband. I could get you to Mexico tonight. You could take half of the money and disappear. I'll do the same with the other half."

Borsky considered the offer. Her mind was working overtime to figure out how to end up with every dime. But so was Mrs. Toohey's.

"Let's get in my car right now," said Mrs. Toohey. "I'll drive us to the airport and get us on the plane."

"What airport?" asked Borsky.

Mrs. Toohey took a chance with her answer. "I'm not going to tell you that now. I'll drive us there."

"Okay," said Borsky. "I can live with that. Except we'll take my car. I'm parked a few blocks away."

"No," said Mrs. Toohey, thinking of her gun in the glovebox of her car. "My car is right here. And I need the stuff in the trunk for the trip. Besides, the folks at the airport have my car on file in their records. I'll be able to drive right in." Mrs. Toohey held her breath and hoped that Borsky wouldn't guess that her car was not registered at the airport. And she hoped Borsky wouldn't look in the trunk because it was empty.

"I guess that makes sense. Your car is right here. Let's take it. But I'll drive." Mrs. Toohey resentfully let go of the duffle bag as Borsky grabbed for it.

This can work, thought Mrs. Toohey.

Chapter 43

Joe watched as the man lifted the heavy duffle and carried it to the car. Mrs. Toohey trailed behind. With ease, he threw the big bag in the back seat. He opened the driver's side door, and noticing the position of the seat, he moved the seat back as far as it would go. He contorted himself to get into the sporty car. Mrs. Toohey easily draped herself into the passenger seat. Joe made note that the car was headed in the direction of the Braxton Airfield and texted Matthew with the developments. Matthew couldn't imagine who the man traveling with Mrs. Toohey could be.

• • •

According to Waze, Torrey had arrived at the small airport. Torrey was skeptical because all she saw was a cluster of small WWII style cinder-block buildings inside a tall chain-link fence, topped with concertina wire. Only one small building was lighted. If there was an airstrip on the other side of the buildings, she couldn't see it. A chain-link sliding gate on rollers was open, leading to an asphalt parking lot with about twenty spaces. The lot, filled with potholes and the occasional weed, had seen better days. The only car in the lot was an entry level Tesla. She recalled that Mrs. Toohey drove a Porsche. The security lights shining onto the parking lot were relatively dim. They didn't illuminate more than a few feet outside the gate. No other cars were parked on the street, so Torrey concluded that she was the first to arrive. She backed up about thirty yards from the gate and parked in darkness alongside the fencing. Whenever a car approached from either direction, she ducked down, so she wouldn't be illuminated by headlights. The eerie silence was broken only by the calls of nearby native coyotes. She hoped Hawk would arrive soon.

• • •

"Where are we going?" asked Edwina as they drove to the Braxton airport. "Did you get Toohey? What's happening?" cried Edwina in confusion.

"You want to go on an airplane ride, little brother?" asked Hawk with a half-smile.

"What are you talking about? I thought we were going on a boat. And in case you still haven't noticed, I'm not your brother anymore."

Hawk looked over at Edwina but ignored the last comment. "Change of plan. Matthew is out. The boat is out. Toohey is dead. We're now going to get Toohey's wife. She's the one behind all of this," said Hawk.

After he had filled Edwina in on the details, she said in a mystified tone, "Based on everything I had heard, I had wondered what she saw in that decrepit old man."

Hawk nodded. "Oldest story known to man. She used her beauty to make Toohey her puppet and to secure her meal ticket. When the walls started to crumble, he was no use to her anymore. She was always about the money."

Edwina said wistfully, "You think anyone will ever pretend to love me for my money?"

"Do you have any?"

"No, not really."

"There's your answer."

Edwina laughed ruefully, but she secretly pouted.

• • •

On the drive to the airport, Borsky peppered Mrs. Toohey with questions. The answers were entirely insufficient to Borsky.

"How much money is in the duffel bag?"

"I don't know. A lot."

"Why were the parents of the sick kids paying your husband so much?"

"He was a good doctor."

"What was in the saline bags?"

"Cancer medicine."

"Why didn't the medicine cure any of the kids?"

"It doesn't work on everybody."

Rather than play Mrs. Toohey's game, Borsky decided to ask more serious questions later, when her hands were free. "You're lying. But no matter. We'll have hours together in the plane as travel buddies. You can tell me the full story then."

• • •

As soon as Mrs. Toohey's car was out of sight, Joe went back to his car and drove into the storage facility. He backed up to the Toohey unit so that his truck was almost touching the door. Mrs. Toohey had closed the door and set the padlock, but it took Joe all of seven seconds to grab his bolt cutters, snip off the lock, and get inside. The storage facility was deserted, so Joe left the door open, while he looked around. The place looked the same as it had when he was last there. He gathered all of the notebooks, ledgers, and statements and put them in his open trunk. He found a couple of empty boxes and used them to load up bags of pills, chemicals, and equipment. He placed the boxes on top of the loose papers. Within fifteen minutes, the unit was cleaned out, except for the bags of pink Fentanyl pills, which Joe left in plain view. In an abundance of caution, he used sterile wipes from the worktable to wipe down anything that he might have touched on either of his visits.

As soon as he was back on the road, he texted Matthew that the assignment was complete. He used a burner phone to alert the police to the shootings at Toohey's house. After the call, he stopped, smashed the phone with a hammer, and then threw it into an open apartment complex dumpster.

After a day of mayhem and murder, he couldn't wait to get home and play with his model trains.

• • •

Matthew saw Joe's text that he was finished in Toohey's storage unit. He knew the police would soon be at Toohey's residence. Then there would be the medical examiner, coroner, and who knows who else. Matthew knew he was going to be stuck at the house until late in the night. He wished with all of his might that he could be with Torrey, Hawk, and Edwina. He took Rocco's hand and held it tightly. "Hang in there, Big Rocky," he whispered.

• • •

As Borsky drove, Mrs. Toohey gave her turn-by-turn directions. Borsky had never been in North County San Diego, so she dutifully followed Mrs. Toohey's instructions. Mrs. Toohey figured that her best chance to get a hold of her gun in the glove compartment was to distract Borsky right when they arrived at the airport. She knew she had one bullet left, and she needed to make it count.

• • •

Several minutes after receiving Hawk's text, a car with its brights on slowly approached from behind Torrey. Her car was awash with light. She thought back to her debates with Matthew as to which superpower would be the best to have. Matthew thought "flight," but Torrey was adamant about "invisibility." She had a friend in grade school whose superpower wish was to be a milkman so that she could give the neighborhood kids rides in her truck. Even six-year-old Torrey thought that was a dumb wish. She didn't have the heart to explain that milk delivery was open to everyone. Through the years, Torrey had hung on to her wish for invisibility. That superpower would sure come in handy right now.

Torrey hunkered down as low as she could. The car passed her and then stopped in the middle of the road, right in front of the airport gate. It was a Porsche. But there were two people in the car.

● ● ●

Borsky put the car in park and looked though the open gate at the airport buildings. "You sure this is it?" asked Borsky. "Where's the plane?"

"This is it," replied Mrs. Toohey. "The runway is behind the buildings. I'm sure the plane is there waiting for us."

Borsky looked at Mrs. Toohey and considered her options. "I don't want to park your car in the lot," she said. "Let's at least make the police work for it, right, partner?"

"Sure, I guess so," said Mrs. Toohey, even though she wasn't sure what Borsky was talking about.

"I'll just go up the road a bit and pull into a side street. Then we can walk from there. Sound good?" said Borsky with a fake smile.

Not that she had any choice, but Mrs. Toohey said, "Okay." She got ready to reach for the glove compartment latch.

Borsky drove another quarter mile and turned up a dingy dirt road. "This street looks like it will do," said Borsky. She crossed over two sets of abandoned railroad tracks and pulled over in front of what appeared to be a defunct railway station. The moment Borsky stepped on the brake, she swung her huge right arm and landed a backward forearm into Mrs. Toohey's nose. Blood spurted like a geyser. Before Mrs. Toohey could scream, Borsky gripped the back of Mrs. Toohey's head. She jerked Mrs. Toohey's head around so that their faces were inches apart. "I asked you some questions before. Now you're going to give me the answers."

After a ten-minute session of question and answer, Borsky was satisfied that she had all of the information that Mrs. Toohey could provide. Then in one mighty motion, she smashed Mrs. Toohey's pretty face into the polished burl dash. After a quick check to be certain that Mrs. Toohey's neck was broken, Borsky used Mrs. Toohey's skirt to clean blood splatters off her face and hands. She found the vehicle registration in the glovebox, along with a handgun, and stuffed them in her coat pocket. No sense making it easy for them.

She picked up Mrs. Toohey's purse and exited the vehicle. She snatched the duffle bag out of the back seat and slung it over her shoulder. While she walked back to the airport, she rifled through Mrs. Toohey's purse and confirmed that she was carrying a valid driver's license and passport. And for good measure, Borsky found a wad of a hundred-dollar bills. She thought about how it was going to be a nice change of pace to be the wife, and not the lackey, of a doctor.

Chapter 44

Torrey was puzzled by the Porsche that had paused in front of the airport gate. She assumed it was Mrs. Toohey's car, but then it drove on. And if it was Mrs. Toohey, she had not been alone.

Torrey was even more baffled when she saw who was walking back in her direction. It was the unmistakable form and face of Mrs. Borsky—the receptionist from Toohey's office. She was alone. Mrs. Toohey and her car were AWOL.

When Borsky got to the gate entrance, Torrey, who was peering over the steering wheel, could see that Borsky was carrying a large army duffle bag and a small dainty purse. With a hollow feeling and a sense of impending dread, Torrey was starting to put the pieces together. She didn't like what the finished puzzle was looking like.

• • •

Hawk and Edwina were making good time, but it was dark, and they were passing through an industrial part of town that, Hawk supposed, had once been a hub of employment. Now, shops were closed, and rusted steel structures were sad reminders of a time when California had been more than a collection of service jobs.

They passed under a bridge that was covered with graffiti. Hawk saw two teenagers hanging over the side of the bridge spray painting KILL ALL PIGS. Hawk slammed on the brakes, rolled down his window, and reached for a Beretta 92 in his coat pocket.

"Hawk," pleaded Edwina, "don't do it. C'mon, we have to go."

"These punks make me sick. I—"

"Yes, we all stipulate that they are punks. If you ask me—"

"I'm not."

"Well you should," countered Edwina.

Hawk was hesitating, as if he were in another world. "Those pigs," fumed Hawk, "put their lives on the line every day for those punks."

"I know," said Edwina, "but Hawk, you've always discounted my opinion. You've never listened to me, even as kids. But I'm telling you now, Torrey is waiting for us. Mrs. Toohey is going to get away if we don't step on it!"

Hawk looked at Edwina. "If I had the time, I'd paint those idiots with their own product."

"Well, you don't have the time. Let's go." Hawk gave the punks one last stare and drove on. Edwina observed, "You know you sounded like Dad just then. That's something he would have said."

"Don't mention that bastard to me," snapped Hawk.

Edwina stared at him in shock. "What? I thought you two were each other's cheering section. You were always his favorite. I thought you idolized him!"

"If I ever did, I regret it. After what he did to you, I told him I never wanted to see him again. He disowned you, so I disowned him," said Hawk quietly.

"You never told me that." Edwina's eyes glistened as she stared at her brother in wonder.

"Why should I have to?" said Hawk as he reached over and squeezed Edwina's arm.

• • •

Torrey called Matthew. No answer. She called Hawk. When his phone buzzed, he saw it was Torrey and handed the phone to Edwina. "You talk to her."

"Torrey, this is Edwina."

Torrey dispensed with greetings. "Edwina, something's wrong. I just saw Mrs. Borsky at the airport."

"What? No! It's Mrs. Toohey who's on the way."

Edwina put the phone on speaker, and Torrey detailed what she had seen. Hawk listened and then laid out a new plan which culminated with a one-way flight for Borsky over the desert southwest. With surprise in her voice, Edwina's first and only comment was, "Since when do you know how to fly a plane?"

Hawk waved off Edwina's astonishment with the motto of the Army Rangers, "Rangers lead the way!"

"Wait a second. You've always said that your unit was an infantry special operations force, not air force."

"That's true enough. But during our training, we had Jump Week, where we had to complete a number of parachute jumps. I enjoyed the flight part of that so much that I cajoled the pilot into giving me off-the-record private flying lessons. He always took off and landed, but he explained everything to me and let me fly the plane when we were in the sky."

"So, let me get this straight. You've never actually landed a plane?"

"How hard could it be?" laughed Hawk.

Torrey interjected, "That's all very interesting you two, but Hawk, aren't you forgetting something even more important?"

Hawk replied, "Yes, I know there's a major flaw in the plan. I'm still working on that."

"What?" said Edwina. "What's the flaw?"

Hawk stated before Torrey could, "How we save ourselves."

"I might have an idea," said Torrey. "Let me make a call."

• • •

Inside the cramped office which passed as a terminal for passengers, Borsky walked up to the only employee around who, dressed in chinos, a blue blazer, and a pilot's hat adorned with gold braids and wings, looked up from a desk cluttered with papers. He rose and offered his hand. "Good evening," he said. "You must be Mrs. Toohey. I'm Tony Mason. I'll be flying you and your husband down to Cabo tonight." Tony looked behind Borsky, obviously looking for a husband.

"Actually, it will just be me. Dr. Toohey got detained at the hospital. He was called in to do a surgery on a young girl. He suggested I go on ahead, and he'd arrange to come down in a day or two," said Borsky firmly. If Tony was taken aback by Borsky's looks or her outfit of tight Adidas sweatpants, an unwashed Nike "Just Do it" T-shirt, and a faded dark trench coat with some sort of stains, he didn't show it. He was often surprised by how shabbily rich people dressed when traveling. And what was with the old army duffle?

"How long before we can depart?" asked Borsky. "I'd like to get to Cabo as soon as possible."

"Just need to finish up with the flight plan," said Tony. "I made some coffee. Would you like a cup for the road?" He gestured to the glass pot full of coffee steaming on a single burner in the corner of the room. Next to the coffee pot was a spartan stack of white Styrofoam cups and a paper bowl of sugar packets.

Borsky looked at the set-up. "No thanks. Where can I sit while waiting?" asked Borsky as she noticed that the few metal-framed, yellow-vinyl chairs in the office were littered with boxes, papers, and trash.

Tony scurried over to one of the chairs and began cleaning it off. "The cleaning crew doesn't come in 'till later," said Tony with an embarrassed look.

"How about if I just wait in the plane? Would you mind?"

"Sure. As I'm the pilot and flight attendant all in one, I'll show you the way. Then I'll come back here and finish up. Can I carry your bag for you?"

"No thanks. I've got it." Borsky allowed Tony to lead the way to the plane.

"You're in luck," said Tony as they walked. "We get to take the Beechcraft Bonanza G36 this trip. It can get us there in comfort without refueling. Much more room than the little Cessna that I sometimes get." Tony continued the sales pitch as if Borsky cared in the slightest. "Yes, siree, did you know that the Beechcraft model has been in service since 1947? This baby has it all, including the Garmin G1000 avionics system." As Tony blathered on, Borsky stepped up on the built-in stairway and considered the four leather seats in the passenger compartment—two forward-facing seats across from two rear-facing. She selected a forward-facing seat next to the door, so she could keep an eye on the pilot in the cockpit. Borsky placed the duffle on her lap, left hand securely on top, right hand in her coat pocket.

Chapter 45

Hawk and Edwina pulled up behind Torrey's car. Because Hawk had turned off his headlights about two hundred meters before the airfield, Torrey didn't see Hawk's truck until it arrived. Torrey jumped out of her car and walked back to meet her friends.

The bed of Hawk's pickup truck contained two stainless-steel footlockers and a heavy-duty backpack. Hawk unzipped the backpack and produced a small Maglite to illuminate what was inside. There were several handguns of different sizes, knives, and lots of ammunition. The outside pockets were filled with gadgets and tools. Torrey's mouth dropped open, but no sound came out. Edwina just said, "Jeez, Hawk!"

"Who wants one?" asked Hawk shaking the loose guns in the backpack.

Hearing no immediate reply, Hawk said, "No takers? Suit yourselves." He opened the footlockers one at a time. There were rifles, night goggles, military-grade flashlights, flares, flash grenades, and many other wartime items that were unrecognizable to Torrey and Edwina.

"You've got your own army surplus store," wisecracked Edwina.

Torrey frowned. "Hawk, what's all this for? We're not going to war!"

"Yes, we are," said Hawk. "Better to be overprepared than under," he proclaimed as he filled the extra space in his backpack with items from the footlockers. "The worst that can happen is that you come overdressed to the party. And never forget, desperate people do desperate things." He opened a separate compartment and pulled out a bullet-proof vest. "You two need to flip for it. Winner puts it on."

Edwina said, "No way! Torrey, you wear it."

Torrey balked. "Hawk, if there is any gunplay, I have a feeling you're going to be in the line of fire long before we're involved. You should wear it."

"Suit yourself," said Hawk. "By the way, Torrey, were you able to fix the hole in my plan?"

"Yes, we're all set. Just need the final coordinates."

Hawk gave a thumbs up. "One more thing before we roll. We need to confirm what happened to Mrs. Toohey. Torrey, you said there were two people in the Porsche when it stopped in front of the gate."

"Correct," said Torrey.

"Are you sure?"

"Yes."

"Maybe you saw two headrests, and you assumed there were two heads on the other side."

"No, there were two people. I'm positive. I saw movement."

"You say you saw the car drive off in that direction," said Hawk while pointing down the street. "And then you saw Mrs. Borsky from Dr. Toohey's office walking back alone and through the gate not more than ten minutes later. Is that right?"

"Yes."

"You sure it was Borsky?"

"Yes. I'm. Sure. I never forget a face," said Torrey with a trace of exasperation in her voice.

"Okay then. Torrey you hold down the fort right here. I'll go find Mrs. Toohey's car. If our collective suspicions are correct, the car must be on a side street not far away. And Mrs. Toohey will be inside the car. Edwina, you make your way to a position where you can see if the pilot is getting ready to leave. If he is, stall him until I get back."

"How?" asked Edwina.

"You'll think of something. Now go!"

"Should I put my disguise back on?"

"No, won't be necessary. Besides, Torrey will need to wear your disguise. Borsky saw her when she went to interview Dr. Toohey. We don't want Borsky to recognize her, at least not right away."

Edwina argued, "Borsky saw me in the office, too!"

"You're not that memorable," countered Hawk as he slapped Edwina on the back.

Neither Torrey nor Edwina was particularly anxious to confirm that Mrs. Toohey was dead. But before either could react or argue the point, Hawk zipped up his black bomber jacket and shooed them away from the truck. He sped off.

Edwina took off jogging towards the gate. She kept low and circled around the perimeter of the parking lot until she had a clear view of inside the office. She squatted in a dark spot created by the poor positioning of the security lights. The pilot was sitting at a desk shuffling papers and finishing a take-out sandwich. He looked to be in his late-twenties and seemed in no rush to finish his meal. Or to get on the plane.

After a few minutes of watching, Edwina couldn't help herself. She felt compelled to find out where Borsky was. Edwina crept down a pedestrian walkway alongside the building which led to the runway. There was only one plane in sight. It was sitting on the tarmac about thirty yards from the back door of the offices. Only the cockpit light was on, but she could clearly see the orange embers of a lit cigarette in the passenger compartment. Borsky was a smoker, just like Dr. Toohey. It had to be her.

Edwina hurried back to her position in the parking lot. The pilot stuffed papers into a flight bag and then filled his thermos with coffee. Edwina was about to call Hawk on the phone, when Hawk tapped her on the shoulder. Edwina jumped. "Aauugghh!" she muffled a cry. "You scared the bejeezus out of me!"

Hawk shrugged. "I found Mrs. Toohey. Dead. Face smashed in.

Broken neck. Borsky shoved her down into the front foot well. She probably won't be found for days. Borsky is crazy strong, and I suspect, just plain crazy."

They walked back to Hawk's truck. Torrey, who was now wearing Edwina's disguise outfit, including the Halloween glasses, and Edwina stood by the tailgate waiting for instructions. Hawk said, "Okay, I'm going in. Has anyone come by while I was gone?"

Edwina swallowed hard, not sure how Hawk would receive the news of her reconnaissance mission. "The pilot is in the office looking at papers and eating a sandwich. Borsky is sitting in the plane smoking a cigarette."

"You went down to the plane? On your own?"

"Yes, I did."

"Good job! Good intel is always helpful! Makes my job a lot easier!" He tousled Edwina's hair.

Hawk looked at his co-conspirators and said, "Okay, you two are on standby right here until I come out." Without another word, Hawk strode towards the office door. Emboldened by her brother's praise, Edwina whispered to Torrey, contrary to orders, that she was going to follow Hawk just in case.

• • •

While Torrey was alone in her car, she texted a short status report to Matthew. She knew he would be anxious about her safety. *M, we r at the airport. Borsky is here. Hawk is going to steal the plane. Wish u were here, T.* She ended with a heart emoji.

• • •

Tony had his flight bag in one hand and his thermos in the other when Hawk appeared. "Sorry, sir. We're closed. If you're wanting to book a plane, someone will be here tomorrow morning at 8:00 a.m. There's a brochure over there listing our planes and rates," Tony said with a smile. "And if you need a pilot, my card is on the counter. I'm available most days this week."

Hawk rested his hands on the counter. "How about right now? Can you take me on a sightseeing tour?"

"No can do. I've got a lady in the plane right now. She's in a hurry, so I've got to get out there."

"Oh, where are you taking her?"

"Cabo. But it's just a there and back for me."

Hawk had a Beretta M9 pistol in his waistband, a semi-automatic handgun in his concealed shoulder holster, a small Glock in the small of his back, and a ten-inch serrated Bowie knife on his hip. He sized Tony up and knew that he would not have to use a weapon to get his cooperation. Between Tony's outfit, his tortoise shell eyeglasses, his perfectly coifed man bun, and a gaudy USC class ring, he looked like an usher at the opera.

Hawk took a few steps towards Tony and opened his jacket. He put his hand on the visible gun handle protruding from his jeans. Tony's smile faded. "Oh, crap," said Tony. "Are you going to shoot me?"

"Nah, nothing like that," said Hawk. "I just need to borrow your plane."

"Hey, man," said Tony holding both hands up, "it's not my plane. I just work for the guy who owns it. You want it, you take it. No skin off my nose."

"Very generous. I also need to borrow your car. That your Tesla that's charging out there?"

"C'mon! It's a lease. If anything happens to it, I have to pay!" Tony looked like he was going to cry.

"Just need it for a few minutes. Keys?" said Hawk as he snapped his fingers.

Tony dug into his pants pocket and pulled out the car fob. He tossed it to Hawk.

Hawk left nothing to chance. "I didn't see any security cameras, inside or out. Are there any that are hidden?"

"No, sir."

"Any security guards that come around during the night?"

"No, sir."

Edwina was crouched, her eyes glued on Hawk and the pilot, as she watched through a small window on the side of the office. Her heart was pounding but skulking around in the dark was exhilarating. She was spellbound by Hawk's performance in questioning the pilot. She marveled at Hawk's ability to confidently control the scene and the pilot with ease, without the use of actual force. It was all implied. Just the rough edge to Hawk's calm veneer had convinced Tony that running, or fighting, was futile. Edwina felt small and invisible as Hawk took charge while she lurked in the safety of the shadows. It was the same feeling she had experienced growing up with their father.

She wondered what she would have done if the pilot had been a macho man with a shotgun who somehow had gotten the drop on Hawk. Would she have had the courage to charge the pilot? Sure, she had helped Matthew to subdue an escaping prisoner at San Quentin, but she knew that she had acted on pure adrenaline with no time to think about the potential consequences. She believed she would risk a bullet to save Hawk, but she realized she would never know for sure until faced with the dilemma in real life. Fortunately, she knew that the question in this case was purely hypothetical because Hawk would never allow a civilian to get the better of him.

"What's your name, son?" asked Hawk.

"Tony, sir."

"Tony, I'm going to walk out the front door. I'll be back in less than thirty seconds. I want you to stay right where you are. Will you do that?"

"Yes, sir."

"I'll be really upset if you've moved. And you don't want that, do you, Tony?"

"No, sir."

"Okay, I'm leaving now. Count to thirty. See if I'm not back before you finish. Will you do that?"

"Yes, sir."

Hawk stepped out the door and was surprised to find Edwina there, but he didn't mention it. "Take the Tesla. Have Torrey drive her car to a public place about a mile away and leave it. Follow her and drive her back here in the Tesla. Then do the same with my truck. Return the Tesla to this parking lot and put the key inside on the desk. Don't get caught speeding but come back as soon as you can." Edwina nodded and jogged over to the Tesla.

When Hawk walked back inside, Tony was on number twenty-six. "See?" said Hawk. "I always do what I say. Now, I need you to do a couple more things for me, okay?"

"Yes, sir."

"The first thing is that I need you to go out to the plane and tell your passenger that you just got a call from the owner of the plane and that he, along with two friends, are going to take the plane to Cabo. The owner will fly the plane, not you. She can ride along if she wants. She won't like it, but she'll agree. Tell her that the owner is going to be here in just a few minutes. Got all that?"

"Yes, sir."

"Repeat it back for me." Tony did, word for word.

• • •

When Tony returned from talking to Borsky, he reported that she was extremely upset but said she would stay on the plane. "Thank you, Tony. As I predicted. Now, one last thing. I need you to go into the storeroom over there," said Hawk. Tony didn't say a word. He just robotically shuffled over without any fuss, opened the door, and stepped inside. He stood like a statue. "Now sit on the floor next to that exposed water pipe." Tony sat right down. "Now give me your hat."

"What? That hat was my dad's," said Tony weakly. "See how it says 'United Airlines' on it? He was a pilot at United for thirty years."

"I'll leave it in the plane for you, I promise," said Hawk. Tony reluctantly complied. His man bun looked less tidy without the hat.

"Hand me your pilot's credential." Tony looked crushed, so Hawk said, "Stop whining. I'm going to give it right back." Hawk took close-up photos of Tony's face and his credential. "Now your cell phone." Tony handed it over without a word. Hawk took photos of Tony's cell number and his contact list. Using two zip ties that had been intended for Dr. Toohey, Hawk secured Tony's right wrist to the water pipe.

"Tony, when does this place open up in the morning?"

"Cleaning crew comes in around five o'clock, first regular employees around six o'clock. The gals that rent out the planes come in at eight o'clock."

"Tony, listen carefully. In the morning, when you are discovered and untied, you will call the police and tell them that the person who tied you up and stole the plane was a 6'5" skinny young man, with a scar on his forehead. He said he had no car or money. He asked you if there was enough gas in the plane to get to Sacramento where his girlfriend lived. He said he would ditch the plane somewhere obvious near his destination. You will not mention my existence by inference or description. And when asked, you will say Mrs. Toohey never showed up. Got all that?"

"Yes, sir."

"Repeat it for me." Tony did, word for word.

"Tony, that lady in the plane is not Mrs. Toohey. She's an evil person who has committed unspeakable acts. I'm going to take her up in the plane and teach her a lesson. I have all of your identification information. I have a good friend in the police department. If I hear that the police are looking for anyone other than a skinny 6'5" scarred guy who was going to Sacramento, I'll come for you to teach you a lesson. Do you want me to come teach you a lesson?"

Tony replied with terror in his voice. "No, sir."

"You need to use the restroom before I go?"

"No," sighed Tony stoically.

"Listen, Tony. I'm going to leave your cell phone on the desk, so you can have it back when the cleaning crew finds you in the morning. I suggest you use the night to reflect on your future. You have nothing to fear from me as long as you heed my instructions. Will you do that?"

"Yes, sir."

Hawk grabbed two bottles of water and a carton of granola bars off the storeroom shelf and set them down next to Tony. He walked out of the storeroom, closing the door behind him. On his way out to collect Edwina and Torrey, he grabbed Tony's thermos of hot coffee. It was going to be a long night.

Chapter 46

When Edwina and Torrey returned with the Tesla, Hawk was waiting outside, drinking Tony's coffee. It was a far cry from his favorite Starbucks special Columbian blend, but it sure beat the sludge he had to drink while hunkered down inside caves and foxholes in Afghanistan. Edwina exclaimed, "Are you kidding me? You're drinking coffee right now?"

"It's freshly brewed. No sense letting it go to waste," said Hawk as he screwed the top back on and stuffed the thermos into an empty water bottle holder in his backpack. "Besides, it would be stone cold soon if I let it just sit inside the building."

Torrey, feeling serious despite wearing Edwina's clown-like oversized men's clothing and Halloween eyeglasses asked, "Now what, Hawk?"

"Now we get on the plane, introduce ourselves to our fellow passenger, and take off."

"Wait!" cried Edwina. "Are we just going to shove her out of the plane? How's that going to work? And then what? We can't just return here with the plane! What—"

Hawk interrupted and asked Torrey, "Are we good to go?"

"Yes, I provided the generalities already. Just need to provide details as soon as you have them."

"Edwina," said Hawk, "do you trust me?"

After the slightest of hesitations, Edwina replied with gusto, "Yes!"

"Then let's do this thing," said Hawk.

No one spoke. No one needed to.

• • •

The three of them marched across the tarmac to the waiting plane. Just before they started to board, a burning half-smoked cigarette flew out of the door onto the ground. Edwina and Torrey shrugged at each other and then gave one another a "here we go" thumbs up. Hawk poked his head into the passenger compartment and said to Borsky, "Good evening, ma'am, sorry for the delay and the change in plans. I know you and your husband booked this flight to Cabo, but my friends and I decided to go to Cabo at the last minute. So, I'm paying the pilot for his lost wages, and of course, your flight will be no charge. Will that be okay?"

"Well," said Borsky, "I'm not happy about the situation, but if the flight is free, I guess it will be fine."

"That's great. Let me introduce everybody. I'm your pilot tonight, and everyone just calls me Hawk." As Torrey and Edwina stuck their heads in the doorway, Hawk said, "And this is Edwina and Torrey. What was your name again, ma'am?"

"Toohey. Hillary Toohey."

Torrey was taken aback when Hawk used their real names. *But*, she asked herself, *what difference could it make at this point?*

As Edwina and Torrey were looking at the seating options, Hawk said, "Why don't we make this a little cozier? That way we can talk and hear each other better." He folded down the seat directly across from Borsky. He then climbed into the cockpit and folded down the copilot's seat back. "There!" Hawk said. "Much better. Everyone get comfortable now. We should be in the air in no time." Edwina took the seat next to Borsky while Torrey sat with her back to the cockpit, kitty-corner from Borsky.

The cockpit was far more sophisticated than the old military plane that Hawk had learned on. But he quickly determined which button to push in order to start the engine. The runway looked short, and the runway lights were old-school incandescent bulbs. Hawk imagined that only small lightweight planes could land here—no commercial or private jets. While he taxied into position for takeoff, he hoped he could get the plane into the air without crashing. He studied the dash and made sure that he knew how to engage the autopilot. With no air traffic control tower to contend with, Hawk taxied to the runway and hit the gas. The plane jerked up and into the dark moonless night.

In the passenger compartment, the awkward silence was louder than the motor. Edwina tried to get Borsky relaxed and talking so that she was not ready for what was to come. "I forgot my smokes," said Edwina. "Anyone got a spare?"

Torrey squinted a questioning look at Edwina and replied, "Sorry, I don't smoke."

Edwina turned to Borsky, asking, "Ma'am, do you have a cigarette I could bum?"

Borsky did not look back at Edwina. She simply said, "No." Borsky sat looking out the window like a silent monolith clutching the duffle bag on her lap. Borsky's loud breathing was audible even over the engine noise. Torrey took sneak peeks at Borsky, wondering how this was going to play out. Edwina thought about how strong Borsky looked. This was not going to be as simple as when the target was tiny Mrs. Toohey.

Torrey wasn't afraid of what might happen. She was more curious as to how far Borsky would go in impersonating Mrs. Toohey. "So, Mrs. Toohey, what takes you to Cabo this evening?" asked Torrey with as much false friendliness as she could muster.

Borsky jerked her head in Torrey's direction and looked hard at Torrey as if she were calculating whether to respond. For just a moment, Torrey thought that Borsky recognized her, even with Edwina's disguise. But that feeling passed when Borsky showed no recognition, so Torrey felt

248

comfortable removing her glasses. Borsky reluctantly replied, "My husband and I were going down for some R & R, but he couldn't make it tonight. He's going to meet me in a day or two."

The small talk continued in spurts and starts for a little over an hour. As Hawk expected, Borsky seemed unaware that they were heading more east than south towards Baja, California. Suddenly, Hawk was climbing out of the cockpit and into the passenger compartment. He casually said as he made his way through the opening created by the lowered seatbacks, "I put us on autopilot for the time being, so I could get in on the conversation." As Hawk was putting the seat into an upright position and getting settled directly across from Borsky, Torrey's shoulders tensed, and her jaw clenched, wondering what Hawk was going to do next.

Edwina, on one hand, was happy Hawk was back here with them. On the other hand, she knew that the moment was near when everything was going to hit the fan.

Hawk glared at Borsky. "You know," he said, knowing that at this low altitude he had about fifteen minutes before they reached the hills and he would have to resume control of the plane, "I've been thinking about it since we took off. You don't really look like a Toohey."

Borsky first looked puzzled, and then she frowned and tried to look unconcerned, as if Hawk had made a comment about the weather. "What's that supposed to mean?" she asked as she clutched the duffle.

As he spoke, Hawk pulled out his ten-inch-long serrated Bowie knife. "I think you look more like a Borsky," said Hawk with a penetrating stare. Borsky used her legs to push herself back into her seat as far as she could.

For a long moment, everyone froze. Hawk was ready to pounce. Edwina was staring at Borsky's right hand which was still buried in her coat pocket. Torrey's breath quickened, and she primed herself for chaos. No one was prepared for bargaining.

"What do you want?" said Borsky warily.

"What do you think we want?" asked Hawk.

"Look, if you know who I am, you know what's in the bag. It's all untraceable. I'll split it with you. Let's make a deal."

"What's in it for us?" asked Hawk.

"My silence," replied Borsky with confidence. "I don't know who you are, but I recognized your two cronies immediately." Then directing her words to Torrey, she added, "Those clothes don't suit you, miss. And by the way, 'Bella Swan' may have fooled Dr. Toohey, but not me. I know it was you who stole the saline bag. Mrs. Toohey admitted to me that she and Dr. Toohey were scamming parents by promising a cancer cure. I presume you discovered that the medicine in the saline bag was phony. But I had nothing to do with that," Borsky proclaimed indignantly.

"Sure, you didn't," said Hawk derisively. "And everyone in prison is innocent."

Torrey jumped in. "If you had nothing to do with it, who else did besides the Tooheys?"

Borsky raised confused eyebrows by the question. "No one, to my knowledge," she said and shrugged.

"What about Toohey's niece, Sunshine?"

"No way. That girl needs GPS to find the bathroom. Dumber than a stump. She was simply a stooge for the old man."

Torrey glanced at Hawk, then reasoned, "So, if you weren't involved in the Tooheys' con game, you'll happily return the money that the parents paid to the Tooheys, right?"

"Look, from what I understand, those kids were going to die anyway, right? So did the Tooheys really do anything wrong? Dr. Toohey simply made the last days less painful."

"How noble," said Hawk sarcastically.

Borsky continued, "Yes, they took advantage of some rich naïve rubes, but no harm, no foul, right? You're here for the money, right? So, let's split it in Mexico. There's enough for us all to live like kings and queens. What do you say?" She looked around at the faces staring at her. Torrey knew that, if there had ever been a doubt, Borsky had just signed her death certificate.

From several feet away, Torrey could feel Hawk's blood boiling. She looked over at him and saw his face harden with disgust. He gave Borsky a withering stare. "Rubes? The parents that were trying to save their kids were rubes?" said Hawk as he slid forward to the edge of his seat. "Hand over the bag, Borsky," commanded Hawk who was seething. Borsky began to fidget, and her right hand twitched in her pocket. Hawk saw the movement and warned in a low growl, "Don't even think about it."

Borsky's eyes skipped wildly around the plane. Like a miser handing out employee bonus checks, she slowly but resentfully began to release her grip on the duffel bag. Then, in one swift motion, she used a lifetime of weight-training strength to push the heavy duffel at Hawk with her left hand. With her right hand, she pulled Mrs. Toohey's gun out of her coat pocket. She extended her right arm, pointed the gun at Hawk's head, and pulled the trigger.

The noise was deafening in the small passenger compartment. The flash of the gun temporarily blinded everyone.

Edwina, who had been carefully watching Borsky's hands, yelled, "Gun!" the moment she saw the handle of the revolver appear. She leapt at Borsky, knocking her gun arm sideways just enough. The good news was that the bullet didn't strike Hawk in the face. The bad news was that the bullet hit Hawk in the left shoulder where his bullet-proof vest provided no protection.

When the gun appeared, Hawk rammed his knife into Borsky's left thigh and pulled lengthwise so that the blade sliced flesh from bone like a fish filet. Borsky's face contorted. She let out a piercing cry, dropped the gun onto her seat, and grabbed her leg with both hands.

Torrey pulled her trusty scalpel out of her pocket. She looked fragile and had the delicate fingers of a surgeon, but Torrey knew how to hold a scalpel to kill an attacker. She positioned herself to stab at Borsky's neck, but quickly discerned that Hawk's knife had done the job. Borsky was effectively disabled. She turned to have a look at Hawk's wound.

Hawk stood over Borsky, looking down as victor. Just as Hawk's adrenaline was starting to fade, Borsky circled her enormous left arm around Edwina's neck. She used her right hand to pick up her gun as blood poured from her leg. Hawk pulled a handgun from his waistband. "Put it down, or I break her neck!" yelled Borsky. "And sit down!" she shouted. Hawk did not hesitate. He dropped his gun to the floor and sat.

As soon as Hawk's gun fell, Torrey turned away from Hawk and towards Borsky. In a single motion, she screamed, "Edwina!" and used the scalpel still in her hand to slash at Borsky's throat. Torrey's blade barely drew blood, but it broke Borsky's concentration enough that Edwina was able to twist out of Borsky's grip. Borsky's head dropped, and her shoulders slumped. She was the picture of a defeated warrior. Then in a last desperate gasp, Borsky felt for Toohey's gun. Hawk's head was close enough to touch. Her hand found the gun. She lifted it, trained the barrel at Hawk's face, and pulled the trigger. Hawk ducked. The only sound was the click of the chamber rotating. The gun was out of bullets. Seeing what had happened, Edwina summoned all of her strength and elbowed Borsky's face with blow after blow.

"Enough!" shouted Hawk. He stood, pulled his Glock from the small of his back, and put a hole in Borsky's forehead. They all stared down at Borsky's body. Her eyes remained open with an expression of surprise. If not for the bloodless hole in her head, she looked very much like the stone-faced statue that had sat quietly for most of the flight.

"That was for my Emily," said Hawk quietly.

"And for Hawk and Angela," said Edwina.

"And for the Tintin girl and the other Toohey patients—past, present, and future," said Torrey.

Chapter 47

"You two all right?" asked Hawk before climbing back into the cockpit.

Torrey checked her conscience and waited for a tsunami of guilt to wash over her. It didn't. She was actually elated. "We're fine," said Torrey. "It's you that needs medical attention. Let me look at that shoulder."

"No time. I need to get control of the plane, so we can dump our cargo. Besides, it was a through and through shot." Hawk climbed into the cockpit and fiddled with the instruments. After he retook control from the autopilot, he said, "These controls are a lot different from the ones I trained on. These aren't analog; they're all digital."

Neither Torrey nor Edwina knew or cared what that meant. "How much longer until we can get rid of her?" asked Edwina.

Hawk's mood, which had been all business since the original plan was hatched, now seemed lighter. Almost as if he had not been ultra-close to becoming a murder victim himself. And as if there wasn't a bloody body in the plane. "About eight minutes," said Hawk. "So, go through her pockets and remove any identification and contraband. I'll dispose of everything later." Edwina and Torrey both put on their big girl pants and searched Borsky from head to toe. "I'm going to lower our altitude even more now," said Hawk. "It's pretty windy out there now. We'll probably get some turbulence. When we get close, keep your eyes peeled for a place to dump her."

Edwina glanced out the windows. "What's that glow way off in the distance?" she asked while looking off to the left.

"That, little buddy, is the Vegas strip—about seventy miles away! I had some good times there!" said Hawk.

"Las Vegas? How did we get out here? I thought we were going to Cabo! Vegas is nowhere nearby! It's not even in the same direction!"

"Right. We're about seventy miles southeast of Vegas, near the town of White Hills, Arizona. Lots of abandoned mines in the hills. No one lives out here anymore, except for hermits and old prospectors still trying to strike it rich. Desert for hundreds of miles. And there are lots of rocky outcrops and ravines. Some of the flash flood erosion cuts are deep. Perfect for our purpose."

"How do you know so much about White Hills? And when were you in Las Vegas?" asked Edwina.

"You were a young, self-absorbed teenager when I enlisted, so you probably didn't pay attention, but I did some of my training exercises at Nellis Air Force Base near Las Vegas. We spent a lot of time marching through and flying over the desert. Once we get rid of Borsky, there are several good spots to land, but considering the wind and the fact I've never landed a plane before, I have a place in mind about twenty miles away that's deserted and flat. We can land there."

"And then what?" asked Edwina.

"Then it's up to Torrey to get us home."

"Torrey?" said a worried Edwina. "How's she going to do that?" She turned to Torrey. "Seriously, how are you going to get us out of here?"

Hawk butted in before Torrey could reply. "First things first. I'm now flying as low as I can through these hills and canyons." Hawk rummaged around in his backpack and took out two pairs of night vision goggles. "Here," he said while tossing them backwards, "put these on, each of you take a side of the plane, and look for a place where no one is likely to wander. And hold onto something. It's getting bumpy!"

They flew in and around the hills for several minutes before Edwina shouted, "There, on the left. There's a rock formation that forms a deep 'V.' Do you see it Hawk?"

"Yes. Good find! It looks out of the way enough so that the body will be hidden from casual view, even from a plane. Of course, the animals will soon take care of that problem anyway."

The next loop around, Hawk instructed Torrey and Edwina to open the passenger door. It took both of them to manage it. Once the door was locked in the open position, the wind howled through the cabin. "Now when I say, 'Go!' you two push her out. Edwina, you may need to brace yourself and use your legs to push. She is one big mother!" A few seconds later, Hawk yelled, "Get ready! I'm going to tilt the plane, so it's easier to push her out." The plane tilted like on a Disneyland ride. It was not lost on Torrey that she could fall out with Borsky. Hawk suddenly shouted, "Okay! Go!"

Torrey helped by lifting Borsky's feet, so they wouldn't catch on the lip of the doorway. When Hawk gave the word, Edwina pushed, and Torrey shoved. Borsky fell like a boulder from the sky. Neither Torrey nor Edwina looked to see where she landed, but Hawk let them know with a loud shout, "Bullseye! The wind and gravity carried her right into the crevice!"

Hawk, with a satisfied smile on his face, turned his head to make eye contact with Edwina. "What are you smiling about?" asked Edwina. "We just threw a dead body out of a plane!"

Hawk nodded. "We sure did. Vengeance is good for the soul, isn't it?"

Chapter 48

"What coordinates did you provide?" asked Hawk.

"Just like you instructed," answered Torrey. "I gave North 35.724, West -114.400. You said those were the geographical coordinates for some general location in White Hill, Arizona. So, my contact will be nearby. You just need to give me the final coordinates of the place you've chosen for pickup."

"Roger that," said Hawk with satisfaction.

"What are you guys talking about?" asked Edwina. "What coordinates? And how did you recite those numbers off the top of your head?"

Torrey felt guilty about keeping Edwina in the dark. Hawk, based on some sort of sibling dynamic thing, had ordered early on in their adventure that Edwina be told each part of the plan on a "need to know" basis. "Mrs. Ed, we knew we had to ditch the plane out here in the desert, where it would eventually be discovered. We needed to have a way to get out of here, in the middle of nowhere, in the middle of the night, without any transportation. I arranged for us to be picked up based on the coordinates of our final landing spot."

"I'm not sure how I feel about another person knowing what we did," said Edwina.

"No worries. He's completely trustworthy, but I didn't tell him anything other than two friends and I needed a ride. I have a fun backstory prepared for when he gets here. Just play along."

After a brief pause, Torrey added with a backhanded wave, "And about the coordinates, the two sets of numbers simply represent latitude and longitude so that any location on the earth can be described." Torrey shrugged. "Sometimes living with a notable memory is annoying, but at times like this, it comes in handy."

"That's eerie," replied Edwina.

Torrey then thought to ask, "What about you, Hawk? How did you recall the coordinates of this landing place?"

"You said you never forget a face. Well, I was in a plane that landed here many times. I never forget landing coordinates!"

Hawk found the landing spot that he was looking for. He thought back to all of the landings he'd watched and all the flight simulators he'd practiced on. He muttered to himself, "Well, here goes nothing." Hawk warned his passengers to hold on tightly as the plane touched down. The landing was bumpy, but successful. Torrey and Edwina applauded.

Torrey texted the final coordinates to her friend. "How precise are these coordinates?" Edwina asked Hawk. "I mean, will he be led to this precise spot, or just to this general area? And if it's the latter, it's pitch dark out there. How will we find each other?"

Hawk laughed off her concern. "Edwina, if we had coordinates to just one decimal point, someone could determine which city we were in. If we had coordinates to five decimal points, someone could tell which tree we were behind, if there were any trees out here. Here, I gave you the coordinates of the landing spot to six decimal points, so someone could tell which tree branch we were sitting on. In other words, we'd lose at hide-and-seek if we were trying to keep from being found."

To avoid any chance of the plane being spotted prematurely by any aircraft or lost campers, the three avengers, splattered with Borsky's blood, turned off all the lights and sat in the dark, not saying much of anything for forty-five minutes. Lost in their own thoughts. The only movement inside the plane was Torrey searching for and finding a first aid kit under the seat. Ignoring Hawk's objections, she cleaned and patched up his shoulder.

In due course, a pair of headlights in the distance got brighter and brighter. Five minutes later, Howard Borden pulled up beside the Beechcraft, stepped out of an old four-wheel-drive Jeep, and called out, "Anybody home?" The blowing sand against the outside of the metal plane made it difficult to hear, but Torrey could see it was Howard.

Torrey was the first out of the plane, followed closely by Edwina. Hawk took his time to join the group, while he made sure the plane was flight-ready, for its eventual return. The bullet hole in the fuselage from Borsky's shot looked bad, but Hawk was sure that the bullet had not struck any of the wiring hidden in the walls. And the bullet from Hawk's gun was buried inside Borsky's skull. The plane would need new seats—blood and leather don't mix—but at least it could be flown back to San Diego. He left the keys on the pilot's console. He almost forgot, but as he was stepping down from the passenger compartment, he removed Tony's hat from his head and tossed it onto the pilot's seat.

"Dr. Jamison!" shouted Howard. "Are you okay? What's going on? What are you doing out here?"

Torrey smiled and gave Howard a loose hug, being careful not to taint his clothes with blood. "Thank you so much for coming to get us Howard. You saved our lives! This is Edwina, and the pilot, who is still in the plane, goes by Hawk."

"But what happened? Your sweatshirt has blood on it!" Howard looked at Edwina's clothes. "And yours, too!"

Edwina was wondering how Torrey would reply. "Remember when I called you?" asked Torrey. "I said I needed to impose on you for a huge favor."

"Yes, yes. And I said, 'Anything you need,'" recalled Howard.

"Then I said I needed this kindness with no questions asked."

"Yes, but—"

Torrey laughed. "Okay, you twisted my arm. Would you believe it if I told you that Edwina is an actress preparing for a part that takes place in the desert? And Hawk is an ex-army ranger who is the film's consultant? And that I'm along in case medical care is needed? And the red stains on our clothes is ketchup? And now the plane is out of gas?"

"No. I wouldn't believe any of that," said Howard dryly.

Edwina didn't want to let go of the actress designation that Torrey had bestowed on her. She shouted at Howard with her best Jack Nicholson imitation, "You can't handle the truth!"

Howard didn't get the humor. He just shrugged and said to Torrey, "I take your point that it's none of my business," he conceded. Howard, a military man from a military family, knew there must be a reasonable explanation for the shroud of secrecy, but he couldn't imagine what it might be. Not even a vague notion.

"The only true part of that story is that Hawk really is an Army Ranger," said Torrey with a glint in her eye.

Just then, Hawk joined the group carrying his backpack and the duffel filled with cash. "I hear you're military. Is that right, son?"

Howard, seeing the military bearing and sensing a superior, stiffened salute, shouted, "Yes, sir!"

"At ease, soldier," Hawk instructed. Then he walked over to Howard and offered his hand. "Nice work, soldier. Torrey told me she knew a Marine who lived in the area who would know about geographic coordinates. You're a credit to the Corp."

Howard was both pleased and taken aback. All he could manage was, "Gee, thanks, sir."

• • •

As the group trudged through the blowing sand from the plane to the Jeep, Hawk pulled Edwina aside. "Thanks for saving me back there," said Hawk.

Edwina demurred. "I didn't do much."

"Like hell you didn't. I was this close to leaving Angela a widow. And you were this close to having to land the plane yourself," laughed Hawk with a slap on Edwina's back.

Edwina hugged Hawk and said in a low voice, "Don't think I didn't notice that you put down your gun the instant that Borsky had me by the neck."

"That's how big brothers roll, little *sister*." Edwina almost crushed Hawk with her hug. Hawk finally had to pry her arms loose, so they could all get out of there.

• • •

Before getting in the Jeep, Howard took off his jacket and handed it to Edwina. "Here, put this on. And give me your bloody shirt. I'll discard it when I get home. And Dr. Jamison, I've got an old sweatshirt in the Jeep that you can wear." He opened the trunk and pulled out a well-worn, Las Vegas High Wildcats sweatshirt. Torrey ducked inside the Jeep and changed into the relic while the men stood outside in the wind. She was glad to have something clean to wear.

Once everyone was in his vehicle, Howard motioned to the plane. "What about the plane? We're just going to leave it?"

"It will find its way back to its owner soon enough," said Hawk.

Howard gave a slight shrug and pointed to a giant Coleman cooler in the rear. "Hey, if anyone's hungry, I stopped at a little diner on the way and picked up six burgers and drinks. Actually, I got eight, but I already ate mine. The food is pretty good there. My friends and I used to come out here during high school and explore the old mines. We always stopped at Rosie's Den Café along the highway. Help yourselves."

The color had finally returned to her face, but Edwina, still recovering from what she had witnessed in the plane, refused the offer. She wasn't sure when she would next feel like eating. Torrey, sitting up front in the

Jeep with Howard, initially declined. But the smell of the hamburgers quickly won out. She had two. Hawk, having no reservations whatsoever, ate his two assigned burgers in less than five minutes. Then he ate one of Edwina's, saving the last in case she had a change of heart.

Howard drove them straight to the Las Vegas Greyhound terminal. They had to wait less than an hour for a bus to San Diego. Hawk paid in cash for the tickets out of his wallet, but he left a handful of money from the duffel in Howard's Jeep with a note, "You done good, soldier. For the Gas. Semper Fi."

• • •

After a long phone conversation with Matthew, Torrey huddled with her compadres in the back of the bus. They had the entire back row, as well as the back half of the bus, to themselves. They didn't talk much about all that had transpired, except that Torrey relayed that Rocco had been transported to the hospital. Matthew had ridden with him in the ambulance. Rocco had lost a lot of blood, but Matthew thought he'd fully recover.

Most of the conversation was about the recovered money. No one had any idea how much was in the duffel. Everyone agreed that the money would be returned to all of the families who paid Toohey. "How will we know who paid what?" asked Edwina.

"Matthew's investigator has all of the ledgers from the storage unit. They should tell us the identities of the patients and the amounts paid," said Torrey.

"I don't want any of that money," declared Hawk.

"Too bad," said Torrey. "You have to think of Angela. And it's not meant to be a payment for the loss of Emily. It's simply the return of money that was fraudulently obtained. Put it in the bank, spend it, donate it—I don't care. But you and Angela are getting your money back just like the other families."

Six long hours later, they were in San Diego. Torrey and Edwina, even with uncomfortable naps on the bus, were exhausted. Hawk seemed as fresh as a daisy and insisted that no one go home until all of the cars were collected. Matthew was at the terminal to pick them up. He dropped everyone at their cars, which were scattered throughout the neighborhoods around the Braxton airport. By 5:45 a.m., Torrey and Matthew were safely home in their condo. By 6:15, both were showered, in fresh scrubs, and on the way to work at the hospital.

Chapter 49

Matthew was exhausted, both physically and mentally. And he wanted to focus entirely on his residency for a change. So, the next day, he called Joe with a change of plans. "Joe, this is Matthew. Thanks again for all of your help last night."

"Did everything work out all right?" asked Joe.

"Yes, thanks to you. But I need more help, if you're up for it."

"No problem, Matthew. Whatever you need."

"You recall that I said yesterday that I wanted you to take all the material from the Toohey locker, so I could go through it at the Palisades house?"

"Of course."

"Well," said Matthew, "I'm swamped and beat. I wonder if you could go through it yourself and give me an easy-to-read report. But before you answer, let me tell you something. You know Dr. Toohey is dead. But so is Mrs. Toohey. There will likely be a bunch of police looking into their affairs. They will likely find out about the storage unit. They will likely go over it with a fine-tooth comb. So, if they find your prints, they will want to talk to you about the Tooheys."

Joe interrupted, "Matthew, let me stop you right there. First of all, I'm not worried about being questioned, if it comes to that. I'll just tell them the truth about my role, but your name will never be disclosed. Second, I wiped the place clean. No fingerprints will be found. Third, I'll go through the documents that I took from the unit, but I'm not that clever with numbers. Give me a clue—what am I looking for?"

Matthew took a deep breath. "Joe, I promised I'd fill you in. Here it is in a nutshell. I have reason to believe that the Tooheys were running a scam where they took large sums of money from the families of pediatric cancer patients, promising a cure. They stashed the laundered money in the storage unit safe. You saw Mrs. Toohey removing the money. I now have it. The paperwork you have should provide the identities of each family and how much they paid to Toohey for the bogus treatment. I need that information in a spreadsheet so that I can return the money to those families."

There was a long silence, so Matthew added an important fact. "And Joe, neither I nor anyone working with me killed Mrs. Toohey. It was the person you saw with Mrs. Toohey at the storage unit. I won't mention that person's name, so you can claim ignorance if asked in the future. But FYI, the person you saw was a woman, not a man."

"Wow, that's hard to believe. But okay," said Joe with a shrug. Joe took a deep breath and a silent sigh of relief. "Matthew, it never entered my mind that you had anything to do with Mrs. Toohey's death. I'll get right on the document review and will let you know when I'm finished. Do you have a plan as to how you'll return the money? I presume you'll want it to be anonymous somehow. Do you want my help with that?"

"I thought you'd never ask!" said Matthew. "Let me know what you come up with."

"Will do."

After the call ended, Joe looked at the boxes of papers in the corner of his basement. He had brought them in from his vehicle for safekeeping. Now he had to organize and analyze them. To ease the pain of mind-numbing boredom, Joe put on a pot of coffee and turned the power on to his model train layout. He set the transformers to three-quarter power. The trains traveled around the track while Joe dumped the papers on an empty worktable. The calming sound of locomotives running over metal track always helped him to concentrate.

• • •

Later that evening, after a full day of work, Edwina, Matthew, and Torrey were sitting in Mabel's Coffee Shop where Edwina had reentered their lives. This time, they sat at a table by a window. Torrey had her standing order of a mocha frappuccino with extra whip. Matthew had black coffee. Edwina had two glazed donuts and a hot chocolate. "Mrs. Ed, those donuts have probably been sitting in the glass case since 5:00 a.m.," Matthew observed.

Through the smacking of her lips, Edwina replied without noticing any irony, "They are so good. Want a bite?"

"Um, no thanks," said Matthew.

Torrey said, "So, how are you doing after last night, Mrs. Ed? I see you got your appetite back."

"If I'm honest, it will take me some time to get back to normal, but it was worth it. We did the right thing, didn't we? Were we courageous, or were we crazy?"

"What do you mean?" asked Torrey.

"Were we right to do what we did?"

Torrey replied, "One thing I've learned is that the difference between right and wrong is not black and white—or even gray."

Matthew was more adamant. "Are you asking if we had the moral authority? Could there be better examples of the need for self-reliance and retribution than us? Look at us. Look how the system and society have treated us so unfairly. We all grew up playing by the rules. My father was murdered in our home, and the system worked to free the killer from San Quentin. Torrey's little sister was on her deathbed; yet politics dictated that she should not be able to die pain free and with dignity. And look at you, Edwina. How were you treated by your co-workers when you decided to transition from male to female? How did society treat you? How did your own father treat you?

"The bottom line is that we three grew up on implied, if not express, promises. Promises that if we followed the Golden Rule and were good citizens, we would be treated fairly. That good would triumph over evil. That our elected officials would care more about doing the right thing than getting reelected. Of course, it would be preferable if those in power were willing to punish those that deserve it, but we know they don't have the willpower, moral gumption, or determination. So, we took matters into our own hands. Undeniably, we did the right thing."

Torrey added a clincher. "Plus, no one knows Hawk better than you. If we hadn't helped with the plan, Hawk would have done something rash, which would have ended up with him in the electric chair or in prison. Angela would have suffered another unbearable loss. Not that our original plan had any semblance to what actually happened," said Torrey while patting Matthew on the hand. "But as I always say, sometimes things work out okay anyway."

Edwina suddenly teared up. "I know I can never repay you for everything you did to help Hawk and me. Hawk is too macho to say this himself, but even he couldn't have done it without you two. The Tooheys' horrific conspiracy is finished, and Borsky has gotten her just due for her murderous plot to steal the money generated by Toohey's scheme. Their three deaths cannot bring back Emily, or the other kids who died during Toohey's treatment, but real punishment has been achieved, and no more families will needlessly suffer."

• • •

While the coffee shop meeting was in full swing, Hawk was tucking his wife in bed. Afterwards, he made a call. The phone was answered on the first ring. "Hi, Tony, you know who this is?"

Tony, at home alone with Chinese takeout, should have been shocked to get a call from Hawk, but he wasn't. He recognized the voice right away. His stomach tightened. "Yes, sir."

"How are you feeling?"

"Just a little sore. And tired," said Tony cautiously, hoping to gain some sympathy.

"Just wanted to check in to hear about your conversation with the police," Hawk said without emotion.

"I told them just like you said. I promise. Call over there if you want!" stammered Tony.

"I already did," lied Hawk. "It's all good. By the way, did you get your plane back?"

"Well, I heard that some ultramarathoners found it out in the desert in Arizona. It's now a crime scene. Not sure when the police will release it. What happened out there?" he asked tentatively.

Hawk ignored the question. "Tony, I'll check back with you again another day." Hawk hung up the phone, smiled, and went to lie down next to his sleeping wife.

Chapter 50

Three days later, Torrey and Matthew were enjoying a Sunday morning at home—their first official day off together in weeks. They slept in late, all the way to 7:30 a.m. Matthew brought the morning paper and coffee into the bedroom, expecting and wanting nothing more than to read in bed and to drink the special blend of coffee he had ordered online from a grower in South America.

"You know," said Torrey, "I've been thinking. With Christmas right around the corner, we should have a big holiday party. Invite everyone. Relieve some stress. Have some fun. What do you say?" she said with a huge grin.

"There's no way this place is big enough for a huge party," said Matthew.

"You're so right!" said Torrey. "If it's okay with you, I was thinking we could have it at your parents' house up in LA. The house is big enough, and if you agree, I'd like to decorate it just like it was when I first came to your home to meet your mother and TJ. Remember that? It was Christmas break during our first year of medical school. There were pink roses everywhere and tons of twinkle lights."

"Of course, I remember. That sounds wonderful. But how do you have time for that?"

"Well, when I said I'd decorate it, what I meant was that I'd hire someone," she said with a grin. "I could arrange it all from here. And I'll be in charge of the guest list. You won't have to do a thing, except pay for it all," said Torrey with a big smile. "What do you say?"

Matthew didn't say anything. He just laughed and said with a kiss, "What did I ever do to deserve you?"

"Just lucky, I guess."

Torrey wasted no time in issuing invitations. She started with family— her parents, who still lived up near Stanford University, and Matthew's Uncle TJ. She invited everyone who she had gotten to know during her residency, including the other amazing medical residents and their significant others. She invited many of the wonderful Kaiser doctors, like Travis McKnight and Anne Peterson, and some of the brilliant nurses who had been so helpful while she was learning the ropes. But mostly, the party was an excuse to be with the friends who were instrumental in her and Matthew's extra-curricular activities.

Edwina RSVP'd yes; she just wanted to know if she could bring a "plus one" and wear something strapless and formal. Torrey assured her with a laugh that she could bring whomever she wanted and wear whatever she wanted.

Joe said he would be there if Matthew would promise that hamburgers from Big Dean's on the Pier would be on the menu.

Hawk and Angela declined. Neither Matthew nor Torrey saw Hawk again after being dropped off at their cars in the early morning hours following the Toohey adventure. According to Edwina, Hawk and Angela had decided to move out of the area and start over in Texas; they were considering adoption. They were going to be house hunting in Waco during the Christmas season. Hawk was going to start an indoor and outdoor shooting range where an ordinary person could learn to handle guns like a professional.

Rocco promised to come if he was released from the rehabilitation facility by then.

Howard said he appreciated the invitation but that he wouldn't feel comfortable because he wouldn't know anyone there, besides Torrey, of course. "Why don't you invite someone to come with you?" asked Torrey.

"You know I don't have a girlfriend. Who would I invite?"

"Anyone!" said Torrey. "Your parents, a friend, anyone at all!"

"I don't know," said Howard slowly.

Torrey tried another approach. "Remember you gave me that mnemonic, along with your phone number? You said you would get a dog if I solved it?"

"Sure, I remember. It was FLNDFFC."

"If I solve it right now, you get the dog, and you come to the party. Deal?"

"I've never known anyone to solve it. So, yes. It's a deal."

"Howard, I hate to tell you, but I knew the answer the moment I looked at it. I knew that, as a military man, you likely would have it be something to do with history and probably wartime American history. Right so far?"

"You're not going to trick me into giving anything away," said Howard suspiciously.

"And LND has to stand for LAND. And C has to stand for sea. So the rest is obvious, right?"

"Just say your guess. If you really have one," replied Howard in a self-assured tone.

"It's all about Paul Revere's lighted lantern signal to his fellow patriots about the route the British troops were taking in Massachusetts on the verge of the Revolutionary War—one, if by land and two, if by sea!"

"OMG," said Howard. "I can't believe it!"

"So, Howard, you owe me. I'll text you the address and the date. You'd better be there with a guest. And bring your new dog!" Torrey didn't wait for an answer. She hung up and went to the next call.

● ● ●

The party was a huge success. Torrey had tried to duplicate the mental image in her mind of how the house was decorated when she first saw it. She trimmed the roof line with miniature white lights, filled the second-story Juliet balconies with poinsettias, and even found a Santa sleigh with reindeer for on top of the roof.

The inside of the house and the backyard were magical, with lights, candles, and flowers. In the living room was a gigantic Christmas tree, with old-fashioned bulbs and tinsel. And in honor of Matthew's mother, Mary, there were pink roses draped over the gazebo. It brought back happy childhood memories. Matthew almost cried when he saw the beautiful setting that Torrey had created.

Couples and small groups chatted and mingled, while waiters circulated with glasses of champagne and exotic hors d'oeuvres. Naturally, Matthew and Torrey, although not necessarily in that order, were the centers of attention. They made sure to talk to each guest privately; good hosts make each guest feel special.

Matthew's uncle TJ spent most of the evening socializing with Torrey's parents, but he couldn't help keeping an eye on Matthew throughout the evening, thinking of how proud his parents would be of the charismatic and responsible man he'd become. Seizing a moment when Torrey and Matthew were not surrounded by guests, TJ hurried over to spend a private minute with the hosts. "I can't believe how you've brought the place back to life!" TJ exclaimed.

"Don't look at me," said Matthew. "Torrey did it all."

TJ chuckled. "Well, that's a given. But Mary is smiling down from heaven right now on both of you."

Without another word, the three of them spontaneously hugged. TJ broke the spell with an unexpected inquiry. "Let's get together, just us, before you head back to San Diego. I want to catch up and hear more about your residencies. Oh, and I want to hear the backstories on the clear liquid you wanted analyzed and on the cellulitis medicine you requested for a VA patient."

The statement hung in the air for a long moment. Matthew just said, "Sure!" At the same time, he shot Torrey a look that said, *Never in a million years*.

• • •

Rocco showed up with a limp and good news. "Guess what?" he said as he approached Matthew. "You sure were right about the Tooheys. The police found the missing Fentanyl in his storage unit. I got the credit in the agency and the promotion I wanted. You're now looking at the Chief Investigator of the Medical Board in San Diego County."

"Big Rocky, that's fantastic!" said Matthew as he patted him on the back.

"I guess getting shot in the line of duty gets you extra points," commented Rocco dryly. "It's a desk job, but I can state with conviction that, after the Toohey experience, I've had enough of working in the field."

"And I've had enough of trying to be a doctor and an amateur investigator. Good luck to you, Big Rocky!"

"Matthew, one more thing. Now that I'm in management, the Big Rocky name is a little too undignified."

"Ten-four! Enjoy the rest of the party, Mr. Chief Investigator," said Matthew with his one hundred-megawatt smile and a bow.

• • •

Joe ambled over to Matthew with a hamburger in his hand and secret sauce dripping down his chin. "Matthew, these Big Dean hamburgers are just as good tonight as they were last time we were here. I mentioned them to Torrey as a joke, but you actually put them on the menu! You two are amazing."

Matthew put his arm around Joe's shoulder and pulled him into the corner of the yard. "How far along are you on returning the money to the Toohey families? I know we agreed on your plan—"

"Say no more. It's all but finished. As we discussed, I've already delivered packages with full refunds to each of the families, except for the Hawke and the Bernstein families. I included an official-looking letter from the Medical Office of Dr. Albert Toohey dated the day before his death."

"We talked about several ideas for the text of the letters. What did you decide on?" asked Matthew.

"I just made it sound like Toohey had to leave the country suddenly, and he didn't feel right about taking money when he couldn't finish the treatment. So, return to your oncologist for further treatment."

"Makes me sick to suggest Toohey had a decent bone in his body."

Matthew then asked about the kids who died. "What about the letters to families who lost children under Toohey's care?"

"Those were a little trickier because I had to imply that each of the several kids in this category was the only unfortunate patient. I said Toohey felt terrible that his treatment did not cure their particular child. He wanted to return the money paid as a token of his regret and sympathy."

"Good job. I hate making this guy out to be some sort of saint, especially if word gets out that he was murdered, but it's worth it so that the families don't feel like they were duped," reasoned Matthew. "And Toohey, the depraved scumbag, isn't alive to learn of his celebrity status."

"Of the remaining two families," said Joe, "Torrey asked me to hold off on the Bernsteins, so she could give me some sort of book to go in the package."

"A book?"

"Yeah, something about a tin boy and his dog." Joe rubbed his chin thoughtfully. "Any idea what she's talking about? She said she'd give me the book tonight."

"Yes, I have a pretty good idea. It must have been a book about Tintin."

"Right. That was it," Joe mused.

"And you didn't want me to handle the Hawke family in the same way as the others. Per your directive, I will fly out to Texas, track the father down, and personally hand him his box of cash. And I haven't forgotten. You want me to say to him when I hand over the package, 'Matthew and Torrey say, "Do whatever you want with this."' I intend to fly out in a couple of days."

"Thanks, Joe. You're the best."

"Anyway, I also wanted to thank you for the generous bonus you gave me. It will come in handy." As Joe walked back over to the hamburger table, he was daydreaming about how he was going to expand his model train layout.

• • •

Howard Bordon was true to his word. He not only showed up, but he also came with a "plus two." When Torrey looked up from her latte and saw Howard, she laughed out loud. Howard was strolling across the patio, arm in arm with Private Biggs from the VA hospital. And pulling on a leash was the cutest Goldendoodle puppy ever. Both Howard and Private Biggs lit up when they saw Torrey. Howard gave her a hug, but Private Biggs gave a mock salute and said with a smile, "Hey, doc, nice place you've got here!"

"So happy you both came! This is my husband, Matthew," said Torrey as she put one arm around Matthew's waist.

Howard shook Matthew's hand. "You're one lucky man!" Howard told him sincerely.

Torrey enjoyed the fact that Howard had brought another veteran and that Biggs was not at all self-conscious about coming to the party with his disfigured face. Torrey loved vets.

The three of them caught up and played with the dog. Both Howard and Private Biggs thanked Torrey multiple times for the help she had given them at the VA. Biggs bent down and pulled up his pant leg to show Torrey that his cellulitis had cleared up. When he did, Torrey smelled the strong odor of whiskey. "Private Biggs," smiled Torrey, "I can tell you stopped at the bar area before I saw you."

"Oh, do you mean the smell of alcohol on me?" He pulled a flask out of his pocket and held it up for Torrey to see. "I always smell like that!" he said as he roared with laughter. "Tell her Bordon! Tell your girl I always smell like that!"

Torrey reflected on how backwards it was that Howard and Biggs were thanking her. In any event, she knew that Howard had already repaid her ten-fold. And Howard looked happy. That was all the thanks Torrey needed.

• • •

Edwina arrived with a splash. She wore a full-length red evening gown, with sequins and sparkles. She held Koa in her arms. Trailing just behind Edwina was her date. They greeted Torrey with air kisses and grins. "Torrey, I'd like you to meet my cute dog-walker friend, Taylor. And of course, you know Koa."

"So glad you could come," said Torrey. "Love your dress! And what did you do to your hair?"

Edwina pointed to her French twist hairdo. "I went into town today and had Mr. Jim do this for me. Isn't it perfect?"

"It is!" exclaimed Torrey as she thought about how her hair, although freshly shampooed, looked the same tonight as it did every day that she was in the hospital.

"Are you carrying Koa because she's too 'big-boned' to walk anymore?" Torrey teased. "You know, her bones seem even bigger than the last time I saw her," said Torrey as she rubbed Koa's bulging stomach.

"It may interest you to know," said Edwina indignantly, "that a company that makes flea and tick medicine is interested in Koa for a TV commercial! And I just auditioned to be a hand model. See how they did my nails at the call-back?"

Torrey looked at Edwina's perfectly manicured and painted fingernails. Then she glanced at her own chewed and uneven nails. She burst out laughing.

"And," Edwina continued, "the pay for the commercials will allow me to move into a two-bedroom apartment. And Taylor might just become my new roommate!" Both Edwina and Taylor beamed.

• • •

The party wound down around midnight. Torrey had offered that anyone driving up from San Diego could stay over in the house. Everyone declined, but most opted to stay in nearby hotels, so they could do some sightseeing the next day.

The candles were still burning, and the backyard was still lit up when the last guest had departed. The croquet equipment that had been set up for the guests was now available. "How about a game?" suggested Matthew.

"Seriously? Now?"

"Well, yes. Unless you're chicken!"

Torrey marched over, picked the green-striped mallet, and readied her ball to play. In ten minutes, she had circled the course, twice knocking Matthew's ball into the bushes. She won handily.

"I thought you said you didn't know how to play!" cried Matthew.

"I read a book," said Torrey evenly. "It's not that hard." They both laughed.

Matthew put on some soft music, and they slow danced on the patio. Torrey pressed her head into his shoulder. Matthew stroked her hair and whispered, "I'm so glad we're finished with all of the revenge stuff. Now we can just concentrate on our residencies and on us."

"About that," said Torrey slowly. "There's something going on at the VA hospital that we need to fix."

Acknowledgements

Thank you to the team at TouchPoint Publishing for giving wings to *Bad Medicine*. Special thanks to publisher Sheri Williams for having faith that I could complete the book with everything else that has been happening in my life over the last year, and to editor Kelly Esparza for her insights and comments.

Thanks to Rozanne, Kristin, and Travis for inspiring me to reach my bucket list goals.

Made in the USA
Monee, IL
03 August 2021